Heart Of

MW00887003

(Huntsman's Fate: Book 1)

Liam Reese

© 2017

Disclaimer

This is a work of fiction. Names, places, characters and events are all fictitious for the reader's pleasure. Any similarities to real people, places, events, living or dead are all coincidental.

This book contains sexually explicit content that is intended for ADULTS ONLY (+18).

Prologue

Duke Moncarthy looked down from his horse at the scene of utter devastation. Pure chance had led his hunting party this far from his keep, where they had encountered the raiding party. His keen eyes had picked out the marauding band of mounted men attacking the caravan train on land under his jurisdiction. Grimly, he drew the sword of Anthorat, the legendary blade gifted to him by his brother, the king.

"Guards on me!" he bellowed, digging his heels into the gleaming flanks of his midnight charger. "Attack!" he added as the horse thundered forward.

At fifty paces, one of the murderers turned – sensing their approach – and called a warning to the rest of the raiding party. Rather than turning to flee, as Moncarthy expected, the attackers faced the duke's small force with determination and drew their weapons.

Duke Moncarthy met the lead marauder, sending his blade swinging at the man's neck. Sharp as a flint knife and heavy to boot, the sword of Anthorat separated the attacker's head from his body in a bloody spray. A fan of black hair flew out as his head sailed off into the oncoming raiders. Unaware its head had gone, the raider's body rode on for a few seconds before slumping in its saddle and falling from its horse.

The Duke's small force found itself heavily outnumbered, each of the duke's men facing three of the raiders. However, Duke Moncarthy, having seen that the raiders targeted women and children, became filled with blood rage and transmitted his anger to his blade. The sword of Anthorat sang as Moncarthy killed five, six, then seven of the attackers in rapid succession. A few of his guardsmen followed, slashing at the dark-haired men and trading blows.

Duke Moncarthy watched as a pair of the raiders brutally murdered a woman and child in one of the caravans, her scream ending in an agonized gurgle. Blocked by men, there was nothing he could do to save her, and with their mission apparently complete, the attackers shouted their retreat.

Moncarthy gave chase. His black horse easily outpaced the raiders' mounts, and he plunged the sword of Anthorat into the neck of one of the fleeing men. Unfortunately, the dead man fell sideways, fouling Moncarthy's horse, and it slowed, panting heavily. The duke watched as the remaining three killers raced away. Turning, he trotted back towards the dead, broken caravans and terrified horses.

"Report," he said, sliding from the saddle.

"Twenty-three dead, Your Grace," Gwakon, his head guard reported, snapping to attention. "All appear to be native families with small children apart from one wagon. They had the appearance of Gazluthians, from across the Wide Green

Sea. We killed seventeen attackers but they managed to exterminate everyone in the caravans."

"So foreign raiders killed the entire caravan to eliminate a single family of their own people?" Moncarthy said, shaking his head.

"So it would seem, Your Grace."

"Burn the raiders and bury the others," Moncarthy ordered shortly. "Which family do you believe was the target?"

"Here, Your Grace."

Moncarthy approached the smashed remains of the wagon. Blood had already soaked into the dry wood, drawing gory patterns in the grain. Six wounds pierced a man sprawled across the harness attaching the wagon to the horses. Sightless eyes pleaded at the unforgiving sky, his long, black hair trailing in the dusty tracks. One weapon had entered his chest, piercing the padded jacket he wore and ending up in his heart. Another lower blow had hemorrhaged several feet of his intestines, and Moncarthy could only imagine how much pain he had died in. Reaching down, he closed the poor man's eyes.

In the darker interior he found the form of a woman. Moncarthy stepped up into the tiny living space, his large frame nearly filling it and blocking out what little light penetrated. His sharp dagger made quick work of the cloth covering the mobile home, flooding it with light. Personal items had been scattered everywhere; plates, bowls, cutlery, foodstuffs, clothing and a small quantity of gold covered the floorboards.

The woman had been beautiful, Moncarthy noted. Flawless pale skin supported by exquisite bone structure had been horribly marred by a sword thrust to her mouth. Moncarthy's palms tingled at the sight of the awful wound, but he forced himself to crouch and close her dark brown eyes.

That was when he heard the infant scream. Radiating from beneath the woman, came the sound of life, muffled but easily identifiable as a baby's cry.

"The gods be praised," the duke muttered. "To me!"

As guards clambered into the small space, Moncarthy grabbed the woman, hauling her corpse aside. Beneath her, soaked with his mother's dying blood, lay a chubby-faced baby. His pale skin and dark hair marked him as the child of the dead couple, and Moncarthy picked him gently up, cradling him and cooing gently.

"Besmir," he mumbled, reading the child's name from his embroidered blankets. "You are safe now, young Besmir."

***

White-hot pain exploded in Besmir's face as Nikros' fist smashed into his nose. His ears rang from the blow, tears springing from his eyes as he fell back. Nikros stood over his fallen opponent, an easy victory as he was twice Besmir's size. The other boys from the orphanage crowding around them, baying for his blood.

Although Besmir could neither see nor hear much, he lashed out with his foot, the stamping action landing a blow against Nikros' knee. The older boy screamed as the joint bent sideways, cracking loudly as it gave out. Nikros crashed to the ground like a felled tree, clutching his shattered knee and moaning insults at Besmir.

The younger boy sat up, wiped blood from his mouth and spat on the ground at the feet of the other boys.

"Look what you've done!" one on-looker cried.

"Nikros, are you alright?" another asked in a panicked voice.

"Of course not!" Nikros snapped. "He's busted my knee. Kill the Pashaq!"

Besmir ignored the insult, having heard it his entire life. In truth, he was nothing like the shaggy, savage, cave-dwelling beasts of that name. Staggering to his feet, he turned to face the first boy to approach him, snarling like an animal and baring his bloodied teeth. Shocked at the image, the other boy hesitated, backing away.

"Break it up now!" Master Winlore bellowed across the yard. "Break it up, I say!"

Round and red-faced, he stormed across to the group who started to melt away from the two injured boys. He carried a stick that had nothing to do with aiding him in walking and everything to do with punishment. He swished it menacingly before him, scything the air to clear it of boys. One, not fast enough to dodge the stick, ended up with a pink stripe across his shoulders, a scream ripping from his throat as he fell to the ground.

Winlore shook his head, grey curls flapping around his ears when he finally reached the pair. His porcine eyes squinted as he took in the sight of Nikros on the floor. The sight of a blood-covered Besmir beside him plowed deep furrows on his brow.

"I might have known it would have been something to do with you, boy," he growled. "It's always something to do with you!"

"I'm sorry I'm the target of these bullies," Besmir said. "Perhaps if you did your job, rather than ogling the cook's daughter, both my nose and Nikros' knee wouldn't be wounded." Besmir wore an expression of complete defiance.

The color drained from Master Winlore's chubby face as if someone had pulled a bung in his neck. His jowls wobbled with the rage that shook his entire body and his lips shrank to thin lines.

"How dare you speak to me like that?" he demanded in a hiss. "Who do you think you are?"

His whisper turned into a bellow and he raised his stick, preparing to whip it down across Besmir's face. Besmir stared back at him, his twelve year old face judgmental and angry. Winlore paused before he started his attack, seeing the expression of a much older soul in the boy's face.

"Get to the nurse!" he snapped, pointing with his stick. "Now!"

Besmir glared at him for a few seconds more but stomped off when he raised his stick again.

The orphanage's nurse, Reileen, gave Besmir her usual look of despair and disapproval mixed with a little pity. Besmir hated it.

"Again, Besmir?" she asked with a tone of resignation. "Really?"

"It's not as if I start these fights," Besmir explained. "I don't go looking to get beaten up."

"I know, lad. I know."

Besmir watched as the only mother he had ever known dipped a soft rag into some hot water and started to clean the blood from his face. Despite the mild pain that flared with each wipe, Besmir felt warmth spread in his chest. Plain, with a kind, round face, Reileen could have easily been his mother. She had darker hair than other Tyrington residents, a close match for his own black locks. Her skin was suntanned and freckled where his was pale, but there could be any number of reasons for that, Besmir thought. Round and padded, she was perfect for the infrequent hugs she gave out as part of her caring process.

"Why do they hate me so much?" Besmir asked in a small voice.

Reileen sighed, resting her hand on his shoulder and running one finger gently up and down his neck.

"Oh love," she started. "Children have any number of reasons to hate each other. They pick up on any silly little thing and make fun of it. You, with your black hair and pale skin, make a really easy target, and the younger ones get led by the older ones." Besmir looked at the floor, shuffling his feet. "And of course," she added, making Besmir look hopefully into her eyes, "they're all incredibly, fatally, ridiculously...stupid."

A smile split Besmir's face, turning into a grin, and then he began to laugh. Relief-filled tears rolled down his cheeks as Reileen took him up in a big hug and made everything alright again.

Hours later, Besmir stood before Duke Moncarthy, Winlore and Reileen. Nikros had limped in with the aid of a crude crutch and been allowed to sit in the duke's presence due to his injury.

"I'm having difficulty, Master Winlore," Moncarthy said, "in understanding whether your problem is with what young Besmir here said," he fixed the youth with a stern, withering look, "or the accuracy of his statement."

Hope filled Besmir's chest when he heard the large man speaking.

Is the duke really on my side?

"Well, I mean, Your Grace... I..." Winlore blustered, reddening.

"Master Winlore," Moncarthy spoke over the other man. "As patron and provider for this orphanage, I am less than impressed with your service. After speaking to Nurse Reileen regarding these two boys, I have come to understand you allow Nikros to attack Besmir whenever the mood takes him."

Winlore opened his mouth as if to speak, but the duke stared at him. "Silence!" he bellowed. "I feel a certain...affinity towards Besmir, as it was I who found the lad, and I will not countenance him being bullied. I expect you to perform your duties without exception, and keeping the boys from beating seven bells from each other is one of them." He sighed. "Should I hear, from anyone, that you have shirked your responsibilities again, I will have no recompense but to allow you to leave my service."

Winlore paled and shrank under the duke's scrutiny, trying to make himself invisible. Moncarthy turned his attention to the other boy.

"Nikros, believe it or not, I was once a boy myself, and I got up to some of the high jinks you boys get to here. Picking on someone because they're different makes you look small, weak, and ultimately reduces you in the eyes of others, despite what they might think of you now. Understand?"

Nikros stared at the older man in wide-eyed terror, his awe at being spoken to by the king's brother plain on his face. All the boy could manage in response was a slow nod.

"And Besmir." The duke turned his attention to the other boy. "You know you have favor in my eyes, but do not think to leverage this. Master Winlore remains the head of this establishment and should always be your first point of contact in case of difficulties."

"Yes, sir," Besmir said.

He'll just go on ignoring me and letting it happen, though.

***

"Get on with it, you worthless gnark!"

The shout echoed through the trees, reaching Besmir's ears as he cut the intestines from a deer the hunting party he had been sent to work with had killed.

"And make sure to clear the guts out this time," the same voice called. "We need them to make bowstrings and the like."

Besmir ran the deer's intestines through his hands, squeezing its partially digested food from either end. Blood covered his fingers along with much less pleasant substances. He hurled the excrement into the trees and looped the empty guts up to dry on a branch. His back ached, his stomach rumbled with hunger and he knew his situation was not about to improve. Taking the tiny knife he had been allowed, he began to skin the deer, scraping the fat from the skin before hanging that from a different tree.

Introna stalked back into the clearing, muttering and cursing that everything Besmir had done was wrong. From keeping the fire lit to how he had hung the intestines, nothing was right.

"Go fetch firewood," Introna barked. "Then refill the water buckets. When you're done with that, gut and clean these rabbits we're going to eat tonight. Be quick about it!"

Besmir trotted off into the forest, losing himself among the trees before the sinewy hunter could think of anything else for him to do.

Life was harder now than it ever had been when he was in the orphanage. While the hunters did nothing to physically hurt him, their gruff indifference and often complete ignorance of him was just as painful.

Besmir bundled branches and logs of varying sizes as he contemplated his life. Wandering around in a half daze, he completely failed to notice the crallcat that watched him intently. His consideration of the events that led up to this moment was violently cut short when the beast exploded from the shadows and smashed him to the leafy floor.

A row of teeth gleamed dully back at his wide eyes, saliva dripping from the sharp tips. Folds of muscular tongue writhed in the cave of her mouth as the crallcat pinned Besmir to the forest floor with both front paws. Panic robbed him of breath and sense as the cat's fetid breath puffed over his face and the stench of rotting meat filled his nostrils. A low, growling hiss erupted from her throat, threatening and fury-filled. Her eyes narrowed, the fur on her face wrinkling as she bared her teeth once more.

With the specter of imminent and painful death on him, Besmir felt an odd calm wash over his psyche – a casual acceptance of his fate.

If this is my lot in life, if this is how it was meant to end, then so be it.

Besmir's body relaxed, his breathing slowed and his heart stopped trying to jump from his chest.

"Come on then," he said gently to the cat. "End it."

The female crallcat tilted her head to one side as if listening to his words. Her own breathing settled a little and she stepped from his shoulders, letting Besmir sit up. With slow, deliberate movements, Besmir silently rose, putting his back to a tree.

He watched in awe as the crallcat paced back and forth in the small clearing, casting the occasional glance at him as if unsure as to what he was or what to do with him. Never in his short life had Besmir seen such a magnificent beast, and pressure grew in his chest at being able to see her so close.

Abruptly the cat sat her hindquarters down, facing Besmir, and grunted.

Is she trying to talk to me?

"What's the matter?" he asked, feeling awkwardly self-conscious at talking to an animal.

The cat grunted again, grumbling as she swung her head from side to side. Besmir smiled in wonder and fascination when the realization hit that she *was* trying to communicate with him somehow.

"Boy!" The hiss came from behind him.

The crallcat's ears jerked toward the sound, her hindquarters lifting and tail twitching as her eyes pierced the gloom just beyond Besmir's shoulder.

"Back away real slow," Introna murmured as the cat began to work itself up again.

Insinuating himself into the clearing, Introna held his bow half pulled, his muscles as tense as the crallcat he faced. Step by slow, careful step, he drew level with Besmir as the cat followed him with her rage-filled glare.

Without warning or giving any sign it was about to happen, the crallcat leaped at Introna, one clawed limb swiping at him, knocking the bow from his grip. His arrow swished off into the shadows of the forest as he cradled his injured arm.

"No!" Besmir shouted, putting himself between the cat and Introna. "Go!" he added, flicking his arm at the forest.

Her muscles twitched beneath the golden-brown and cream fur covering her hide as she studied him with curiosity in her eyes. Almost casually, the five-foot beast turned and trotted calmly into the trees, disappearing in the space of a heartbeat.

***

"I'm telling you," Introna hissed later to his hunting companions. "It was a crallcat and he told it to go."

Besmir sat apart from the others as normal, his back to their group as they ignored him but discussed him as if he were somewhere else completely.

"A crallcat?" one of the others asked. "You sure? They usually attack on sight and don't leave much behind after."

"I know," Introna said. "But I swear to the gods when I caught up with the lad it was sitting facing him as calmly as I'm talking to you now."

Besmir listened as the hunters chatted about him, speculation and guesswork an ample substitute for actually asking him what had happened. Anger simmered low in his belly when he realized these men would never accept him as one of their own. Rejected at the orphanage and now rejected by these hunters, Besmir decided he would be better off living a solitary life. Determination pressed against the back of his skull.

I will learn everything I can from these morons then petition the duke to allow me to venture out alone.

"When he shouted at it, I thought I was dead, but it just looked at him as if it was confused," Introna said. "Then it ran off into the forest...just like he told it to."

Besmir felt their eyes on his back as they muttered about curses and demons, his chest tight with suppressed emotions.

I'll show you. I'll show you all!

Chapter One

Besmir stretched and twisted in his saddle as his gelding snorted, tossing his head and stamping. A scent drifted to the hunter – brine and salt – as the small group headed for the port town of Nirsdon. His keen eyes took in the forest of masts waving gently at the far side of a group of squat, wooden buildings, many of which had been smeared liberally with tar. The whole town looked dark and oppressive, making Besmir glance back at the rolling, verdant hills they had come from.

"Not the most welcoming appearance, is it?" Zaynorth asked when he noticed Besmir's expression.

Besmir shook his head slowly.

"I never really thought of Tyrington as attractive," he said. "But this place makes it look like a polished jewel. Is this the best option we have?"

The old mage chuckled and stroked his beard, glancing at the monochrome town before them.

"It might appear unpleasant, yet Nirsdon has some of the most agreeable and welcoming inns in Gravistard, as well as fine wines and spirits."

Besmir grunted at him and clucked his horse forward.

Lacking any kind of defensive walls, Nirsdon almost grew from the landscape as they approached. Shacks started to appear at the sides of the dirt road, giving way to cheap cabins that, in turn, were replaced by larger buildings of stone and lumber. Smoke from hundreds of fires added to the overall stench assaulting Besmir's nose, contributing to the odor of rotting fish and human waste. Piles of decaying trash lined both sides of the street, and Besmir looked on in disgust as children as young as two or three played in the filth left by others.

Zaynorth led them through twisting streets that looked to have been laid at random. With space at a premium, businesses crowding the docks, the buildings started to press in, making Besmir feel like an animal in one of his traps. Throngs of people, either on horseback or foot, shoved and jostled each other, shouting and grunting as they tried to complete their various tasks. Besmir tried not to stare at the variety of people swarming around him. His isolated life in Tyrington had shielded him from the mass of cultures that mixed here, and it was as much as he could do not to gawk at the brightly colored feathers and scaled skins of those he had never set eyes on before. He turned to watch an obviously female creature with a plume of red and pink sprouting from her head as she passed. He caught sight of Keluse watching the same creature, squeaking in some language he could never begin to understand, and grinned. Keluse looked as awed as he felt. She turned and caught sight of him, returning his grin with an edge of childlike delight.

Immense warehouses lined the waterfront, some with savage-looking guards posted outside. Opposite these were dozens of taverns and inns, almost all featuring someone outside proclaiming their establishment was the best and almost all full of drunken sailors.

Dusk had fallen as Besmir's party threaded their way through the town, and a chill breeze nagged at them from the sea. Zaynorth headed for one of the larger buildings, a stone-and-wood place that resembled the prow of a ship, even down to having a large-breasted figurehead without. Three young men materialized from a narrow side alley and approached.

"Take yer mounts mister?" one asked.

Besmir saw he had little in the way of clothing. Most of what he did have was ripped and worn. Dirty, with greasy hair and spots, Besmir thought him around fifteen, the other two younger.

"It's free if you stay at the Sunken Mermaid," one of the younger boys chimed.

This was obviously something they had been told to say and made to practice over and over until it was right. Besmir wondered if this might have been his fate if not for the duke, while Zaynorth gave them orders to care for the horses and headed inside.

The Sunken Mermaid featured rough wooden furniture, sailing accoutrements – nets, an anchor – and was populated by the same varied mixture of people as the streets outside.

Zaynorth threaded his way through the crowd, most of whom were in the middle of singing a bawdy ballad, and reached the bar.

"Jondras." A large man thrust his hand out for Zaynorth. "Proud owner of the Sunken Mermaid."

A grin split the man's face, far wider and with too many teeth for him to be native. He was squat and round with dark red skin over his angular face and hands. Besmir looked down to see he had six fingers on each hand and five knuckles on each.

"Pitcriss?" Zaynorth asked. "You are a ways from home. Have you rooms for us?"

Besmir watched as the Pitcriss cast his eye over the group, evaluating them for wealth and the potential to cause trouble before smiling again.

"Is the lady with one of you?" he asked.

"No, she'll need a separate room, the rest of us can share," Besmir told the creature.

Jondras's eyes cut to Besmir and he noticed they had oval pupils surrounded by a light green iris.

"I was conducting business with your father," the Pitcriss said dismissively, misreading their situation. "Younglings should know their place."

Besmir heard Morcath and Ranyor hiss as they caught the innkeeper's words.

"Please, allow me to deal with this, Lord," Zaynorth said to Besmir, declaring his deference publicly. "The Pitcriss is obviously unused to being in the presence of high-born."

Besmir smirked as he watched Jondras re-evaluate his position in the group.

"No offense meant," he apologized in his ever so slightly accented voice. "I get all manner of people through here and many of them are less than trustworthy. I shall order rooms prepared for you all, and please, if there is anything I can do for you, just ask."

"We require passage across the Wide Green to Gazluth," Zaynorth stated. "We also have several mounts to sell and obviously want the best price."

Jondras drummed his fingers against his belly as he thought, producing a hollow sound that set Besmir's teeth on edge.

"The horses are not a problem, not a problem at all," he said. "The passage, however, might prove a little more challenging. With the war in Gazluth there are few trading opportunities and little profit to be made, so ships seldom journey there."

"Still, that is our destination," Zaynorth said. "So make it known we are seeking passage."

The Pitcriss folded his long-fingered hands beneath his chin and offered what looked like a small bow to Besmir. It became obvious to the hunter how different Jondras was when he turned and Besmir saw the tail that swung from side to side as he stomped off.

"Let us be seated," Zaynorth suggested. "And have some food not cooked by Ranyor."

"If my cooking offends you so much," Ranyor said with a sniff, "feel free to prepare your own meals."

Zaynorth chuckled. The week or so it had taken them to get here from his cabin had been spent riding all day and sleeping almost as soon as they had eaten. Although there had been little time for much conversation, Besmir had seen them working as a cohesive unit and knew they could all depend on the others in a crisis.

"You're dragging me into the middle of a civil war, then?" Besmir asked once they had all settled around a pair of tables. He, Zaynorth, Keluse, Ranyor and Morcath sat beside a large fire pit that glowed with heat, leaving the others to claim a second table. Although they appeared to be relaxed, Besmir noticed their hands were always free to access their weapons and one or another would glance around the Mermaid every so often.

"The war is over," Zaynorth said. "Tiernon took the throne when your father disappeared and conquered the rest of the populace by force." He shook his head. "Thousands died, but without a leader, a figurehead for everyone to follow, the rebellion was doomed to fail. Now there is a vast split in Gazluth. Those loyal to, or fearful of Tiernon live their lives to the fullest. Those who opposed him have ended up in the basest of squalor. Wives without husbands and children without fathers are denied the basic essentials for life." Besmir watched the old man's face shift, the set of his features becoming angry. "So no, no war, but plenty to put right." Zaynorth excused himself and left to discuss something with the Pitcriss.

"Zaynorth can be a little touchy when it comes to your da," a voice rumbled from the other table.

Besmir saw it was Herofic, and the surprise must have shown in his face, as the thickset warrior laughed. Herofic had said almost nothing to Besmir since they had met, showing none of the deference the other warriors did, for which Besmir was grateful. A stout man of around five feet in height, Herofic carried a battle axe that looked as if it could cleave mountains. He had bushy eyebrows with long hairs jutting at odd angles that gave him a stern expression, but the eyes that sat beneath them twinkled with merriment.

"Does he blame him for the war?" Besmir asked.

"Blames your father, blames himself," Herofic said in a quiet rumble. "Guilt eats at Zaynorth daily, and only healing his homeland will begin to assuage it."

Besmir grunted, wondering what path he had rashly decided to follow.

"The mix of people here is amazing," Keluse said. "That fellow who runs this place, did you see his tail?"

"And the one with the feathers earlier?" Besmir said, ignoring his future for now.

"She was a Corbondrasi from the deserts of Boranash," Ranyor told them. "All have colored plumage. It is an incredible sight to behold."

"Have you been there, then?" Keluse asked a little self-consciously. The tall man nodded, rubbing his chest.

Besmir nodded to the healing arrow wound he himself had accidentally inflicted.

"How is that?"

"Fine, Lord," Ranyor said. "I heal at an incredible speed."

"Still, I am sorry," Besmir said. "Again."

Ranyor shrugged. "No matter," he said amiably. "I am sure you will be as forgiving when I shoot you in the back."

"When?" Besmir asked with a grin.

"When," Ranyor said with a smirk. "To answer your question, Keluse, yes I traveled to Boranash to witness their celebrations. Each year, for three days, the entire population ceases normal activities and holds a festival to their god of rebirth, Loranus."

Keluse stared longingly at Ranyor as he lost himself in the past.

"Men and women dress in the finest of clothes and adorn their plumage with jewels and fine paints. Everyone is included, royalty mixing with peasants without judgment.

Everyone donates what they are able, even if it is a single piece of fruit or lone fish, and everything is freely available to all."

"It sounds beautiful," Keluse said.

Ranyor nodded, his expression changing subtly.

"It is. Yet some things I find more enchanting."

Besmir watched as the tall warrior held Keluse's gaze just long enough to make her realize of whom he was speaking. She blushed and looked away as the information sank in.

"Of course, once the festival is over, they all go back to scheming and back-stabbing each other," Ranyor said with a chuckle.

***

Later, once a filling meal of roasted meats and vegetables filled his belly, Besmir watched a man approach them. Cloaked in a ragged yet heavy coat that may have once been blue, his long hair exploded from beneath a floppy hat lying at an angle. Heavy, black boots with wooden soles announced his approach as effectively as a fanfare, and the ballooned trousers he had tucked into them looked well used also. His face had the appearance of tanned leather, the vicious elements having taken their toll, and a scar ran horizontally across his forehead as if someone had attempted to remove his scalp. Mud-water eyes grazed over the group before lighting on Zaynorth. Yellowed teeth formed a nasty smile, and Besmir saw several of his companions' hands move towards sword and dagger hilts.

"Word has it ye be seeking passage," the stranger said in a voice like granite splitting.

"Maybe," Zaynorth said. "For the right price."

The stranger thrust out a hand as brown and callused as cow hooves. Gold rings adorned the first and middle fingers.

"Toras," he said. "Captain of the *Dawn Singer*." Without invitation, he grabbed a chair and reversed it, folding his arms across the back. "Fleet, she be, sleek and fast as a dolphin."

"How impressive," Zaynorth said with as little enthusiasm as he could muster. "We need passage to Gazluth for ten."

"Ten to Gazluth," Toras muttered as he grabbed a serving girl and demanded ale. "That be a dangerous place to find port to begin with. And the *Singer*, she's not quite large enough to take on ten more people."

"Oh well, as unfortunate as it is, I am confident we shall find that which we seek. Good day, Captain, please accept the refreshment at our expense." Zaynorth dismissed him.

The group stayed relatively silent as Toras drained the tarnished mug that was brought to him. Other patrons in the Mermaid were getting progressively louder as the beer flowed, hiding any embarrassing silence from the group.

"Well, good luck to ye," the captain said, placing the mug before Zaynorth. "Thanks for the drink," he added as he stood.

Besmir noticed he wore a sword beneath the heavy coat. A serrated, nasty-looking thing with thorn-like sections jutting from the blade's edge. Turning with a flourish, Captain Toras thudded his way across the room and left the Sunken Mermaid.

"Strange," Besmir said, frowning.

"At least we have secured passage across the Wide Green," Zaynorth muttered, sliding the captain's empty mug across towards him.

"Call me odd, but didn't you just tell him to go?" Besmir asked in confusion.

"Sire, you are odd," Zaynorth whispered.

Dipping two fingers into the empty mug, the mage pulled out a small slip of parchment and unfolded it. Besmir looked at the scrawl there but had no idea what it said.

"Sneaky," he muttered. "What does it say?"

"It appears he was not inventing the number of passengers he could take," Zaynorth said, tugging his beard. "This is an inflated price for six."

"So we'll have to find another ship," Besmir said.

"If it were only that easy," Zaynorth said, pursing his lips. "The Pitcriss was not making things up when he mentioned it being difficult to get passage to Gazluth. Many will not sail unless there is profit, and ships are expensive to run. Plus there is the added danger of having your ship seized."

"Seized?" Besmir asked. "Why?"

"Trading opportunities are limited due to the aftermath of the war, and Tiernon is in need of vessels to carry troops and supplies. Any captain willing to sail there is either foolhardy or…"

"Or?" Besmir quizzed.

"Or engaged in piracy," Zaynorth said.

Besmir's mind flashed to the evil sword the captain had worn. Definitely something a pirate would carry.

"How many crew is this ship likely to have?" Besmir wondered.

"Twenty to thirty depending on the size," Herofic rumbled from the other table.

"Against six?" Besmir said. "So there could easily be a nasty accident as soon as we're out at sea?"

Keluse paled at his words, shifting closer to Ranyor unconsciously.

"Possible but unlikely," Zaynorth said. "If we are to leave four people behind as witnesses, even a pirate would be unlikely to risk throwing us over at sea."

"Possible. Unlikely," Besmir muttered.

"I am confident I am able to deflect any unwanted attention, Besmir," Zaynorth said. "If necessary, I can create the illusion we never existed in the captain's mind."

"Magic?" Besmir looked at him uncertainly. "I'm not sure I trust it all that much."

"My brother is more than gifted in the illusory arts," Herofic said, nudging Besmir. "You were sure he was a lizard creature to begin with, after all."

Besmir recalled the moment when Zaynorth had first appeared, searching for him and looking like a horrific reptilian creature as a test. Only someone with Fringor royal blood would have been able to see through the illusion he cast on Besmir's mind, proving he was the rightful heir to the throne of Gazluth.

"What else don't I know?"

"Much," Herofic replied. "Two or three weeks at sea might help with your education, though."

Besmir stared at the rough table.

Two to three weeks?

Anticipation and nervousness rippled through Besmir then. Anticipation at sailing to a new land and nervousness at going to sea for the first time.

Chapter Two

Besmir discovered a number of things aboard the triple-masted schooner, *Dawn Singer*. The Wide Green Sea was more of a dark grey color, pirates were more interested in keeping their ship afloat than murdering them, and he suffered from horrible seasickness.

After six days of near constant vomiting over the side, his stomach ached so badly it felt as if he had been beaten. He felt weaker than a newborn foal and his lips had split, attacked mercilessly by the salt air. Worse still, none of his friends seemed the least bit bothered by the constant rocking.

Keluse appeared happy, dancing up and down the deck without a care. Zaynorth, Herofic, Ranyor and Morcath idled around, sleeping for much of the time and fishing with borrowed lines just as often. Most of them gave Besmir a wide berth, as his temper had worsened by the hour as soon as they had cleared the harbor. Only Captain Toras seemed immune to Besmir's caustic, sarcastic comments, paying him a little attention every so often.

"Ye should feel less sick in the middle of the ship," he said as he stomped past on his way to do something Besmir could not begin to understand.

"I hate this ship," Besmir moaned as he dragged himself level with the main mast. Toras laughed heartily and slapped

Besmir on the shoulder, jolting him forward and sending another wave of nausea rolling through his stomach.

"Ye should be used to the feeling by time we reach Gazluth," the captain said sarcastically.

Besmir groaned.

By the second week at sea, however, his body had gotten used to the constant rocking and he managed to accept the incessant creaking sound that filled his ears from every direction. Besmir stood at the terminus of the bowsprit, hanging on to one of the rigging lines that thrummed as if alive in his hand. Below that, he could just see the back of the figurehead, the Dawn Singer herself, a beautiful woman who supposedly represented the sea goddess, Sharise. Somewhat oddly for a water goddess, the carving had wings with the feathers clearly defined. Besmir mentally shrugged this off and hoped she brought good luck and a quick crossing.

"Besmir," Zaynorth said, approaching. "How are you feeling today?"

"I was lucky enough to be able to drink some water without being violently ill," Besmir said with a tired smile. "A bonus in my opinion."

"Excellent. May I speak with you?"

"It looks like you already are," Besmir joked as he turned back out to sea.

"I wanted to discuss the possibility of you having powers, granted to you with your royal blood," the older man said.

"Like I told you before, I can't do anything like that," Besmir said. "Only..." he glanced up to see a gull soaring overhead.

"Yes?" Zaynorth asked eagerly.

"It didn't occur to me until you said anything, but I can sense animals, where they are and what they're doing," Besmir admitted.

"See?" Zaynorth said with a cry of triumph. "I knew there must be something."

"I fail to see how that's going to be of any help at all."

"Yet it is a beginning point," Zaynorth said. "If your parents had lived, your father would have taught you how to use and develop your magical abilities from an early age."

"Pity they're dead, then," Besmir said shortly.

Zaynorth gasped and stared at the young man with wide eyes and thin lips. He tugged at his beard nervously.

"Your father and I were good friends for many years before he chose to exile himself," Zaynorth said with a trace of anger in his voice. "Do you feel nothing for their loss?"

Besmir shrugged, looking away from his accusatory stare. "Two people I never met?" he asked. "People I don't know die every day, should I feel for them too?"

"Yes, Besmir!" the older man shouted. "It is normal to feel sorry for people who die, whether they were known to you or not. If you cannot, then why did you agree to come with me?"

"Greed," Besmir lied. "You said I was going to be king and I like the idea of that."

"I do not believe you are speaking the truth," Zaynorth said. "And you are the rightful king, but Tiernon is a battlemage with incredible powers, so there is no guarantee you will be able to defeat him."

"A battlemage?" Besmir asked, incredulity stretching his face. "All I can do is tell you there are rats eating the grain in the hold and the ship's cat is about to give birth so she's nesting rather than hunting, and this Tiernon is a battlemage?" Besmir stared into Zaynorth's grey eyes for several heartbeats before pushing him aside. "Where is Toras? I need to get this ship turned around."

Besmir heard the old man following him as he stalked along the deck towards where Captain Toras should be manning the large wheel.

"Take us home," he demanded as he almost jumped up the small flight of stairs leading up to the aft deck.

The first mate stood there, burly and savage, his arms folded, protecting his captain with his bulk. A long, flat-bladed sword hung openly at his side, and Besmir had no doubt he was proficient in its use. He regarded Besmir with the cold eyes of a predator as he approached.

"Little chance of that," Toras said, tapping the first mate on the shoulder and giving him the wheel. "We have crossed the halfway mark and don't have the supplies to go back."

"Fewer supplies than you might imagine," Zaynorth said, telling them of the cat and her lapse in ratting duties.

Toras yelled at his men and a pair of sailors opened the hatch behind the middle mast, dropping below decks to kill the rats.

"So you see, young sir, ye is stuck with us," Toras mumbled through a rotten-toothed grin.

Besmir curled his fists and clamped his mouth shut, jumping back down to the lower deck and storming back to the prow.

"What are the chances I'm just going to die when we get there?" he asked when Zaynorth caught up with him again.

"I will not let that happen," he assured.

"You couldn't save my father, so what makes you think it's going to be any different with me?"

Zaynorth's mouth worked, trying to form the words that would make Besmir understand, make him believe. Yet they would not come, and he watched as Besmir turned away, staring out to sea once more.

"That's what I thought," Besmir said dismissively as Zaynorth left.

***

Keluse looked at Besmir's back rocking with the motion of the ship as it cut through the tops of the waves like a sword. She had been close enough to hear the argument between Besmir and the older Zaynorth the day before, and given both men a wide berth since. Now she approached the man she had come to respect, even love, with fear gnawing at her. Ranyor had explained some of the situation to her, but she had no idea how Besmir felt about it all and was afraid to ask.

The second she approached, Besmir turned, and his smile dissolved all her fears immediately.

"You do know I can't teach you to hunt if you're hiding from me, right?" he asked.

"I know," she said. "It's just... I thought you might want to spend time on your own. To think about things."

"Spending time considering my impending doom is probably not the best idea," Besmir told her. "I need to take my mind off that and do something else."

"Why are you doomed?" Keluse asked.

"Dear old Uncle Tiernon, remember him? Apparently he's some all-powerful wizard who can probably melt my head with a thought," Besmir said bitterly. "But it's all fine because I can tell the cat's just about to have four kittens."

"Kittens?" Keluse said, sidetracked. "Where?"

"In the hold, behind a stack of cloth."

"What did Zaynorth say?" she asked.

"About the kittens? Surprisingly unconcerned," Besmir said, sarcasm lacing his voice.

Keluse looked at him with her head tilted and one hand on her hip, her mouth set in a disapproving line.

"It's fine to be scared," she said. "I'm scared nearly all the time. Of everything."

"It's not even that I'm scared," Besmir replied. "It just feels like a complete waste of time. Uprooting everything I had in Gravistard to travel hundreds of miles and get squashed like a bug as soon as I get there." He kicked his boot against the railing. "Dragging you along..."

"I chose to come," she pointed out. "What did Zaynorth actually say?"

"Just that I'd be able to use the same sort of magic Tiernon can if he hadn't murdered my parents," Besmir said.

Keluse watched Besmir rub at his chest as if he could remove some pain there.

Guilt? Sorrow?

"Have you tried to use it?"

"No idea how," Besmir said with a shake of his head.

"I expect Zaynorth could help," Keluse said quietly. "Would it be worth finding out?"

"Maybe," he said noncommittally.

***

Besmir stared out at the stars as day faded into night, turning events over in his mind. Ever since the strange old man had turned up looking for him his life had been in turmoil. Now Zaynorth expected him to believe he himself had powers that could equal or even best Tiernon.

Maybe Keluse is right. Maybe I should ask Zaynorth about it.

"So, magic then?" Besmir said as he approached Zaynorth the following day.

That got the old man's attention, and he looked up from the book he had produced from somewhere. "What about magic?"

"Well, if I'm going to get turned into a frog or something, I want to be able to at least try and put up some kind of resistance."

"Turned into a frog?" Zaynorth started to laugh. "Is that what you think Tiernon is about to do?" Besmir shrugged. "To begin with, it is unlikely Tiernon will be turning anyone into frogs." He stood, closing his book. "Fire and lightning are more likely, fear spells and illusion."

"Just fire and lightning?" Besmir said. "Is that all?"

"You realize he thinks you dead? Tiernon has no idea you even exist, so no reason to be expecting your arrival."

"For some reason that doesn't make me feel much better."

"Come, let me see what you can already do," Zaynorth said, leading Besmir to one side of the schooner. "So, cats and rats? What else can you sense?"

Besmir concentrated, opening his mind so he could feel the presence of the animals around him. From almost immediately under their feet he could sense the ship's cat, cleaning her four kittens as they nursed from her. In the main hold diagonally to his right, a lone rat nibbled through a sack to get to the grain inside. He described it all to Zaynorth.

"Try to think further out," the old man said. "Down through the hull and into the water. Is there life there?"

Besmir frowned and closed his eyes, gripping the railing tightly as he tried to move his attention from the cat down. Sweat beaded his forehead as he struggled to make himself go through the wooden hull and into the cold waters below. Something stopped him, however, and no matter what he tried, his mind refused to penetrate the wood. Eventually he huffed a breath out and gave up.

"I can't do it," he said, defeated. "It's too hard."

"What is the hardship? Can you explain it?"

"I can see the cat, but when I try and get through the wood into the sea, I'm blocked."

Zaynorth nodded, stroking his beard.

"I would hazard a guess it is your rational mind causing the issue," he said. "Are you able to enter the sea over the side?"

Besmir tried and.found himself suspended in the surface layer of the sea. A few fish swam along beneath the boat's hull surrounding his conscious mind, shoals of fish danced in unison, mindlessly following the one in front as they hunted for food. Larger fish swam in lazy circles around the smaller, hunting and feeding. Smaller things floated around, minute creatures carried on unseen currents, filtering food from the water they lived in.

Something immense and dark drifted past deep beneath the hull, and Besmir's mind shied away from it, scared that something so huge could exist without him knowing it was there.

"Yes," he said, smiling. "Easily."

"It must be your rational mind in that case," Zaynorth observed. "Telling you it is impossible to penetrate the wood."

"But I can see through the decking," Besmir told him.

"Because you *know* you could go there through the hatch. Your mind tells you it is impossible to proceed through the hull, as you would not be able to do so physically. The first thing you need to train your mind to do is realize it has no physical limitations. Your thoughts are able to travel through solid rock if you choose to do so, never forget that," Zaynorth advised. "Now, have you ever been able to affect an animal with your thoughts?" Besmir shook his head. "Are you willing to try?"

Besmir let his thoughts reach out to the rat, approaching it quietly.

Why am I trying to be quiet?

He drifted close, unsure of what to do.

Shall I touch it or can I…

Without knowing how, Besmir flowed *into* the rat, feeling what the rat could feel.. Whiskers twitched with every movement and hunger gnawed at his stomach. Odd sensations rose from behind him and he realized it was the rat's tail as if it grew from his own spine. A squeak erupted from the rat when he laughed. Besmir spent a few minutes exploring the hold, scampering along wooden beams and through holes that had been chewed through planking.

Freeing himself from the rat proved to be more difficult than taking it over. He thrashed and jerked, the rat rolling and squirming as if in pain. Panic gripped Besmir's mind as he fought desperately to free himself of the furry prison he had sentenced himself to.

Think, man!

Calming his thoughts, Besmir tried to recall what the old man had told him.

Forget the physical and let your mind be free.

An odd sensation of disconnect flowed over his mind as he drifted up out of the rat, watching it scamper off in fright. Existing as thought alone, he drifted back up through the decking to see Zaynorth shaking his body.

"By the gods, man, wake!" Zaynorth yelled as he shook Besmir again.

"I'm awake. I'm here," Besmir said, turning to see Zaynorth's worried face.

"What happened?" he demanded. "You were like a statue."

"I...somehow I managed to take over the rat." Besmir tried to explain what had happened, but the expression on Zaynorth's face was complete puzzlement.

"I suggest you do not do that again," Zaynorth said, still ruffled by what had happened. "At least until we can figure out how to get you back."

"Something like that must have happened to you, though," Besmir said.

"Illusion mage," Zaynorth said shortly. "The strangest thing that ever happened to me was having an illusion fail." The old man thought for a second. "Can you feel people in the same way as animals?"

"No, it's different with people," Besmir said. "I can feel them all the time. I have to search out animals.

"I wonder if it is related to size?" Zaynorth mused. "With people being much larger than most animals. Can you affect people as you can animals?"

Besmir shrugged.

"I don't know," he admitted. "But I didn't know I could affect animals until today."

Besmir looked up, high in the rigging, balanced among the ropes, masts and cross -pieces, sat one of the sailors, idly carving something from a small piece of driftwood. Besmir concentrated, freeing his mind and floating up towards where the sailor reclined. He flicked his thoughts at the man's arm, knocking it. The sailor jumped, dropping his infant carving to the deck twenty feet below. He pulled his mind back, darting back into his body as a commotion erupted.

"Who be throwing bits of wood?" the captain roared, rubbing his head as he searched the sails aloft.

Besmir grinned at Zaynorth's confused expression.

Chapter Three

"Land ho!" one of the sailors bellowed from aloft.

Besmir raced over to the port rail, searching the horizon for anything that might be his apparent homeland. Eventually he noticed a darker smudge through the morning mist and his heart leaped to see land.

Finally I can see Gazluth for the first time.

Captain Toras started bellowing orders, bringing the ship to life around him. Men appeared from bolt holes and hiding spaces, jumping to tackle the first task they could find. Besmir waited impatiently as the smudge darkened with infuriating slowness, features eventually growing along the coast.

Forests sprouted above the rocky shoreline, verdant and lush and teeming with life. Dotted at various points, he could make out lone buildings that eventually gathered into towns. Toras turned the *Dawn Singer* to run parallel with the shore, demonstrating just how fast the boat cut through the water.

"Best ye leave any talking to me," Toras growled from behind him.

Besmir turned to see a much larger ship had approached them, unnoticed by him as he studied the shore. At around thirty feet away, Besmir could see the new vessel towered above the *Dawn Singer*, the main deck at least five feet higher. She was longer, wider and carried far more men. Her red sails struck a chord of doom in Besmir's heart as he read the name *Imperius* on her bow.

Besmir's companions joined him as he watched to see what was happening. He saw Herofic had taken the time to don his plate armor, his immense battle axe strapped to his back. His eyes flicked to the little storage area where his bow and quiver of arrows lay.

"Leave it for now," Zaynorth grumbled from his side. "Let us see what unfolds first."

Besmir nodded slowly, keeping an eye on the huge ship. Strange looking men lined the railing as it grew ever closer, and something gnawed at Besmir's stomach as he watched.

"Lower sail and prepare to be boarded!" a clear voice reached from the large ship. "By order of His Majesty Tiernon Fringor!"

"Here we go," Toras grunted. "*Imperius!*" he bellowed. "The *Dawn Singer* is on official business for King Portala Moncarthy of Gravistard and cannot be accosted."

"You are a long way from home, *Dawn Singer*, and in these waters King Tiernon decides who is accosted and who is left alone."

"Then we'll have to wait until His Majesty arrives!" Toras bellowed in return.

"I speak with His Majesty's voice," drifted across the dwindling space. "Drop sail and prepare to be boarded."

Imperius remained abreast of *Dawn Singer*, the schooner slowing as ordered.

"How likely are we to get out of this?" Besmir asked.

Toras looked at him, his leathery face shifting into an expression of unease.

"Can ye swim, lad?" he asked. "Likely we'll all be put over the side."

"Not I," Herofic mumbled, reaching back to loosen the ax.

Besmir shuddered when he thought of Herofic being dragged to the bottom, struggling in his cocoon of metal. His own leather clothing would be difficult enough, and he glanced at the shore again to gauge how far it might be.

Never going to make it.

"I can't swim," Keluse whispered nervously from beside him.

Besmir grabbed her hand, squeezing gently to reassure her. "Something else I've got to teach you?" he said in a playful voice.

Keluse smiled weakly, glancing over at the massive ship at the same time as the two vessels met with a hollow *thump*. She jumped and stepped closer to Besmir as a long plank was lowered to the *Dawn Singer*'s deck and several heavily armed men stumped down it, taking up positions at the end. Once a defensive wall had been set up, Besmir watched another man descend the plank. Dressed in a dark blue and maroon uniform adorned with silver trim, he had an unusual hat atop his curled hair. Although effeminate in appearance, he also wore a sword at one hip and looked to have the physique to wield it.

"Captain?" he asked.

"Toras."

"Rear Admiral Whermod, Gazluth Navy. Have you your seal and paperwork?"

"To be sure," Toras said, reaching into his heavy coat.

Whermod gestured to one of his men, who trotted obediently across, took them and returned. The rear admiral made a show of examining the written papers before approaching Toras, surrounded by his men.

"Captain," he began. "I believe these to be forgeries." He fixed the other man with a determined stare as he waved the paperwork before his face.

"Then ye are mistaken," Toras growled. "Send word to King Portala, he will verify their authenticity."

"Oh, I shall," Whermod said in a falsely obsequious voice. "In the interim, I shall have to insist your vessel is impounded and thoroughly searched. My crew will come aboard to secure your compliance." He began to turn.

"That I cannot allow, Rear Admiral," Toras said, completely unshaken by the other man's words.

Whermod snapped back round, white-faced and pale-lipped, shaking with rage. His guards loosened their weapons as tension flooded both ships. Hopelessly outnumbered, the crew of the *Dawn Singer* gathered behind their captain as Rear Admiral Whermod spat his words through clenched teeth.

"You are in Gazluthian waters and have been issued a royal order by a ranking member of the navy, Captain. You will obey my order or face the consequences. Now prepare to be boarded and escorted to Port Vartula, where your vessel will be searched and your crew kept aboard."

Silence settled over both ships as Toras considered the Rear Admiral's words. Scores of bows had been drawn on *Imperius*'s deck, and he scanned them with a keen eye. Everyone there knew the archers could shred the *Dawn Singer*'s crew in a few heartbeats if given the order.

Besmir swallowed and felt the crush of defeat before he had even set foot on Gazluthian soil when Zaynorth stepped forward.

"I do apologize, Rear Admiral," he said politely. "However, I believe your ship to be aflame."

"What insanity is this?" Whermod demanded, spinning to look back.

A croak of horror escaped his lips when he saw the flames licking greedily up the masts, along the ratlines and bursting out across the sails. He sprinted for his ship, bellowing commands to his men, who started milling about like confused chickens.

Besmir squinted at the *Imperius* as she rocked gently in the swell, untouched by the fire her crew was valiantly trying to extinguish. Buckets were drawn and thrown at the fire which refused to go out, as Zaynorth had conjured it in the minds of them all. Sweat broke out across his brow with the effort of beguiling so many minds.

"Time to leave, Captain," he said through clenched teeth.

Toras needed no second prompting and dashed about, howling orders and extorting his men to unfurl the sails. Besmir dashed over to the gangplank and started to heave it over the side, his burden lightening as Ranyor and Keluse joined him. Herofic and Morcath were happily slashing at the lines holding both ships together, securing their release.

As *Dawn Singer* pulled away from *Imperius*, Besmir heard the crew's groans of misery change to roars of anger as the flames faded from their minds. He turned to see Zaynorth slumped against the railing, a hand pressed against his head where one of the ropes under tension had lashed at him when cut. .

"Pile on every scrap of sail ye can!" Toras screamed. "Hold out yer shirts to the wind if it helps!"

The *Dawn Singer* leaped forward as soon as her crew secured the lines holding the sails in the optimum configuration. Besmir heard a thunderous clap as the mass of sails bellied out, catching the wind and propelling the ship forward away from *Imperius*.

"Might be lucky enough to outrun them," Toras said as he studied Zaynorth's prone form. "What did ye do?" he asked. "I was not seeing any fire."

"Just a little trick I learned a long time ago," the old mage said breathlessly.

Besmir offered his hand, helping the other man to his unsteady feet.

"Ye's a mage, then," Toras observed.

"Sometimes," Zaynorth said. "Will we outrun them?" he asked.

Captain Toras looked above him then into the water, considering their speed.

"*Dawn Singer* be one of the fastest ships afloat," he said with pride. "And that *Imperius* be a bulky great tub. But she got something the *Singer* does not."

"What's that?" Besmir asked.

"Slave rowers below decks. Did ye not see the ports along her side, ready for oars to be lowered?"

Besmir shook his head. Chill shock clutched his chest at the captain's words. "He uses slaves?" he asked, subdued.

"Aye, that he does," Toras grunted. "Prisoners taken in the war. His own citizens Tiernon uses."

Besmir looked from Zaynorth to Herofic and Ranyor, turning back to the old mage again. They all nodded slowly, confirming Toras's words. Hollow sickness grew in Besmir's chest, similar to his seasickness but subtly different.

***

The coast of Gazluth slipped past his unseeing eyes as *Dawn Singer* tried to outrun the *Imperius*. Besmir could smell the heady mix of pine forest and salt water that tantalized his nose, but it meant nothing. The cry of gulls reached his ears, but his brain refused to register their presence. The men around him muttered in low tones while the sailors yelled to each other and sang shanties entreating Sharise to afford them more speed.

Besmir shut it all out. His mind rolled over the same point: Tiernon condoned the use of slaves. That felt bad enough, but for Tiernon to sanction the use of his *own* people set a fire in Besmir's belly, unquenchable and fierce.

"What kind of man is he, to do that?" he asked no one in particular. "A king is supposed to protect his people, not use them as slaves."

"Exactly why we spent years searching for you," Herofic said quietly.

"Tiernon was always seduced by the lure of power, but your father's abilities and skills always outshone his," Zaynorth said. "Not until he married and sired an heir did his brother have any kind of power over him."

Besmir heard the sadness ringing in the old man's tone and wondered how close Zaynorth had really been to his father. Something inside Besmir grew a little at that point. A hardening of his resolve to help those who suffered at Tiernon's hand.

"Sail!"

The cry from aloft made heads turn to see who had called, turning again to look in the direction he pointed. At first Besmir could see nothing save for grey-green rolling waves, a few isolated sea birds bobbing around, diving for fish, and the occasional floating tree. Tense minutes passed as he scanned the horizon along with his companions and he started to believe the lookout had been mistaken or seen a different vessel. Dismay crawled through his chest when the mass of red sails resolved in his vision, revealing the *Imperius* was, in fact, gaining on them.

Captain Toras stomped across to where they had all huddled at the aft rail to watch the immense warship grow ever closer. He looked at the ship and then at Zaynorth.

"If ye have any ideas, mage, I'll be more than happy to hear 'em."

"Were those papers forged?" Besmir asked when his friend shrugged without speaking.

Toras stared at him as if he was simple, his eyes wide and yellow teeth revealed in a savage grimace.

"Of course they were fake, boy," he growled. "Where would the likes of I be getting hold of a royal letter of marque?" The grizzled captain stared at Besmir for a few heartbeats before adding, "If ye have no more simple questions for me, I have me ship to save."

With a final glance back at the ever-growing *Imperius*, Captain Toras strode away to scream orders at his men. Besmir felt heat flaming in his cheeks as he faced his friends, but the feeling soon drained when he saw the warship had sprouted a bristle of oars that dipped into the water in unison over and over. Carried on the breeze, they could all hear the crack of a whip and the screams of men whose entire lives had become a living hell. In Besmir's mind, a desperate plan began to form.

***

Zaynorth watched Rear Admiral Whermod standing calmly as the *Imperius* bore down on the schooner. He cast his eye proudly over her crew as they toiled silently to catch the smaller ship. Every piece of equipment was in its rightful place, properly maintained and functional.The triple-masted ship was almost in range, and he turned to his right.

"Arm the forward ballistae, Captain," Zaynorth heard clearly."Admiral." Captain Serwall addressed him formally. "The slaves are tiring."

"Replace them, Captain," he said, turning a disapproving glance on his subordinate.

"We have, sir. They have been beaten until they drop, then replaced with others. Now we have no more to replace them with." The captain tried to hide his terror.

"Then I suggest you find a way to get more from them, Captain," Whermod told him in a friendly voice. "Unless you wish to man an oar yourself, that is."

Serwall paled and turned to his first officer barking orders to have the slaves replaced with fresh sailors from his crew.

Imperius jumped forward with every stroke of her oars, closing on the *Dawn Singer* inexorably, sending ripples of nervous anticipation through his belly. At twenty feet, when he was able to see the whites of the terrified eyes aboard the schooner, Whermod gave the order.

"Wind forward ballistae."

Zaynorth watched in horror as the cranking of gears and creaking of stressed wood reached his ears. The world went abruptly silent and Whermod prepared to give the order to fire, smashing and shredding *Dawn Singer*'s sails, when the sea between the two ships bellied up.

Gallons of water formed a dome slowly rising from the sea. At four feet above the water's surface it broke, sluicing off the head of a creature from a nightmare. Ice-cold panic rooted Zaynorth to the deck as he watched the thing grow ever larger. The *Imperius* gave a massive jolt, knocking Whermod and his men to the deck. Some of those aloft lost grip, their screams cut short when they smashed into the decking. Whermod hauled himself up, staring in horror as the thing's head hovered into view.

Eyes the size of cart wheels stared mercilessly down at the fleeing, panicking men and a mouth that could easily hold a building opened to reveal a razor-edged tongue and teeth the size of horse heads. Zaynorth could see down the creature's throat, its huge muscles easily capable of crushing a man flat. An appendage exploded from the sea, dark red and multi-jointed, slamming to the deck and splintering the wood like kindling. Muscles as thick as a man bunched, gripping hold of the *Imperius* as the monster tried to haul itself aboard. The warship gave a sickening lurch as the hull shattered under the weight of the creature and terrified screams echoed up from the oar deck as water and monster invaded the ship.

"Hold!" Whermod bellowed. "Hold there! It is nothing but illusion as with the fire!" Zaynorth watched as a few of the men around him paused, turning towards Whermod in comprehension.

Savage grins spread over their faces as the realization sank in. They turned at his order and ran along the shattered decking towards the ballistae. Zaynorth could see the look of satisfaction on Whermod's face as he watched his men. They would fire the bolts, and the chains holding them together would cut through the masts and rigging with ease.

"Fire!" Whermod bellowed.

Multiple twangs split the air as the ballistae fired simultaneously. Zaynorth watched as the bolts shot forward, chain stretched between them. His eyes cut back to Whermod again watching his expression as his rational mind refused to believe what happened then. Rather than sailing through the illusion, the chain bit into the creature's face, wrapping round it, the pointed iron bolts digging into the red and purple flesh. Its bellow of rage-fueled pain slammed into Zaynorth's ears like a hammer, dizzying and felling him again. Further limbs exploded from the sea, some wrapping round *Imperius* while others flapped at the chain, freeing it from its head.

Sailors scrambled away from the thrashing beast as it tightened its grip on the warship, throwing themselves into the cold sea rather than be eaten. Horrible, final, explosive booms resounded as the ship gave way, timbers splitting and splintering as sections arced high into the air. The main deck tilted to such an angle that men and cargo tumbled towards the beast's gaping maw. Sections of the rigging and masts leaned slowly, groaning as the damp wood snapped under the weight before smashing down into the sea. Another multi-jointed arm erupted from the sea, wrapping around the broken stump of a mast and dragging the ship inexorably down.

Below decks men scrambled to escape as the pressure grew, stabbing painfully against their eardrums as the holds flooded. Confused and scared beyond belief they clawed at each other in their desperate need to escape the rising water. Barrels and crates tumbled from where they had been stowed, slamming into the men and knocking them into the roiling waters.

Zaynorth watched Whermod grab onto the main mast, looking down into the blood-red gate to hell. Captain Serwall had managed to grasp one of the massive teeth, desperately trying to halt his impending doom. Zaynorth watched in fascinated horror as another of his crew fell from the deck, grabbing Serwall as he passed and dragging both men screaming to their doom. Darkness crowded in at the edges of Zaynorth's vision as he watched both men disappear in a red spray, the sea monster's peristalsis crushing them.

Whermod snapped back to full alertness when he found himself tipping towards the mouth, fear making his fingers clamp tight to the wood. An explosion of air blew out from *Imperius*'s below decks as another compartment gave way under the immense pressure the creature exerted. Zaynorth could see bodies and pieces of bodies floating up in the boiling sea before being swept back down in the current.

Whermod's final breath was snatched away as the mast beneath his feet jolted sideways, throwing him into the sea. Something massive and hard smashed into his skull with a sickening *crunch* even Zaynorth could hear. Blood covered his face as he drifted into the deeps.

Chapter Four

The crew of the *Dawn Singer* stared in horror at the monster that was systematically destroying the *Imperius*. Limbs and muscles wrapped round what was left of the ship, dragging it down as it sank back into the water. Dark red flowed up from the horrible wound the chain had inflicted, but it had not stopped the creature from demolishing the larger ship completely. Barrels and crates floated on the surface along with hundreds of dead, their pale faces fixed with expressions of horrified fear.

A few survivors had managed to scramble into the longboat and were already rowing away as fast as they could . One of the red sails billowed to the surface like a ghost beneath the waves before sinking once more.

"Raise cloth!" Toras screamed, slapping and kicking at his stunned crew. "By the nose of Sharise get us out of here!"

Dawn Singer lurched as her sails caught the breeze and Toras threw himself at the wheel.

"By the gods, man!" Toras shouted to Zaynorth in a voice that trembled. "What did ye do?"

"Not I," Zaynorth said, pale with horror. He cast about, searching for clues.

"Besmir!" he cried, noting the younger man's vice grip on the rail, his closed eyes and rigid stance.

Zaynorth, Keluse and the others crowded round Besmir, touching and shaking him without response, shouting in his ear to try and wake him up. Herofic pried his fingers from the wood, gasping at the deep gouges Besmir had made from gripping so tightly.

"What ails the lad?" Toras asked. "Be he petrified through fear?"

"I do not believe so," Zaynorth said with worry in his voice. "Let us get him below decks and warm him up."

***

Besmir felt himself drift through the depths. Searing agony throbbed through the creature's head, pain such as it had never felt before, but it would feed once at the bottom, filling its belly with meat from the floating wooden box. Besmir thrashed vainly at his prison of flesh, struggling to free himself of the primitive beast he had taken over.. Besmir could tell the creature would hide, feast and heal before venturing out again. It had never occurred to it to crack open the floating boxes and feast on the meat inside, but they proved tasty, although the pain had been great..

Home. Familiar rock formations cradled the creature's massive body and held the wooden box down as it threatened to escape in the current. Besmir felt the creature work its limbs inside the remains of the ship, ripping at the wood until it opened, giving it access to the feast inside. Besmir felt something soft and grabbed the morsel, dragging it towards his mouth with anticipation.

Stop! This is wrong.

That was an odd thought. Why would eating meat be wrong? Bones crunched as the creature tipped the morsel in his mouth and swallowed. Another. Then more. Trapped within, Besmir screamed and screamed.

***

Besmir screamed, jerking up straight and clawing at his mouth as he tried to clean the feeling of men from inside there. His fingers encountered nothing and he stared about, trying to comprehend what was happening to him.

A young woman stared at him in shock.

Keluse. She's called Keluse.

Fine, blonde hair cascaded round her shoulders, falling over her chest and flowing down her back. Besmir concentrated on his feelings where she was concerned: companionship, love?

Is she my wife? My sister?

"Besmir?" Keluse asked in a half-whisper.

"I think so," he said, frowning. "Am I?"

"Don't you know?" Keluse narrowed her eyes, frowning. "What happened Besmir?" she asked. "What can you remember?"

Thoughts tumbled around like flotsam in a stream, confusing Besmir. Sometimes he was a man, hunting and sailing, while other times he was something else. A massive sea beast that lived at the bottom of the ocean and ate...

Besmir retched when he recalled what had happened.

"By the gods, Keluse, how long have I been here?"

"Four days," she replied solemnly, unable to meet his eyes.

"What? How can that be?" he asked, unable to understand how he had been trapped in the sea creature for four days.

It felt as if he had used the beast to sink the ship before drifting back to its lair then started to feast. Almost as soon as horror had overtaken his mind, Besmir had woken up here.

"Where are we?"

"In the hold aboard the Dawn Singer," Keluse replied. "What happened? Zaynorth said you...somehow called that thing."

"It was worse than that, Keluse. Far, far worse."

Something in his voice, or the way he looked made Keluse worry, and she rose, telling him she would be back with the old man before long. Besmir lay back on the makeshift bed of sacks and straw, trying desperately to wipe the feeling of devouring humans from his mind.

"Besmir?" Zaynorth shook him gently awake. "Sire? Are you well?"

Besmir sat up, wiping his eyes.

"I was trapped," he said. "Inside that creature as it...it..." He huffed a breath out and Zaynorth laid a hand on his shoulder, squeezing gently.

"Please, please do not *ever* do anything like that again, at least until we understand how to get you back safely." the old man begged. "We have no idea what melding with such an alien creature might do to you."

"I've got no problem with that," Besmir said. "None at all. Where are we?" he asked, just then realizing the constant creak of masts and rigging was suspiciously absent.

"Moored in the harbor of Port Vartula on the southeast coast of Gazluth. My brother has ventured out to secure mounts and what provisions he can purchase."

"Are we safe here?" Besmir asked nervously.

"Captain Toras dropped anchor in a sheltered cove and changed the ship's name to *Whistling Mermaid*, altered the rigging and swapped the sails. I fear he may be a pirate after all, but I think we are safe." Zaynorth watched Besmir nod. "Are you able to travel?"

"Yes," Besmir said. "I'm fine. Now."

***

"Ye be departing then?" Toras growled when he saw Besmir, Zaynorth and Keluse climbing from the hold.

"Yes, Captain," Besmir said. "Thank you for getting us here."

Toras reached out and guided Besmir aside, leaning in close to murmur in his ear.

"I be wondering if it is I who should be offering ye thanks," the captain said, flicking his eyes to the water and back to

Besmir. "Some think I just be an old pirate." He tapped the side of his head. "But I be thinking you be something special. Look up the *Whistling Mermaid* if ye be needing a reliable ship." He grinned. "Or be wishing to adopt a kitten."

With that, Captain Toras gripped his hand, shaking it firmly before stomping off along the decking. Besmir watched him go, wondering what the old pirate had managed to overhear of their conversations and if he had been eavesdropping. Deciding he would never know, Besmir trotted down the gangplank, leaving the *Whistling Mermaid* to set his first foot on Gazluth.

***

King Tiernon Fringor looked at the man kneeling before him with a mixture of distaste and ridicule. Fleet Admiral Sharova was a small man, compact and short but a powerhouse nonetheless. This story he had brought before the throne, however, made Tiernon smile as well as inciting rage within him.

Is he attempting to make me look foolish? Why would he risk it knowing I would likely have his head?

"Tell me, Sharova," Tiernon said in a deceptively calm voice. "Do you actually expect me to believe my flagship was dragged to the bottom by a *Torasner*?"

Sharova looked up into his king's eyes with utter fright carved into his features. Tiernon re-evaluated what he was being told as soon as he saw it.

"Yes, Your Majesty. According to the survivors, it was some kind of massive thing with numerous limbs that grabbed the *Imperious* and sank it with almost all hands aboard." The fleet admiral's voice shook as he made the report.

Tiernon stood, pulling his ermine-trimmed red and purple robes around him.

"Join me in my chambers," he ordered. "I would hear this tale in private."

The king stroked his gaze around the room, looking for any sign of a challenge from the assembled nobles and visiting ambassadors.. Not one of them even had the courage to meet his eyes, and he sneered as he stepped down from the dais, letting his guard form up around him.

Throughout the palace, servants and other lowly creatures darted into side passages as he approached, hiding from his potential, unpredictable rage. Statues of his ancestors watched him pass with sightless, marble eyes until he reached the far end and looked with pleasure at the gaping hole where his brother's likeness once stood. Tiernon had allowed the plinth to stay but blasted the rest of the figurine through the granite wall when he had left.

"This is probably one of the most satisfying spots in the entire palace, Sharova," he said, pausing at the empty alcove.

"Yes, sire," the other man said in a defeated voice, stumbling when one of Tiernon's guards shoved him along after the king.

Once inside his quarters, surrounded by expensive luxuries and priceless artworks, Tiernon shrugged off his heavy robes and threw himself into a comfortable seat, hanging one leg over the arm. Sharova glanced around, his face going pale as he looked at the terrified faces of the women caged around him. Tiernon snapped his fingers and a young girl appeared, a gold-jeweled goblet in her hand. Although she had been pretty once, the way her jaw hung open, drool freely running down her face, changed her appearance into a gruesome parody of beauty. Vacant, empty eyes stared from her head without seeing anything, and Sharova stared at the poor thing.

"Like my pet?" Tiernon asked as the girl squatted beside his chair like a faithful hound.

"Yes, sire," Sharova said,swallowing hard..

Tiernon regarded him with cold, unfeeling eyes, the minutes drawing out until the naval man thought he was sure to die.

"So, Admiral," the king said eventually. "Tell me again of this sea beast."

Sharova swallowed hard before relating the story he had heard from eight men, collating all the stories into one account. Once finished, he waited for Tiernon to pass judgment. The king sat, staring at the wall while the mindless girl beside him urinated on the floor as if unaware she had company or was in the king's chambers.

"How many aboard?" Tiernon asked.

"One hundred and seventy souls, sire."

"How many survived?"

"Eight, Majesty."

"Have them brought here," Tiernon said. "Their families as well."

"Their families, Majesty?"

"Oh, yes," the king said absently. "Nothing makes a man more likely to speak the truth than sawing off his wife's fingers. I will discover what really happened to the *Imperius* and I will punish all those who have lied to me."

Sharova swallowed

"By the way, how are the slaves I generously provided working out?" King Tiernon pinned the other man with his insane glare.

"Excellent, Majesty, they have proved their worth in capturing further vessels to swell your navy. However, some of your lower-ranking officers have seen fit to work them until death, so we are running low on stocks." Sharova spread his hands apologetically, noting how they trembled.

Tiernon scratched the head of the girl squatting beside his chair and drained his goblet, handing it back to the pathetic creature that had once been someone's daughter. Sharova watched as she trotted obediently off, his mind trying not to consider what had been done to make her that way.

"It is your responsibility, Fleet Admiral, to ensure the assets I have granted are well looked after. I do not possess an endless supply of fresh slaves yet."

"Of course, sire," Sharova answered. "I shall see to it those officers are punished." It took a few seconds before Tiernon's words registered. "Yet, Your Majesty?"

The king grinned, a savage and cunning smile that sent spears of ice into Sharova's belly.

"Yes, Sharova, yet. I have plans in place to ensure enough bodies to swell the army ranks as well as provide more slaves to row the fleet." Tiernon looked incredibly happy with himself.

"Are we to go to war then, sire?" Sharova asked in confusion.

Tiernon shot forward, leaning in close to the other man, who only just managed to halt his natural reaction to flinch back. Sour, rotten breath puffed over his face, and Sharova gagged. Tiernon, unknowing or uncaring, carried on speaking, excitement making his breath puff out in little waves. Iron fingers grabbed Sharova's shoulders, squeezing hard as Tiernon explained his plan.

"No war, Sharova, not yet anyway, no. Breeding." Tiernon's mad eyes searched Sharova's to see if he understood.

"Breeding....people?"

"Exactly!" Tiernon shouted, snapping to attention. "Exactly." The king threw one arm out towards the caged women, who flinched as far back as they could. "Some of these will give birth to my new soldiers," Tiernon exclaimed, bringing groans and whimpers from the cages. "I will personally sire the first generation and they will sire further troops in the space of thirty years I will have hundreds, thousands, of trained men ready to do my bidding."

Sharova swallowed again, pure fright clawing at his insides as if a hellcat were trying to escape. Such a plan had to come from a broken, insane mind. Not only to consider breeding humans, but to use his *own* children?

Pack and leave. Run to another country and become a farmer.

Sharova's mind began planning his escape from this living hell until his eyes raked over the desperate faces of the caged women. Dressed in little more than rags, beaten and starved, some barely out of childhood, they stared at him with pleading faces.

What if it were my sister? My niece?

These had been proud Gazluthian women once. *His* people.

How can I leave them to face this future?

"What say you?" Tiernon asked, drawing his attention away from the women.

"Sire?" Sharova asked, confused,

"Do you like my plan?"

Revulsion rolled through Sharova at the very thought, but he managed to fix a placid mask over his features, smiling sickly at his king.

"Of course, Your Majesty," he forced himself to say. "It is an excellent idea."

Sharova found himself considering various poisons.

Chapter Five

Besmir saw a similar mix of cultures and people in Gazluth to those of the land he had left. The differences, however, were numerous and stark. People here were quiet as they bustled from place to place, heads bowed so their eyes did not meet the gaze of any other. Hooded cloaks covered at least half of the people in the streets, and tension made the air thick. Besmir could feel the oppression clamping down on him with every footstep he took into Port Vartula. Glancing over, he saw the same expression of distaste on Keluse's face that he could feel on his own.

Gravistard had been vibrant, colorful and loud, but the image and atmosphere Gazluth presented was one of depression. Of the buildings that were actually in use, few were well maintained, and many of the abandoned ones had been destroyed by fire. Piles of blackened timber and wet ash spilled into the streets, left to the elements. Horror slapped Besmir when he saw ribs – obviously human – partially buried in one of the gaps.

"Why haven't they been buried?" he demanded.

Zaynorth looked over, his own face a mask of rage.

"It would appear things have changed since I left my homeland."

Besmir looked at the set of the mage's jaw, tense beneath his beard, the deep lines furrowed at the apex of his nose and how stiffly he walked.

"This manner of sacrilege would have never been endured before," he grunted. "This is an affront to Mraginar," Zaynorth spat, invoking the goddess of love and family. "I cannot believe things have devolved so far."

Zaynorth led them through the vile streets from the somewhat civilized waterfront into the darker backstreets. Citizens here were even more secretive, shutting doors and ducking into alleyways as soon as the small company approached. As they came to what had once been a busy market, now abandoned, stall frames broken and canvas flapping in the breeze, a group of armed men filtered in from the far side. Besmir saw they wore uniforms which, although unkempt and dirty, identified them as soldiers of the watch, and he breathed a sigh of relief.

"Hold!" the obvious leader ordered. "Prepare to be searched."

"On what authority?" Zaynorth demanded rudely.

The one who had spoken stepped over to Zaynorth, hand on the hilt of his sword, as his men loosened their own weapons. Besmir and Ranyor stepped closer to each other, in front of Keluse. Besmir laid his fingers on the hilt of his hunting knife, the only weapon he had apart from the bow which would be useless at such close range.

"Captain Lefruse," the soldier said. Someone had snapped his nose at one point. Poorly set, it pointed off to his left as his red-rimmed eyes locked onto Zaynorth. "And on *my* authority. What have you got to pay for passage?"

Besmir could feel Keluse shaking beside him, her fear obvious. Determination hardened in his chest as he stared at Lefruse. There was no way he was about to let these men intimidate her.

"Since when did the city watch demand payment for passage?" Zaynorth asked.

"Since I decided so and since no one cares if a few strangers go missing," Lefruse said with a dismissive gesture. "So I will have a look through those packs and relieve you of some valuables, or my men will be forced to relieve you of your lives."

Besmir tensed, a ball of hot acid growing in his chest at the threat. Zaynorth laid a gentle hand on his arm when he noticed. Lefruse saw the gesture and grinned, revealing blackened teeth as he turned to Besmir.

"Fancy yourself, do you, boy?" he growled.

"Against a drunken waste like you?" Besmir spat. "There's no competition." Ranyor tutted beside him as Lefruse's grin faded.

"As you wish," the captain said. "You have chosen death and I am more than happy to oblige."

He stepped back, dragging his sword from its scabbard awkwardly, and Besmir smiled. Years of brawling with the other orphans, fighting off more than one assailant at a time, had hardened Besmir's muscles, and further years of hunting had kept him lean and fast. He snapped forward, grabbing Lefruse's wrist and twisting it savagely. The captain yelped as his fingers jerked open, dropping the poorly maintained sword with a clatter. His eyes widened when he felt the kiss of cold steel against his neck, and they could all see the muscles in his throat working as he swallowed.

"Call off your dogs," Besmir growled into the other man's face. "Or draw your last breath."

He kept hold of Lefruse's wrist, squeezing and twisting it so the bones ground against each other painfully until beads of sweat formed on the soldier's forehead.

Around them, Lefruse's six men finally reacted, pulling out swords and springing clumsily into action as Ranyor pulled his own sword to meet them. Two fell back within the first few seconds, clutching the bloodied faces the warrior slammed his fist into. The remaining four slowed, their eyes flicking between Ranyor and their two companions, one of whom spat a tooth onto the street.

"Wait! Wait!" Lefruse cried in a panic as Besmir lifted his blade, forcing his lead back and drawing a single drop of blood.

"I want to speak to your commanding officer," Besmir said, staring hard into Lefruse's eyes.

"I-I have no superior," he said. "We found these uniforms and saw an opportunity. Please, let me go."

Disgust filled Besmir at his admission, and he threw Lefruse to the ground in disgust. Kicking him savagely once he was down, Besmir shouted at them all.

"You're the lowest sort of scum in this forsaken hole. Preying on the weak and hopeless, using watch uniforms to accost people rather than working to earn an honest living." He stared down at Lefruse in disgust.

"Work?" one of the other men said. "What work? I have not been able to feed my family properly since the war. I do not know what life is like where you hail from, but it is filled with starvation and misery here." He sheathed his sword again, turning away in disgust.

"Where is the real watch?" Besmir asked.

"Them? They left as soon as King Tiernon stopped paying them. A few stayed just in case the gold started flowing again. Eventually the final few had had enough and left along with the rest," Lefruse said. "We broke into the guardhouse and took these uniforms, what else are we supposed to do? I have three daughters to feed." The defeated man looked down.

"There's no law enforcement in the town?" Besmir asked.

"None," the other man said.

"So…don't you think it might have been a good idea to start your own?" Besmir asked. "Instead of fleecing weak travelers, you could have called a meeting, gathered some of the local business owners and asked if they wanted to fund a local police force?"

The seven men looked at each other, embarrassed at not even considering the plan.

"With just us few?" Lefruse asked. "There were hundreds in the watch before."

"Maybe so. However, even a small force would have been able to secure the harbor and waterfront. I'd wager men would join you once they saw you making a difference. Then further people and businesses would begin to pay for the service you provide."

"But the king stopped all pay to the watch, what would make it any different for us?"

Besmir looked at the man, unable to understand how someone so simple could even have sired children. Slowly, as if talking to a child, he explained, "The local businesses would pay *you* directly, Lefruse. As long as you were all honest and true to each other, there would always be pay."

Lefruse scratched his broken nose, considering Besmir's words as if they were a revelation.

"What do you think, boys?" he asked. "Could we make a go of it?"

The men looked at each other, as if unsure of their own abilities, kicking their feet and muttering incoherently.

"Gods, men!" Besmir thundered. "Have you no self-respect? Do you enjoy petty thievery, or would it be better to earn an honest living by carrying out a job your children can be proud of you for?" He shook his head, stalking back and forth before them as he had when choosing Keluse as apprentice. "Just go before I decide to beat you as an example."

Besmir turned his back on the men, giving them a perfect opportunity to attack. None did. With slumped shoulders and attitudes of defeat, the seven men slunk off back to wherever they had been hiding.

"What are you grinning at?" Besmir demanded as the small group started up the hill that led from the port town.

"Your speech and manner with those men reminded me of someone I once knew," Zaynorth told him. "Your father."

***

Zaynorth led them to an inn situated at a crossroads a few miles outside Port Vartula. A light, misty rain had soaked them all as they walked the last mile. A chilly breeze whipped wraiths in the mist and sent snakes of shadow wriggling off through the grass. The squat wood-built inn was nestled back in a grove of ancient oak trees, providing shelter and building materials. Single-story and thatched, a curl of smoke crept from the stone chimney only to be whipped away by the wind. With dusk approaching, both Besmir and Keluse felt pulled toward the warm sanctuary offered by the inn. A golden glow shone from within, and it was as if they could feel the heat from the fire sure to be blazing in the hearth.

Herofic met them inside, and Besmir found he was smiling at being reunited with the stocky fighter.

"Welcome to the Hrolmarch Inn and Tavern," he said, spreading his arms. "Come and warm yourself by the fire. I managed to buy us a horse each, but pickings are slim." Herofic turned to his brother. "Did you see the state of Port Vartula?"

"We did," Zaynorth replied sadly. "I fear the state of the kingdom is far worse than we expected it to be. We were accosted in the open, in plain view of anyone who happened by."

"Are you all well?" Herofic asked with real concern.

"Yes. Besmir handled the situation," Zaynorth replied, smiling again.

"Anything to eat around here?" Besmir asked, ignoring their comments.

Herofic grinned, signaling the barmaid.

"My friends have finally arrived," he told her, wrapping an arm round her waist. "My brother, Zaynorth. This is Besmir, his apprentice Keluse, and someone called...um." He tapped his finger against his cheek, pretending to think.

"Ranyor," the rangy man said. "Age has obviously addled his brains."

"Well, seeing as how you are my only guests at the moment," she said, leaning against Herofic in a familiar way, "make yourself at home."

"Food! Ale!" Herofic cried out.

Besmir had not heard him say more than thirty words before, and found himself warming to this new side of the man.

"And later, you," Herofic added, squeezing the barmaid's bottom.

Besmir shared a look with Keluse, eyebrows raised in surprise.

"Have you known her long?" he asked of the fighter when she had waddled off.

"Carlise? No, I only arrived here a couple of days ago. Came up here while you were recovering in that ship." Herofic replied. "There happens to be a horse trader a ways down the road...what?" he asked on seeing Besmir's look of disapproval.

"It's just...it seems a little...free."

"Things are different in Gazluth," Zaynorth said. "If two people find each other attractive and have no marital ties, it is not frowned upon if they are intimate."

Besmir saw the mixed glance of apprehension and desire that crossed Keluse's face when Ranyor caught her eye.

"Here we are, gentlemen," Carlise said, laying a tray of meat and bread on the table before them. "Keluse, if you want to, I'll heat some water so you can bathe."

"Oh, that would be incredible," Keluse said gratefully. "Thank you."

Besmir speared some slices of meat, using them as topping for the bread.

"So what's the next step?" he asked around a mouthful of food.

"I had thought," Zaynorth said, "to venture north and begin to gather support against Tiernon."

"Support?" Besmir asked. "For another war?" Zaynorth nodded sadly. "You think this land can survive another war?"

"I can see no other way, Besmir," Zaynorth said. "I am open to ideas, but without a force behind you..." He spread his hands.

Besmir frowned, chewing his meat thoughtfully. As a lone soul, he had always operated best on his own, and hated the idea of relying on others. "I don't want to drag the whole country back into a war."

"What else do you suggest? Confront him alone?" Ranyor asked.

Besmir looked at him, chewing. "Why not?"

"To be blunt," Zaynorth said. "As we wish to prevail, confronting him alone would seal your doom."

"What was the point of seeking me out, Zaynorth?" Besmir asked. "Why did you spend years searching for someone to bring over here just to start another war?"

"What other choice do I have?" Zaynorth thundered, his rage boiling over. "Sit back and watch Tiernon destroy the whole country? No! Never! I will fight him until I draw my final breath and utilize any means needed."

"You will, will you?" Besmir asked calmly. "I thought you brought me here to lead."

All the fight seemed to leave Zaynorth then. He slumped back in the chair, chin down, avoiding the gazes of the others.

"Have you the leadership skills?" the mage asked quietly. "The years of training needed to run a country? A kingdom?"

"Of course," Besmir replied sarcastically. "In the Garvistardian orphanage. They tutored us all in statecraft and warfare." Ranyor glared at him with hostility. "Did you want a figurehead or a leader?"

"I grew up alongside your father, in the great capital. We were as close as brothers, so I had similar training. I would advise you faithfully, Besmir, you *would* be king."

Besmir grunted and carried on eating. "So, what *is* next?"

"I still believe we should travel through the heartlands," Zaynorth said. "Start to gather support, even if you do not plan a war."

Chapter Six

Steam rose in small curls from the surface of the hot water. Keluse stared in awe at the massive wooden tub Carlise had filled. Easily large enough to fit two people, the pool sat in the center of a room at the rear of the inn and had been lovingly crafted from tightly fitted planks, sealed with waxed wadding. Keluse felt heat seeping in through her clothes and started to disrobe eagerly, desperate to feel the kiss of hot water on her skin.

Lowering herself slowly, Keluse moaned as the hot water soothed and eased her muscles, kneading away the aches and pains of travel. She leaned her head back, soaking her hair in the water and sighing deeply. The deep sounds of water in her ears deafened her to the sound of the door being slipped open. She lifted her head, loving the feel of water sluicing down her neck.

"Keluse?"

Her terrified scream split the air at the sound of Ranyor's voice. Her heart beat doubled and a lump grew in her throat.. Spluttering bathwater, she crossed her arms and ducked below the surface.

I can't stay here forever. What does he want?

With burning lungs, Keluse rose to the surface, just poking her head out of the water.

"Ranyor, get out, I'm in the bath!" she shouted.

Relief released the tight bands that had clamped tightly round her chest when she saw he had his back turned to her.

"I was wondering if I might join you?" Ranyor asked in a deep voice.

"No!" Keluse squealed.

"Only to bathe," he said quickly. "I promise,"

"Ranyor, I don't bathe with other people!" she said.

"However, it takes a great deal of effort to heat the water, and it may be cold by the time you have completed your ablutions."

Keluse sighed in frustration. Torn between her desire to soak in the hot water and plagued by the fear of what Gohran had put her through years before.

"Don't worry, Ranyor, I'll just get out and you can have the water. If you would just step outside," she said in a disappointed voice.

She watched as he began to disrobe, stripping his sword and dagger off and laying them aside before unlacing his shirt and pulling it over his head. Her eyes grazed over the muscles in his back, writhing and twitching with every movement, and her hands twitched involuntarily.

"Ranyor..."

"Trust me, Keluse," he said gently. "Whatever has befallen you in the past, I will *never* treat you with anything but respect.

Keluse tucked herself against the side of the tub as Ranyor climbed the steps to get into the bath, silent tears joining the water as she averted her gaze. He gasped when the hot water cocooned his body, and she almost turned her head. Minutes passed in silence as she huddled against the wood, shaking, but as time passed, her fear began to subside and she turned her head.

Ranyor sat across from her, arms spread along the edge of the tub and head back, ignoring her nude form completely.

Maybe he's nothing like Gohran. Maybe not all men are like him.

Keluse considered that as she let her arms unfold gently. Besmir had never once made an attempt to bed her despite their spending months alone together in the same house.

Can I trust Ranyor? Do I want to?

She studied him, his chest heaving as he breathed in the steamy air. His muscles glistened in the candlelight, the play of shadows on his chest making him look immensely strong, and warmth spread through her belly. His raven hair had plastered to his skull, altering his appearance completely.

"Is this all right?" he asked abruptly, making her jump.

"Y-Yes," she said after a second's thought. "It's just really strange, bathing with someone else. Especially a man."

"I have missed this," Ranyor said with a chuckle. "There is great beauty and culture in your homeland, but your bathing practices are strange."

"Not as strange as this," Keluse said, making him chuckle again.

"I have often found it odd that people are so ashamed of their bodies," he said. "All are born naked and only really need clothing for warmth."

"So we should all wander around naked?" Keluse asked with an arched eyebrow.

"Not necessarily," he said, lifting his head to stare into her eyes. "Yet this constant embarrassment over nudity is ridiculous. I, for one, cannot understand it."

"It's just the way we are," Keluse said. "Gravistardians don't flaunt their naked bodies, that's something for a husband or wife to see. It's private."

"Life is too short, Keluse," Ranyor said, using his hand to cup water over his hair. Reaching over, he lifted a bottle, sniffing the contents. "Wash my hair?" he asked.

Shock chilled Keluse. This was too much. It was one thing to remain at opposite sides of the pool, safely out of reach of one another, but to get close enough to touch him? Ignorant of her internal battle, Ranyor handed her the bottle – lavender – and turned his back. A scar ran down his right shoulder blade, long healed but puckered, making her wonder what had happened to him.

Without realizing what she was about to do, Keluse found herself tipping some of the oil into her hand and massaging it into Ranyor's hair. Her hands trembled, but she could no longer tell whether it was fright or anticipation that made them so.

"That feels incredible," Ranyor rumbled. "Are you sure you have never bathed with anyone before?"

"I'm sure," she said, chuckling nervously.

Rinsing Ranyor's hair with water from a wooden bowl, she ran her fingers through the midnight strands, relishing the silken feel like quicksilver over her skin. Ranyor turned, staring into her sapphire eyes with his dark brown ones. At this close distance, Keluse could see honey-gold flecks in the mahogany.

"Turn around," Ranyor told her.

Keluse's breathing sped up, heart hammering as what felt like a small bird tried to break out of her chest. She gasped, surprising herself as she turned away, presenting her naked back to him. Warm water flowed over her scalp and down her neck, making her jump. His hands followed, gently massaging her scalp with the lavender oil, sending shivers of delight down her spine. Keluse sighed gently as tension flowed from her with the warm water he rinsed her hair with.

"You are beautiful, Keluse," he said, leaving the bath and wrapping a towel around his waist.

Keluse turned, expectation and disappointment plainly evident on her face. Worry gnawed at her belly while need burned in her chest.

Where's he going? Why doesn't he want me? Am I damaged? Can he tell?

Snakes writhed in her belly then. Poison filled her mind as self-hatred consumed her.

"What's wrong?" she demanded. "Not good enough for you?"

Ranyor frowned, his confusion evident.

"Keluse..."

"No!" she screamed. "Just go. Go on. Get out!"

Despair carved lines in Ranyor's face as he gathered his belongings, slipping from the bathing hut and leaving her to cry.

***

Chilly water swirled around her shivering body when Keluse heard the door open once more. The tapers were low, some burned out completely, throwing deep shade into the corners as Keluse looked up to see who had come to invade her privacy this time. Carlise, the barmaid Herofic had become friends with, stood inside the door, hands clasped beneath her ample bosom.

"Are you well, dear?" she asked in a concerned voice.

"No," Keluse whispered with a choking sob. "Why are you here?"

"I came to check everything was in order. You have been in here for quite some time."

"I'm freezing," Keluse admitted.

Carlise grabbed a heavy towel and crossed to the bath.

"Come on, little one," she said. "Out you get."

Keluse stood and climbed out of the cool water, letting Carlise wrap her in a warm grip.

Carlise led her back through to the main hall and into a back room filled with her personal items. The young woman looked around, taking in all the soft furnishings and female touches that marked this as her space. Flowers sat in a jug on a nightstand, perfuming the air and creating a welcoming atmosphere.

"Have a seat, dear," Carlise said, pointing to a chair and handing her a plate with a huge piece of cake on top. "And tell me all about it."

Haltingly to begin with but with increasing speed, Keluse explained her past. Her abuse at the hands of Gohran and the shame it had filled her with. "You are from a different country, love," Carlise started. "Ranyor knows that. He also knows you are quite shy and would not want to pressure you. I would wager he has no idea about what has happened to you, but is being a gentleman because he has feelings for you."

Confusion and pleasure washed through Keluse then. "Did he tell you that?" she asked.

Carlise laughed, a deep, warm sound that made Keluse feel at home. Growing up without the benefit of a mother had left her with a massive hole in her heart, one that Carlise was beginning to fill.

"He need not speak a word, dear, I have eyes," she explained. "I see the way he looks at you when you are not looking. My husband once looked at me the same way."

"Husband?" Keluse asked. "But Herofic?"

"Is a good man and fun to be with. I have been lonely since Borlas died in the war."

"Oh," Keluse said, embarrassed and sad. "What do you think I should do about Ranyor?"

"Let things take their course," Carlise said. "You both have feelings for each other. I am sure nature will take the lead."

"But I feel bad now. I shouted at him and—"

Carlise held her hand up. "Talk to him," the barmaid said. "Tell him what happened, I am sure he will understand. From what Herofic has told me, he is a good man."

"Herofic talks to you?" Keluse asked in confusion.

"It cannot all be bedroom fun, dear," Carlise said, making Keluse's cheeks burn.

Chapter Seven

The small party plodded northwards, swapping stories and learning about each other. Zaynorth and Herofic had some amusing stories and a longer history, as they were the oldest in the group.

"So your father told him if he could eat his own face, he would be welcome to try and best him with practice staves," Zaynorth added with a chuckle.

The old man had been reminiscing for days, telling stories about his past, growing up with Besmir's father and life in the palace.

"Did you know Tiernon as well?" Besmir asked, guiding his horse nearer the old man.

"I did," he replied solemnly, "and should I have been able to scry the future then, I would have ended his life without giving it a second thought."

Besmir looked at his lined face, noting the set jaw under its coat of hair. Keluse looked shocked at his admission but remained silent.

"What was he like then?"

"Strange," Zaynorth said. "Secretive and withdrawn. He never made any attempt to hide the fact he believed he should be king, but your father could best him at combat, magic and just about anything else they competed at. It was not until he fell in love with your mother that Tiernon had leverage over him. No one believed he was dabbling in the darker side of magic, summoning demons to do his bidding."

"Demons!" Keluse gasped, making a protective sign in front of her face.

Herofic and Ranyor exchanged a glance while Zaynorth continued.

"As his power grew, Tiernon's mind deteriorated, becoming distracted and seeing things that others could not. He started increasing taxes to pay for the gods only know what, and life became so difficult for those at the bottom of society that they organized a revolt. Tiernon raised his own armies, and—" Zaynorth paused. "You know the rest."

As they crested the top of the hill they had been climbing, Besmir's horse whinnied, his fear growing as the scent of smoke and ash hit his nostrils. Besmir soothed him with his mind, not even considering how dangerous it might be, and the animal calmed a little as they all stared down the far side of the hill in horror.

Dozens of tents had been burned, their charred, blackened remains a testament to what had happened here. Besmir nudged his horse towards the devastation even though he did not want to see it up close. Sick sadness crawled through him when he drew near. Hundreds of bodies lay twisted and burned, the stumps of their fingers held out in silent pleas of desperation. Besmir forced himself to look at them, their pained masks of horror staring back at him with bared teeth. Here and there signs of animal predation marked where various creatures had feasted on the cooked meat available.

"By the gods!" Zaynorth whispered as Besmir dismounted. "What happened here?"

"Someone slaughtered these women and children," he said, crouching to examine a huddle of bodies burned beyond recognition. "I can't see many men here."

"They died in the war," Ranyor said in a quiet voice. "My sister lived in a similar situation to these people before I left." Sorrow carved lines in his face, and Keluse laid a hand on his shoulder. "Scraping a living where she could after her husband died fighting Tiernon's army. I hope she lives still," he added in a choked voice.

"Tiernon had these people murdered...as revenge?" Besmir asked, staring at the decimation around him.

They must have been terrified.

The stench of wet ash and the sweet smell of decomposing bodies combined with the thoughts of what these innocents must have been through slid cold fingers of hate around Besmir's chest, and his determination hardened.

"I'll make him pay," he vowed, looking into his companions' eyes one at a time.

Herofic nodded his approval while Ranyor gave a tightening of his mouth.

Tears rolled openly down Keluse's face. "Can we leave, please?" she begged.

***

Rolling plains of grass gave way to woods and gentle hills as they continued north. What few supplies Herofic had managed to buy, Besmir boosted with fresh meat from the wilds. Keluse watched one evening as he felled a deer with a single arrow, sprinting across to end its agony with his razor-sharp knife. He whispered to it as the life drained from its throat into the ground.

"Thank you for this gift. For giving your life to sustain mine, I bless your soul. You shall be welcomed into the Great Forests of Cathantor."

Keluse watched as Besmir stroked the deer's neck gently while it died. His gentle words and kindness touched her heart, and she found herself warming to him even more.

"Do you always say that?" she asked as they hung the carcass up by its hind legs to drain.

"Yes," he said with a little embarrassment. "It's important to me. Nothing should suffer more than it needs to, so you've got to make sure you kill as quickly as possible."

"And Cathantor?" she asked.

"God of the afterlife, he's said to have endless forests where the spirits of animals can spend eternity," Besmir explained as he opened the deer's belly, spilling its entrails to the ground.

"We should save some tendons to twist you some strings for your bow," he added, skinning the deer.

***

Four days farther north, they came across another settlement, this one thankfully untouched by violence. The evidence of hardship, however, met their eyes at every glance. The tents were tatty and patched, with dirt and animal waste splattered up the sides. Dirty children dressed in little more than rags stared as the mounted group passed. Women, wide-eyed with fright, darted out of their tents, grabbing children and dragging them inside for safety.

"This is no life for anyone," Besmir muttered as a group of five old men armed with farming tools confronted them.

"That is far enough!" the youngest, still around sixty, grunted. "What is your business here?"

"Just passing through, sir," Besmir replied respectfully. "What are you called?"

"Suranim," he said, relaxing a little at Besmir's tone. "Where are you headed?"

"North to Quilith," Zaynorth said. "I have friends there."

Besmir felt the anxiety rise in the group of old men when the mage mentioned that name, a few of them whispering and muttering. Suranim stepped forward, lowering the scythe he carried to the muddy grass.

"Quilith is gone," he said in a sad voice. "Razed to the ground by Tiernon's soldiers."

Besmir watched Zaynorth and Herofic look at each other, white-faced and tight-lipped.

"When?" the mage demanded. "Why?"

"Two years past," Suranim said. "And as far as I am aware, he wanted to demonstrate his power to us."

"Fun!" Besmir cried as a small group started to form around them.

"Some of the survivors came through here not long after it happened. Poor souls. Most of them young women with children and no husbands. Blank faces and empty stomachs. We had to move them along," he said apologetically. "We can barely feed the people we have now." Suranim looked down. "They said Tiernon was there, casting his spells, burning things left and right, homes and businesses destroyed and people murdered in the streets."

"We saw something similar," Besmir said tightly. "Tents burned with children in them."

Muffled cries of fright rose from the crowd of gathered women and children as they glanced at their meager possessions in utter terror.

"I am unsure what to do now," Zaynorth said. "If Quilith is no more. I had thought that we would make our start there."

"Start of what?" one of the other old men asked.

Besmir glanced around at the sad, sick faces, fear and terror writ large on every face. Zaynorth spoke with his brother in low tones while Keluse stayed close to Ranyor.

These are my people. This is what I've come here for.

Besmir looked at Zaynorth, a small smile crossing his lips.

"It has to start somewhere," he said. "Why not here?" Without waiting for an answer, he raised his arms for quiet. "People of Gazluth!" he cried in a booming voice. "I am called Besmir and I have traveled for months from a distant land to bring an end to Tiernon and his tyranny!"

Besmir waited for the cheers and rapturous applause. Disappointment cut him when none came, just a few jeers and catcalls. He frowned, realizing how it must look to these hopeless souls.

"Go home!" someone shouted.

"Leave us alone!" another called.

"We have already lost enough!"

"Who are you?"

"I am Besmir!" he shouted back at them. "Son of the rightful king and heir to the throne."

Laughter met his words.

"The *rightful* king?" someone shouted sarcastically. "He turned tail and ran years ago!"

"What are you willing to do for us then, Your *Highness*?" another sarcastic voice demanded.

Besmir strode over to his horse and mounted as the catcalls and shouting continued.

"Keluse, with me," he ordered before guiding his horse through the jeering crowd and out of the tent town.

"Besmir!" Zaynorth bellowed from behind him.

The hunter merely raised his arm and carried on riding.

***

For the following two days Besmir hunted, ranging farther and farther away from the tent town in pursuit of fresh game. Nothing was off the menu for him. He had Keluse set traps while he used his abilities to sense and follow larger spoor.

The effect on the people of the tent town had been remarkable. However, their attitude towards him and his apprentice changed to grudging approval as soon as the first stag had been dropped in the middle of the small group of tents.

"Zaynorth is in charge of making sure all have a fair share!" Besmir had shouted. "Herofic is in charge of beating anyone who tries to get more than their fair share!" With his words still ringing in the air, Besmir had turned his horse and trotted back out to hunt for further meat.

Now tired and cold, he found himself missing the easiest of shots, cursing when his fingers fumbled an arrow or slipped from the string. He broke the vow he had made to himself after being joined with the sea creature by reaching out and attempting to take control of a massive stag he had narrowly missed with three arrow shots.

Defeated and worn from two days of constant hunting, Besmir sat with his back against a tree and let his mind drift free. Silvery light suffused the forest, highlighting the thousands of lives surrounding him. Trails of ants, beehives, individual birds, a few rodents and then the stag. He drifted towards the animal, flowing into its brain without a thought, feeling its lungs heaving and the fear it felt from his own arrows. He took a few deep breaths, pausing to let the fright drain from the stag's body before wandering towards his human body.

Besmir stared at himself through the eyes of the stag he possessed, wonder curling around in his mind. As he watched, his mouth twitched up into a smile and he felt the most unusual sensation as his human eyes opened. He was Besmir but at the same time he was somehow the stag also. His brain struggled with the overload of information his eyes took in. He could see the massive antlers of the stag as well as the outline of his human body, clad in dark leather and fur.

***

Arteera's belly ached with a pleasant sensation she had forgotten existed. An ache from being filled with fresh, roasted meat. She smiled as her friends and neighbors cavorted around the large fire they had all helped to build, the old man Zaynorth and his muscular brother handing meat out to anyone who asked for it. The laughter of children filled the air, another thing she had almost forgotten, and she reached up, wiping something from her face and staring at it. Reflecting the firelight as it dangled from her finger, her tear glistened in the near dark.

Tears? For a little food?

Yet Arteera knew the stranger who proclaimed himself king had done so much more than feed them. In the week since his arrival he had brought hope and revived people who were so close to death from lack of food, she had expected to discover they had passed away one morning. Even in such a short time the people around her had changed, their attitude of scorn towards Besmir morphing into a grudging respect.

"He might not be the rightful king, but at least he has kept his promise to feed us."

Arteera had heard similar comments coming from the tents surrounding her own.

He can call himself whatever he wants as long as he continues feeding us.

Arteera sensed the change in atmosphere before the crowd even fell silent. Struggling to her feet, she stepped forward to see what had caused the hush. The fire crackled, but it was the only sound as everyone watched Besmir ride slowly into the middle of them all and dismount. After three days of near constant hunting, he looked exhausted but satisfied. Yet there was something about him Arteera could not define; something was different, but her mind could not pin it down at first. When the realization hit, her stomach dropped.

He was empty-handed.

Arteera waited for the crowd to moan when they saw his lack of food and silently cursed herself for it. Why should they rely on a stranger to feed them? Now they had been fed, they could start to fend for themselves once more. Turning her attention to Besmir again, she saw he was staring out between the tents, beyond the firelight.

As more heads followed his gaze, the gentle pad of hoofed feet on grass reached her ears.

He has betrayed us!

Panic gripped Arteera's chest at the thought, locking her limbs and rooting her to the spot even though her mind screamed at her to run.

That makes no sense. Why would he spend three days hunting to have us all slaughtered?

Rationality loosened her muscles and she gasped in a deep breath.

Twin points of light appeared, reflected firelight, and Arteera gasped again when the massive stag walked calmly into the circle of people. Gasps and mutters, punctuated by pointing fingers, rippled through the crowd when they saw what had happened. The magnificent beast looked around, his rack of antlers impressively large as he studied them all.

Besmir stepped over to the stag, laying his hand on the creature's shoulder gently and stroking its flank. Arteera watched as the stag took a deep breath, his chest heaving and steam puffing from his nostrils as he blew the air out.

"This is my gift to you." His quiet voice still managed to reach every ear. "A token of the power I can wield."

Arteera felt her mouth open as the stag knelt before them all, bowing its head to the floor in a human gesture.

Is he making it do that?

"Whenever any of you see this stag," Besmir called to them all. "Remember my name. Remember the promise I make to you this night. I will end Tiernon's rule of terror and brutality. I will free Gazluth!"

A few weak cheers erupted from the crowd. Women, children and old men waved and clapped as they started to chant his name over and over while others muttered under their breaths, complaining he was a madman who Tiernon would slaughter like a lamb..

The hunter leaned heavily on his horse and shook his head as if clearing it. The stag appeared to wake from a trance, realizing it was surrounded by people, and it bolted from the tent town, leaping high into the air over obstacles before being swallowed up by the night.

Chapter Eight

Besmir opened his eyes and found himself staring at a woman who's beauty was hidden by the dirt and hard living she had seen. Long black hair fell around her shoulders, shining in the early morning light like silk despite the mud that clung to it.. Flawless skin had once been laid over a bone structure that equaled any of the classical beauties he had seen depicted in books and statuary. Her pink-lipped mouth was pursed in concentration as she worked on something. Besmir took a deep breath and her eyes flicked over to him, pools of hazelnut-brown peering at him through thick lashes.

Besmir had the sensation he was falling from a great height. His stomach rolled and he flinched in anticipation of hitting the ground. Her lips curled into a sensual, yet demure, smile, and he felt the same expression on his face.

"Good morning, my Lord," she said in a musically sweet voice that dripped warm honey down his ears. "Are you well?"

"I... uh... I think so," he replied groggily. "Not to be rude, but who are you and where am I?"

"I am Arteera and this is my tent," she replied simply.

Twin dimples appeared beside her mouth when she smiled, making Besmir desire to make her smile more so he could see them. The tent was fairly small, barely large enough for the two of them, especially as he was stretched out across the floor, covered in blankets, his head propped on a pillow.

"And I'm here because...?"

Arteera smiled – dimples appearing – and put her work aside.

"You collapsed after the incident with the stag, my Lord," she said. "As mine was the nearest tent, this is where you were placed."

Besmir nodded, seeing for the first time how poor Arteera was. He could see barely any possessions of any kind. A few small piles of cloth occupied one corner, presumably her wardrobe, and apart from a wooden plate and cup, he could see nothing to indicate she had anything of value.

"Thanks for letting me sleep here," he said. "I think I may have overexerted myself somewhat."

"That, my Lord, is probably the greatest understatement I have ever heard."

Besmir chuckled, smiling at her dry wit.

"You can stop with all that 'my Lord' business," he said. "Just Besmir is fine."

He shifted in Arteera's bed, the covers falling away to reveal his bare chest. Arteera looked away, but not immediately. Besmir caught her eyes roving over his body.

"So, who has my clothing?" he asked.

Arteera lifted the clothes she had in her lap and he recognized them as his own.

"I was making a few repairs," she said, her eyes still averted. "And adding this."

Besmir leaned towards her, taking his shirt from her delicately fingered hands. She had embroidered a stag on his right chest, capturing the likeness of it in mid-leap. Using simple thread, she had rendered the creature so completely, it looked almost real.

"That's incredible," Besmir muttered, rubbing his thumb over the stitches.

"Thank you," Arteera replied quietly. "My mother was a seamstress."

"Was?" Besmir asked without thinking as he slipped his shirt back on. "What does she do now?"

"She is dead," Arteera said bluntly. "My father also."

Her matter-of-fact attitude was tempered by the agony he could hear in her voice, and he wanted to reach out, comfort her, hold her and promise everything would be all right.

"I'm sorry to hear that," Besmir said gently as Arteera wiped her eyes and sniffed.

The silence between them grew, neither one knowing what to say to the other, when Besmir heard voices outside.

"I should go," Besmir said. "Thanks again for letting me sleep here. And this," he stroked the embroidered stag again before dressing quickly.

"Are you really the king?" Arteera asked, looking up through her lashes again.

"That I am," Besmir replied with a grin before slipping from the tent.

***

"Your Majesty," the figure on the stone floor spoke.

Tiernon stared down at General Marthius from his throne. Disheveled and dirty, his robes of state showed stains that had been there for some time. Surrounded by the six guards who were always present and he knew, chilled the souls of any who saw them, the king grunted as General Marthius dared to glance up, his eyes filled with dread as he stared at the silent creatures behind the king.

Each guard wore a full face helmet, steel with small triangular slits to see through, chain mail coats over thick padding, and leather trousers tucked into black boots. Each carried the same weapon, a broadsword at least four feet in length strapped to their hip. Imposing as all that was, along with the fact that each of the guards was six feet in height and sturdy as an oak, it was what he could not see that made the general nervous.

Tiernon's guards never spoke, never made a sound of any kind, and stood motionless as if they had been carved from granite until he twitched. No breath stirred their chests, no sound made them turn. "Get up, Marthius," Tiernon snapped. "I can barely hear you when you mumble at the floor." The general stood, eyeing the guards suspiciously.

"Repeat what you just said," the king ordered.

"We have an informant in one of the tent towns south of Quilith, Majesty," Marthius reported as sweat trickled down his back. "She is reporting there is an uprising led by someone proclaiming himself the rightful king and calling himself Besmir."

Tiernon's head snapped up, his expression curious and suspicious at the same time. His eyes bored into Marthius's, making him tremble. The king's attention slid away from the general and he muttered to someone only he could see.

"I will!" he snapped. "Silence!" Turning back to Marthius, Tiernon added, "This Besmir is an impostor. Take a squad and make an example of him. Leave his head on a pole in the center of the tents, burn a few and kill the occupants. Make sure they all understand the price of standing against me."

"Your will, Majesty," Marthius said, bowing.

"Marthius," Tiernon called as the general was making his escape. "They have told me you should be one of the few to sire the new generation,"

Marthius frowned up at his king, confusion crashing through his mind as he tried to figure out who the king was talking about and what the subject was.

"Who, sire?"

Does he mean the guards?

"My advisers," Tiernon said, waving his hand at nothing, "have decided you should father some of my soldiers."

"Of course, Majesty," Marthius said, puzzlement playing over his face.

"Let me take care of this uprising and I will return, sire."

King Tiernon waved, grinning at Marthius, who backed away in obvious fear.

***

Word spread fast that there was a man who offered free food to any who asked for it, and the small tent town suffered a massive influx of new people. Besmir and Keluse tried to hunt as much as they could as well as getting some of the others to start fishing in the nearby lake and river. Game began to get scarce, and Besmir worried the situation might return to how it had been before they arrived.

On one of the rare occasions both he and Keluse were in the camp at the same time, Besmir called an informal meeting to discuss the situation.

"The problem is we've hunted and trapped just about every living creature within a day or two's ride of here," he said, yawning. "With so many mouths to feed and just the two of us hunting, we're likely to have to start traveling farther and farther out to find game. I was thinking we ought to set up some kind of delivery system to relay animals back here. If Keluse and I concentrate on hunting while others clean and prepare the meat, we—"

Zaynorth held his hand up, stalling Besmir in mid-sentence. The older man stood, pacing before them with a troubled expression on his face.

"You have performed an honorable, noble thing, Besmir," he said gently. "And the people that live here love you for it, but feeding them is not the reason we came here," he said. "If you really wish to help improve their lives, we should be looking to get you on that throne. That is where you can make the greatest changes."

Besmir sighed as feelings of resignation thudded through him.

"We both know that's never going to happen," Besmir said. "Even if I agreed to lead these poor souls into another war, who would fight? Old men and children?" He glanced guiltily at Suranim, who looked at the muddy floor. "What do you think Tiernon's going to do when he finds out someone's trying to raise an army against him?" he demanded of them all. "Wait for it to happen? You've all seen the horrors of which he's capable. Burning children in tents and destroying whole towns."

"But that is exactly why we must continue and try to find a way to beat him!" Zaynorth added in a pleading tone. "To release the grip of terror and violence he has on the whole country."

"No, Zaynorth," Besmir said gently.

"We must at least try," the mage said.

"No, Zaynorth."

Sorrow cut Besmir's heart when he saw the tears brimming in the older man's eyes. Zaynorth had spent years searching for him, seeking out the rightful king and bringing him back to Gazluth only to discover the land he had left had changed completely. Besmir watched as hope drained from Zaynorth's eyes, adding years to his complexion. He slumped into a rough chair, defeat wrapped around him like a shawl.

"I want to end Tiernon," Besmir said. "I just don't see how."

Silence dropped over the little gathering like a veil of depression. None were willing to speak. Each person was contemplating their own thoughts. Oddly, it was the normally taciturn Herofic who finally broke the silence.

"Arm the women," he said.

Several heads whipped round towards him and a small smile played around his lips.

"You heard me right," he rumbled. "As fighting men are lacking in numbers, there is only one possibility remaining to us. Gather as many women as will agree to do it and train them to fight."

Astonished silence greeted his statement as they all thought on his words. Besmir glanced at Keluse, who wore a little smile as she stared at her feet.

Would that work? Could I lead an army of women against Tiernon?

"What about training? Weapons?" he asked.

"You cannot be serious!" Zaynorth sputtered. "Your uncle has an army of battle-hardened, fully armed soldiers and you would face them with a few women carrying sticks?"

Besmir frowned at the old man, wondering where this attitude had come from.

"Have you ever seen a female protecting their young?" Besmir asked. "Not just women but any mother?"

Zaynorth nodded.

"They would attack with teeth and nails if necessary. I've spent most of my life as a hunter and I can tell you now, the most dangerous, fearsome and downright scary thing to face is a female with young to protect."

"This will never work, Besmir," Zaynorth said finally. "You will doom the entire country."

"Not five minutes ago you were advocating war yourself," Besmir retorted hotly. "Now you don't like the idea because it involves women? It was your brother's suggestion," he added.

Zaynorth stared at Herofic with disapproval on his face, tugged at his beard and scratched one ear.

"Yes," he said. "It was Herofic who suggested this and he knows why I am so against it." The old mage got out of his chair again. "It seems there is not much more I can offer in this council, so I shall take my leave."

Besmir watched the space where the old man had been, his brow furrowed with confusion in his hurt expression.

What's that all about?

The young hunter watched as the man who he had come to regard as a friend stalked off and he thought back to his childhood. In the orphanage, the other boys had either ignored him completely or saw him as a target to be picked on. Later in life, his experiences with the hunters had left him as even more of an outsider and he had eventually exiled himself, preferring to live alone. Friends had been an afterthought, unnecessary, pointless. Zaynorth's words had hurt deeply, and Besmir found himself wondering when he had become so attached to the old man..

"That might have gone better," Herofic observed bluntly.

Besmir stared at him, daggers in his expression. "Might be worth you explaining what that was all about," he said in a tone laced with anger.

Herofic scratched his cheek, looking a little embarrassed.

"It was...uh...a long time ago," he began. "Zaynorth was deep in his studies, becoming a mage. The gift is a rare thing, as you know, so your grandfather was more than willing to support us all financially."

Besmir let his mind drift as Herofic spoke, imagining the family he had never had the chance to meet, to be part of.

"I was in training to be part of the royal guard, The White Blades, responsible for protecting the royal family, palace, and anything else seen fit by the royal family." Herofic sighed. "Women trained alongside men and we all served without consideration of what that meant. I was assigned a partner, to train and serve with, Yorain she was called, from a minor noble's house. I saw her as nothing more than a friend and fellow soldier, but Zaynorth," Herofic paused, looking back in time, "Zaynorth fell for her hard."

"As his brother and her shield brother, I ended up covering for both of them during their secret little trysts." Herofic smiled. "It was a pain at the time, but I would give anything to return to it." Besmir heard the subtle catch in his throat as the warrior spoke. "And I endured hours of them just sitting, staring into each other's eyes, like moonstruck children. Yorain and I were to travel with the king and his family on a tour, visiting some of the garrison towns along the northern border, and Zaynorth begged her not to go." Herofic bowed his head, silent for a time as the past caught up with him. "Of course she said she had to go, it was her duty and there was no way she could leave me, her shield brother, to go on my own. She would see him soon and she loved him." Herofic sniffed. "I had never seen my brother so happy before," he said sadly. "And never since."

"It was an easy tour. The old king was so kind and friendly to all. He never put himself above anyone, taking time to speak to any he encountered with respect. I do not recall ever hearing a bad word said against him."

Pride filled Besmir then, an odd sensation to feel for an ancestor he had never met, but he languished in it regardless.

"In the highlands sits a little town, not much more than soldiers and their families, but it protects the Anver pass from marauding Oskapi."

"Oskapi?" Keluse asked, turning red when they looked at her.

"Oskapi were human once but have somehow devolved into animal ways," Ranyor explained. "They have become brutish and violent, grown larger and more muscular than others, probably due to the harsh conditions they live in up there. Attacks on Gazluthian settlements are rare, but when they do occur, the Oskapi come in number. A lone male is nothing and can be picked off with arrows, but a hoard of them wielding clubs and crude shields becomes an overwhelming force."

"It must have been a hard winter or something, as they attacked the garrison at Anver pass," Herofic said. "Throngs of them, as far as the eye could see, poured down from the mountains like a wave. Tusks jutting from their lower jaws, their beady little eyes filled with greed and gluttony." Herofic's words came out laced with hate and pain. "Filthy animals almost overwhelmed the whole town. Were it not for the fact the garrison commander had strengthened the walls during the summer, it would have been lost."

"King Runalf ordered us all to join the soldiers in defending the town and repelling the Oskapi," he said with tears brimming in his eyes. "There was no denying him, of course, and so Yorain and I ventured out onto the wall. We slaughtered hundreds that day. The catapults and ballistae decimated them with fire and massive boulders it took two men to lift." Herofic paused as he recalled the details, the pain evident on his face. "It was as they were running that it happened. A lone Oskapi had managed to climb a mountain of the dead and surprised us. He grabbed Yorain before anyone knew he was even there and smashed her head open on the stonework." Herofic swallowed, his voice thick with emotion as he struggled on. "She still looked as pretty as she always had, even in death. I hacked that...that thing to pieces, but it was too late."

Keluse sniffed and rose, walking over and hugging the big man in a surprising display of feeling. Herofic looked utterly shocked but patted the young woman's back gently.

"There, there, lass," he said gruffly. "I had to be the one to tell him when we got back," Herofic mumbled. "I saw something die inside Zaynorth that day and he has never been the same since," the warrior added. " Because he lost Yorain, the great love of his life."

Chapter Nine

Life continued in the tents, the residents gradually beginning to carve out a life for themselves until panicked screams tore the dawn, one day as women and children ran through the gathering of tents.

Besmir stared toward the commotion with cold dread filling his chest. More and more people had come to the tent town looking for the new leader of the resistance in the hopes of being fed.

One such had been a farmer and he had driven his herd to join them, bringing cattle, goats and pigs along with a wagon filled with chickens. He offered milk, eggs and the possibility of making cheese. Besmir was about to worship him.

A few enterprising souls had begun to earn a small living from Besmir and Keluse's kills, curing and stitching the furs from rabbits into small, useful items. These were traded for other items and a thriving market for various goods blossomed. There had been peace and happiness.

Until now.

"What's the matter?" Besmir demanded as one girl ran past.

"Soldiers!" she screamed, her head flying around in wide-eyed panic. "Soldiers come to burn us all!"

Besmir grabbed her by the shoulders, swinging her to face him, and shook her hard enough to make her head flail about.

It had the desired effect. The girl stopped shaking and looked up into Besmir's eyes with her green ones.

"Go find Zaynorth," Besmir said slowly. "Tell him to meet me in the gathering place and bring his brother. Understand?" Besmir demanded.

The girl nodded and darted off in a new direction. The tattered rags of her dress ended just below the knee and Besmir watched as her muddy feet cycled with her pale legs, flashing like the tail of a rabbit or deer in flight.

Besmir waded through the sea of fleeing people, trying to calm them as he went, without success. Some people were even trying to take their tents down, hurriedly throwing their meager possessions into the bale of cloth before dragging the whole thing away. A child of around a year old sat on the muddy ground, bawling at the top of her lungs. Besmir sprinted over to her, snatching her up and out of the path of the herd of feet headed directly for her.

"Who do you belong to, then?" he asked, searching around as the baby carried on screaming.

Wrapped in warm clothes that were surprisingly clean for anyone living in the tent town, the baby carried on yelling for her mother as Besmir yelled for anyone who knew her. A girl of no more than fifteen faced him, tear-streaked face a mask of worry as she held her arms out.

"Please, sir," she said in a voice that trembled with utter fright. "She is my baby sister but I am all she has now."

Besmir's heart melted at the emotion in the girl's face and he handed the child back to her sister, who engulfed her in the protective cage of her thin arms. He watched her disappear into the swirling mayhem of people and animals, waiting for a few seconds until the reality of the situation crashed back into him and he dashed for the center of the tent town and the impromptu gathering place.

Zaynorth, Herofic, Ranyor and Keluse were already there, all searching for clues as to what was happening, who was coming. Besmir noticed that while Herofic was not wearing his armor, he did have his heavy battle axe at the ready, arms bulging with tensed muscle.

"Who's here?" Besmir asked. "What's going on?"

Zaynorth turned, looking pale and more worried than Besmir had ever seen him.

"Tiernon has sent men," he said quietly. "Apparently word has spread. As you predicted."

Besmir turned as mounted riders trotted into the clearing, trampling anything in their path, causing chaos and further panic. One woman took a glancing blow to the temple from a hoof after being smashed to the ground by a horse. Besmir screamed at them to stop, throwing himself at them in a vain attempt to stop them from trampling people to death.

Ten riders sat atop muscular horses ranging from a midnight black to a chestnut brown, their sleek sides flashing in the sunlight as they breathed. Each of the soldiers wore a polished steel breastplate, helmet, greaves and gauntlets, carried a long, curved sword, and a shield hung from each saddle. Besmir heard more commotion and shouting from behind him and spun to see a further group of men hacking through the tents and shoving people aside.

Besmir felt his chest burn with rage and found his bow in his hand, an arrow against the string. He pulled back and released in a single movement. His arrow cut the air, punching through the hand of one of the attackers, who screamed and fell to his knees clutching his injured wrist.

"Halt!" A voice cracked across them all from behind Besmir. "I carry a message from King Tiernon Fringor."

Besmir cast his narrow gaze at the man who had spoken. He had guided his horse a few steps forward of the others and looked down at them all through the eye slits of his helmet.

"Your king ordered me to convey his best wishes. He would also like to know the whereabouts of the one calling himself Besmir." The soldier cast his glare over the crowd again. Women and children cowered before him, increasing Besmir's hate. "Your merciful king wishes it to be known that should the whereabouts of Besmir be made available to us now, you all shall remain unharmed. However, should anyone be discovered harboring or hiding Besmir," he paused for effect, "the whole of you shall suffer a horrible fate."

Besmir started forward, about to challenge the soldier, when Zaynorth stepped in front of him, his hands raised in a show of peace.

"Please, sir," he said in an obsequious, servile voice. "He left days ago, ran away he did. Up north."

Besmir watched as the information sank into the mounted man, his eyes narrowing in suspicion beneath his helmet. Around them some of the tent-town residents started to mutter.

"He stands right there," one mumbled. "Why should we shield him?"

"He has fed us, Nincarly," another more reasonable voice said. "Where was Tiernon as our children starved?"

Nincarly mumbled something Besmir could not make out. He heard similar conversations around him as whispers rippled through the crowd that ringed him.

"Lies will ensure your death is slow and painful, old man," the lead soldier shouted down at Zaynorth.

Herofic walked up beside his brother, hefting the large ax without any outward malice. The soldier's eyes swung to him.

"Fancy yourself with the ax then, old man?" he sneered. "One of my men favors that weapon also." He turned to his right, nodding at one of his companions. "Arlon could fell an army with his ax, could you claim to be as good?"

Herofic looked up at the lead soldier, shrugging wordlessly.

"Arlon!" the soldier shouted, gesturing toward Herofic. "Now we shall have some fun."

Herofic tapped his brother's shoulder, guiding him from his side and pushing him towards Besmir.

"What's the meaning of all this?" Besmir hissed at the old mage. "No one should have to die for me!"

"Who is about to die?" Zaynorth asked.

"Herofic," Besmir hissed incredulously, nodding to the warrior.

Herofic himself stood calmly in the center of an increasingly wide circle of people. He looked impassive as he rolled his shoulders, loosening his muscles and swinging his keen-edged ax.

"He will not die," Zaynorth said with a grunt and devilish grin.

"What are you up to? Is this all an illusion?"

"No illusion, Besmir," he whispered in reply. "Watch. Herofic will take this boy down a peg or two."

Besmir turned to watch the armored soldier swagger over to Herofic, kicking the meager possessions of tent town residents aside as he did. Arlon sneered down at the slightly shorter Herofic, removing his helmet and shaking his dark brown hair free.

"Worry not, oldster," he said in a tone dripping condescension. "I will go easy on you."

Herofic looked up at him, silence spreading from his expressionless face. Besmir watched Arlon's face shift, his confidence slipping but changing to rage. The younger man grabbed his battle axe from its position slung over his back and swung it ferociously at Herofic's face.

Herofic never moved, maintaining eye contact with the younger man as he swung the ax within inches of the other. Besmir heard hisses of surprise and approval as well as a few squeals of fright.

"You have spirit, old man, I will not deny you that," Arlon said.

Without speaking, Herofic set his left foot back, turning his side to the younger man and bringing his ax to bear. Arlon tilted his head, smiling in anticipation of an easy fight.

"Make him pay, Arlon," the commanding soldier said.

"Yes, sir!" Arlon cried.

Without warning, he launched a blow at Herofic, aiming for his chest. Besmir's heart felt as if it stopped beating when he saw the ferocity of the blow. Yet Arlon missed. Somehow, Herofic had anticipated the blow and flinched out of the way. His own ax flicked out in a blur, catching the overbalanced Arlon in the ribs with the needle-sharp points.

Arlon bellowed in pain, rage and embarrassment, backing off a step as he swiped blood from his side. Herofic had managed to pierce his skin just behind the breastplate he wore, jabbing through the leather behind with ease.

Arlon attacked again, another savage blow, cutting diagonally down at Herofic's shoulder. The older man flicked his own twin-bladed weapon, sending up a ringing *clang* as the two axes met. Arlon stumbled forward, his ax burying itself in the soil before Herofic's feet. Herofic hammered a savage punch to Arlon's face. The audible crack of his nose breaking made Besmir feel sick.

The armored soldier screamed this time, clutching his face with both hands. Herofic reached down and grabbed the handle of his opponent's ax, hefting it in appraisal. A few voices in the crowd started to cheer as the younger man stumbled back from the older. Besmir watched the mounted leader's face fall at seeing his man bested so easily. Savage joy swelled his chest to see it.

Yes! People will not just let you bully them into submission.

Herofic swung both blades lazily before him, drawing patterns in the air. With increasing speed he twirled and spun both blades until they disappeared in a blur. Besmir watched in awe as the man he had joked with over the last few months changed into a murder-filled killing machine. Both battleaxes whistled as they cut the air, and Besmir realized they made a shield that even arrows would not be able to penetrate. Abruptly Herofic started forward, determination on his face as he approached the lead soldier.

Arlon ducked out of the way when he saw the smaller, older man performing the movements, his mouth open and eyes wide with shock.

Herofic's chest heaved, sweat beading his brow as he spun the battleaxes. The crowd bayed and cheered to see this lone man face up to a group of mounted soldiers, but Besmir wondered what the outcome would be. There was no way these men could leave Herofic alive and return to Tiernon. Their lives would be forfeit as soon as he heard the news.

Herofic's left arm shot out, pointing straight at the lead soldier, who exploded backwards off his horse and crashed to the ground, his helmet and face split open. Shocked silence dropped over all gathered there as they watched Arlon's ax fall slowly to one side, leaving the soldier's head split in two.

Chaos erupted then as milling citizens tried to dodge the frightened attacks of Tiernon's mounted soldiers.

***

Fleet Admiral Sharova paused in the shadows of the dark corridor, patting the pouch that he had secreted inside his clothing to make sure it was still there. Not a sound reached his ears save for the cooling breeze that whispered over the palace stonework without. Pressing his back to the cold stone, Sharova considered the absolute stupidity of his idea. Yet his dreams had been haunted by the faces of the women and girls Tiernon had caged in his quarters. Most harrowing of all was the face of the young girl who behaved like a faithful dog, squatting beside her master and fetching things at his behest. Sharova had woken from many a nightmare, sweating and shaken, the image of her slack-jawed face drooling and so close to his own. His mind had tortured him relentlessly over what might be happening to those women, eventually leading to his hiding in the shadows in the early morning.

Sharova sighed quietly, knowing if caught, this would cost him his life, but he could no longer look at his own reflection without the taloned claw of guilt raking through his guts. No matter they had been enemies during the war, no matter they had been engaged or married to those who stood against Tiernon. They were Gazluthian women, and he could no longer bear to think of their suffering at the hands of his insane king.

Silently Sharova padded along the Hall of Kings. Their statue eyes followed his progress blankly, but he thought he saw approval there also. He paused at the ruined statue of the rightful king, shivering at the amount of power Tiernon must be able to wield to hammer a whole statue through a wall.

He offered a prayer to Sharise for protection and laid his ear against the door to the king's private quarters. Silence greeted him, and he let out a shuddering breath as he took hold of the gilt handle and twisted it gently. Every click, every tiny sound that came from the door felt as if it heralded his demise, burning alive as Tiernon focused his power against him.

Yet with a final muffled *thump* the door swung inward freely and silently enough to allow him entry. Inside, he had to pause to allow his eyes to adjust to the lower light there. He wrinkled his nose as the stench of human waste crept up his nose, acrid and vile. Muffled breathing and gentle sobs hit his ears, squeezing his chest at the piteous sounds. His eyes started to pick out various shapes as they adjusted.

Far from being what Sharova remembered, the room had been cleared of the riches, treasures and art, all furniture was gone and the statues were suspiciously missing. Sharova stepped gently across to the thing that apparently dominated the room now. Six feet long, waist height and three feet from front to back, the table had been constructed from some dark wood. Silver inlay crawled across its surface, making patterns that drew Sharova's attention at the same time as repulsing him. Horror threatened to crawl up his throat when he saw the bloodstains, dark and frightening.

What has been happening here?

"Help!" a high voice cried quietly from his right.

Sharova snapped his attention to the cages and the pale, scared moon of a face that stared out at him. He danced over to the cage, trying to calm her before she raised the alarm and they all died.

"Help! Oh please, for the love of God, help us!" she cried again.

"I shall, but you must remain silent!" Sharova hissed in panic.

She had a ragged and filthy scrap of a dress, stained and virtually useless as clothing. Dark hair that could have been any color – matted and filthy, twisted – framed a face that could have been anywhere from twenty to fifty. It was impossible for Sharova to make a guess due to the poor state of the girl.

Shapes moved in the darkness, more of the women waking up and turning to look at him with bleary eyes. Some were filled with dread, expecting more horrors to be inflicted on them, while others were well on their way to being as slack and empty as the dog-girl Tiernon had. Sharova's heart beat faster as the girls and women crowded the front of their cage, all begging for him to help them.

"Please," he begged as loudly as he dared. "Please, you must try and calm yourselves. If the king hears you, he will come."

The effect of his words was not lost on Sharova as most of the captives fell silent, cowering against the back wall and whimpering quietly.

Dear gods, help me free these women.

Without knowing if his prayer was even heard, Sharova crouched beside the gate and pulled a roll of oiled cloth from a pouch at his side. Within sat a collection of lock-picking tools that had cost a small fortune. He smiled as he considered the fact he had paid for the instruments with gold paid from the treasury and now he was about to use them to steal from the king.

The tip of the torsion wrench skittered over the surface of the lock as his hands shook. Sharova took a few deep breaths to calm himself, closing his eyes for a second. He barely managed to choke back a scream when something touched him. His entire form jerked, ripping his hand away from the lock and scattering his picks. Swearing, he stooped to collect them.

"I am sorry," a female voice whispered. "I really did not mean to scare you so."

"Really?" Sharova hissed back. "And you thought touching my hand in the near darkness of Tiernon's chambers would be the best way to achieve that?"

Sharova's anger helped to calm his trembling hands, and he slipped the torsion wrench into the lock with ease. A hissing sound came from inside the cage, making Sharova think she was crying.

"Look, I apologize," he said, his chest aching in sympathy. The last thing any of these captives needed was to face his anger. "But I am already on the edge of my nerves and your touch...well, you know."

It was as he was slipping the hooked pick into the lock that Sharova realized the woman was laughing, not crying at all. He felt a ridiculous grin spread over his own face, tension draining from him rapidly. A mad chuckle threatened to explode from his chest, ending this insane venture before it had properly begun.

"Try to control yourself, woman," he snapped, using false anger to control his own fear.

Whoever was within started to snuffle, her muffled laughter infectious, and Sharova had to bite his tongue hard enough to draw blood to stop himself. He sighed and started the process of feeling the tumblers inside the lock.

Minutes stretched out, each feeling like a decade, as the gentle clicks and occasional squeak leaked from the lock. Each tiny sound was like thunder in his ears, and Sharova found it impossible to understand how no one had been alerted to his activities. The woman just on the other side of the ironwork had finally fallen silent but gripped the bars close to the lock, her hands deathly pale in the wan light.

"Thank you for this," she breathed as sweat broke out on his forehead.

"You...are not...free yet," he replied, trying to maintain pressure on the wrench.

"I thank you...*we* thank you, for even making the attempt," she said. "Everyone else thinks we are traitors, betraying king and country. I have heard them speaking as if we are not here, saying we deserve our fate..." She trailed off into silence as he worked.

"It matters not to me whether you are traitors or innocent," Sharova said haltingly. "No one *deserves* this fate." He heard a long, shuddering sniff from inside the cage. "Once I heard his plans for you, I knew I had to take action…yes!" Sharova hissed as the lock gave with an audible *click*.

The gate swung inwards on silent hinges and a sea of dirty, smelly women, dressed in rags, poured out into the room. Sharova's heart beat a little faster when he realized his insane plan might actually work. One of the women had laid her head on the massive altar, silent tears running down her face and onto the surface. Sharova watched in disbelief as her tears melted into the numbing symbols inlaid there, the silver glowing a pale blue.

"Come," he ordered. "Be as silent as you can, stay in the shadows and do not move unless I do so first."

He scanned the small group, counting seven in all and wondering where the rest had gone, as he recalled there being many more during his initial visit. Some of them met his gaze with frightened but hopeful eyes, others looked away, trying to cover themselves as much as possible with crossed arms. Sharova made sure each woman nodded they had understood his instructions before turning towards the door again.

"In case we do not escape," the laughing woman said, "I am Thoran,"

"Sharova," he whispered in reply.

"I know, Fleet Admiral," Thoran said. "I recall your visit."

"Fleet Admiral no more," he said. "Grand treason is a good way to hand in one's resignation, however."

Thoran smiled, the expression lighting her features, and Sharova realized she was beautiful beneath the layers of filth and depression. He smiled in return and was about to speak again when the door to Tiernon's inner chambers opened, admitting his pet dog-girl.

Her eyes went wide with horrified surprise when she saw the women outside their cage. She dragged in a deep breath and opened her mouth to scream.

Chapter Ten

Keluse's body refused to move. Her mind screamed at her to run, hide, get away, but her limbs felt leaden and would not obey her commands. As soon as Herofic had killed the lead soldier, his men had attacked. Herofic had thrown himself at the man nearest to him, cannoning into his horse and knocking it off balance.

She watched as the other horses bucked and threw their riders, some trampling their former masters.

Besmir. Besmir did that.

As if her thoughts summoned him, she watched an arrow appear through the throat of one of the men about to stab Herofic in the back. He stiffened, clawing at his throat as his eyes rolled madly, looking for one of his comrades to help.

Ignorant of his being saved, Herofic hammered his battle axe into the soldiers who had formed into a rough fighting group. His immense strength, combined with the weight and sharpness of his ax, rendered their armor next to useless, his blows ripping through metal as easily as their bodies.

Cold sickness dribbled through her as she watched them screaming and bleeding. Herofic cut them down mercilessly, felling them like a farmer cutting hay. Tears streamed down her face as she watched the soldiers die or fall, so injured they could never hope to live. One stumbled past her, holding the severed stump of his right arm and mumbling as his lifeblood sprayed out between his fingers. Hot drops hit her face as he passed, slowing and falling to his knees before slumping forward to the ground.

Screams of agony and panic smashed into Keluse's ears, and she turned to see the nightmare scene of the other soldiers mercilessly hacking their way through unarmed tent-town residents. One blood-soaked man grinned maniacally as he slashed his curved sword at a fleeing child.

"No!" Keluse screamed.

Her body performed the action of raising her bow before she even realized what was about to happen. An arrow punched through the breastplate and into the chest of the soldier, pitching him backwards to be trampled by fleeing citizens and advancing soldiers.

Keluse's mind whirled, thoughts tumbling in her brain. Did he have a family? Children? Were there those who would miss him? What even was his name? Rooted to the ground, betrayed by her own mind and racked with guilt, Keluse could only watch as the horrible battle raged around her.

Herofic and Besmir had killed the formerly mounted soldiers; their hacked, broken bodies lay in various poses of anguish. Nightmare injuries marked their bodies where the axman had cleaved into them viciously. In all the time Besmir had been teaching her to become a hunter, Keluse had never felt squeamish, but seeing inside these men made her palms tingle, a pain growing in between her breasts. Entrails had spilled from one man, and she watched in abject sorrow as their owner tried to gather his guts, the loops spurting through his fingers as he sobbed and begged.

***

Besmir let another arrow fly, watching as it slammed into the back of a soldier, knocking him forward. Ranyor slashed his sword at his neck, severing his spine and killing him instantly. He watched the sinewy man whirl, slashing at another man and catching him across the face.

Turning, Besmir watched a group of women and their older children jump on another man, dragging him down by force of numbers. One little mob grabbed his sword arm, pinning it to the ground and wrenching his weapon free, while one of the women – a mother, Besmir was sure – drove a crude knife just beneath the edge of his helmet. Even at such a distance Besmir heard his gurgling scream.

Herofic was leaning on his ax, breathing heavily as he scanned the battle ground for danger. Besmir darted across to him.

"What ails you?"

"Why did you start all this? Killing the lead soldier like that?"

Herofic stood, grunting in disdain, and hefted the ax again.

"You would have preferred it if I had waited for them to start the slaughter?" he asked, anger coloring his face.

"I'd have preferred it if you'd have given me a chance to speak, to give myself up before chopping his head in half."

"And achieve what?" Herofic demanded, spinning to face Besmir. "You would be dead and the hopes of everyone finished." His eyes bored into Besmir's own, filled with rage.

"But these people would be alive!" Besmir cried. "Women, children. They'd be able to live another day."

Herofic slammed his ax down into the neck of a moaning soldier as he writhed on the ground, clutching at his belly. Besmir watched coldly as he died.

"They would be dead and more besides had I not attacked first," Herofic grumbled. "And you know it. You saw the dead at the first camp we found. The other women and children? Burned beyond recognition? That is exactly what they would have done here."

Besmir knew the stocky fighter was probably right, but the horrifying truth was that every person there, every dead child and mother, had died because of him. Besmir scanned the scene of violence before him. Dead soldiers lay side by side with the people of the tent town as if they had been defending rather than murdering them.

What manner of man is Tiernon to do this to the poor and starving?

"I'm sorry," he muttered to Herofic.

"I knew your father and grandfather, lad," Herofic said gently. "Good men both, and it seems the old saying about seeds and trees is not far wrong. Trust in Zaynorth and I, Besmir, trust we have the best interests of Gazluth in our very hearts." He offered his hand and Besmir took it. "My king," Herofic added.

The younger man grinned.

"Let's end this," he said, searching for any remaining soldiers.

***

Ranyor slashed his blade across the face of one soldier as a ragged group of women and children hauled another to the ground, butchering him brutally. Ranyor watched them defend their home from these attackers in his peripheral vision as he faced the other man. The king's soldier wrenched his damaged helmet off, hurling it at Ranyor and growling through his pain.

Ranyor saw his blow had dented the man's helmet, mashing his nose and shredding his lips. Ranyor stabbed at him, not wishing to give him an advantage, but he danced back and brought his sword up, feinting at Ranyor before reversing his cut and slashing at his chest. Ranyor stepped back, reassessing the man before him.

"One of Tiernon's better-trained dogs?" he goaded.

"Better a king's dog than servant to a Pratak like him." The soldier thrust his blood-coated chin at Besmir.

"What?" Ranyor asked with a grin. "It looks as if you have some kind of injury to your face."

His opponent roared and charged Ranyor, slashing at him wildly. Ranyor parried one blow, turning the man's blade so it caught in the dirt at his feet.

"No!" the soldier roared when he realized he was finished.

Ranyor slammed his blade into the man's unprotected back before twisting it and wrenching it out again. Blood pumped from the soldier's back, a thick fountain of crimson gore spreading over his clothing. Ranyor crouched beside him as he died, gripping his hand in brotherhood.

"We are all men of Gazluth," he said. "Be at peace, brother."

The downed man coughed out his final breath, the light fading from his eyes. Ranyor sighed, shaking his head.

"Are you injured?" he asked the group who had killed the other soldier.

"We...we are well, my lord," one of the older women replied.

Ranyor saw the younger children were gathered around their mother, leaning into her skirts, while her slightly older children stood by, weeping. The eldest boy was pacing around, glaring up and down as if searching for something. Red-faced and with his teeth bared, the young man raged as Ranyor watched.

Sadness welled up inside Ranyor at seeing the bloodlust in the boy's eyes and the utter burning hatred pouring from his every gesture. How many of the younger generation would never know how great Gazluth could be? Now that Tiernon had fractured the land, rending families apart and turning countrymen against each other, Ranyor feared for the future of his homeland.

Crying people milled around him, gathering what meager possessions they could find and attempting to repair what was left of their homes. The brief but brutal battle had damaged or destroyed around thirty tents, scattering the occupants' personal items and trampling them into the mud.

Ranyor made his way through the crowd, dodging people looking for loved ones and stripping the dead soldiers of anything of value.

"Damn Tiernon to the Pits," someone moaned as he wandered. "Sending his men here."

"I wish that Besmir fellow had never come," another voice complained.

"You would have starved without his aid, and you know it," someone replied.

"Still, he is the cause of all this. We should have given him to them."

"And you really think Tiernon would just let us be? Do you even recall the war?"

Ranyor walked on, ignoring the acid comments and soul-destroying wails as people recovered their dead. Arriving at the tent he had been sharing with Herofic, he found Keluse sitting cross-legged at the entrance. Her head was bowed, a curtain of blonde hair cascading over her slim shoulders.

Relief flooded his system at the sight of her, and he longed to brush back her hair so he could see her face, lose himself in her sapphire eyes.

"Keluse," he breathed. "I lost sight of you. What happe—"

Ranyor's words failed in his throat as she looked up at him, the sight like a hammer to his gut. The Gravistardian woman's face was screwed up, creased with guilt and pain, fear and horror. Tears had reddened her eyes, and her nose was red from wiping it repeatedly. She sucked in a breath, the air jumping in her throat, and sighed it out again.

"I-I-I...killed a man," she wailed. "Sh-Sh-Shot him in the chest." The pain in her voice tore at him. "I-I-I'm a killer!"

Ranyor squatted beside the sobbing girl, concerned for the gore on her face.

"And you, Keluse, are you injured? Where has all this blood come from?"

Keluse, however, was in no state to answer, muttering that she was sorry over and over again. Ranyor lifted her easily and she wrapped her arms around him, clinging on as if for her very life. He could feel her shaking, even through the thick clothing she wore, and Ranyor wondered how much this would change her. He ducked inside the surprisingly spacious tent, sitting them both down on his crude bed.

"All I can see is his face," she said. "The pain and fright as he fell back." She turned her wet eyes to him. "Do you think he had a wife or, or children?"

Ranyor considered lying to her but had made a promise to himself not to do so. Whatever she had suffered in her homeland, telling her lies would be to perpetuate that crime.

"I hope not," he said gently, cupping her chin. "But many soldiers marry and have children before leaving for war."

A low moan escaped from Keluse then, a wail of pain and sorrow that folded her in two. Ranyor laid a hand on her back, feeling the breaths expand her chest as he stroked her spine.

"His face," she muttered. "I can't forget his face."

"What led you to shoot him?" Ranyor asked. "It might help to speak about it."

Keluse sat up, turning her face to him, the pain still there.

"You think so?" she asked, hope filling her voice. Ranyor nodded. "When I saw him he was...was just about to kill a little girl. I-I-I don't even remember pulling an arrow out or drawing my bow...but then he was dying with my a-arrow in his chest and I had my bow up. I can still see his face," she added.

Ranyor held her hand, drawing invisible symbols on her skin and relishing how soft it felt.
"Look at it this way, then," he said quietly. "If you had not stopped him, he may have slaughtered that girl and many more before someone else managed." He studied her face to

see if his words were having an effect. "He was killing *children*, Keluse. No matter what side of this conflict you are on, killing children is evil, heartless. It is Tiernon's fun. In my opinion you are a savior, a heroine that protects children from evil men."

Ranyor's heart beat faster when a tiny smile crossed her lips, the tiniest hint of color returning to her cheeks.

"A heroine?" she asked. "Me?" Ranyor nodded, twining his fingers through her own. "I don't think so," she said.

A little of the pain left her voice, relieving Ranyor's concerns somewhat. Warm pressure hit his chest abruptly and he stared into her eyes, a feeling of completeness washing over him.

"I can still see his face, though, I just can't forget it," Keluse muttered, staring at Ranyor's lips. "Make me forget, Ranyor," she begged. "Please," she breathed, pressing her lips onto his.

Chapter Eleven

Tiernon's dog-girl prepared to scream the alarm.

Sharova had other ideas, however. He slipped the thin blade of his knife into her soft throat. Thoran slapped her hands to her mouth as the girl's young body started to spasm in Sharova's grip. Wrenching, choking noises came from her throat as she died, and Sharova felt a horrible sense of despair swell in his chest at having to kill her. Yet whatever Tiernon had done to make her the way she had been had been worse than him ending it.

Sharova hugged the dead girl to his chest as the jerks from her body got progressively weaker. He stroked her hair and whispered to her as she died, lifting her small frame with ease when it was over.

"I will not leave her here for him to defile further," he explained when Thoran questioned him with her eyes.

Her face changed at his words, the deep creases at the apex of her nose vanishing, her eyes becoming round. She reached out and gripped his arm, squeezing gently in approval, then turned towards the door.

The Hall of Kings stood as silent and empty as it had earlier as the small group slipped from the king's room, bare feet slapping on the stone floor and the sound of their combined breathing loud in the dark.

Sharova turned toward the throne room at the head of the corridor, staring at the gaping maw of blackness that was the hall itself. Thoran grabbed his arm as he was about to start forward.

"It is madness to go through there!" she hissed.

"It is also virtually unguarded and a good conduit to the outside world," he whispered back.

The atmosphere in the great hall was markedly different to that which he remembered. When empty and only lit by celestial light, the massive room echoed hollowly with their combined footsteps. To Sharova, it sounded like thunder rolling through the hall, and he expected guards to appear and cut them to shreds at any moment. Although slight, Virine's body was a constant burden, making Sharova's back and arms ache. Sweat streamed down his back and his breathing came in pained gasps.

"Hand her to us," one of the other women mumbled. "We will share the burden."

Sharova reluctantly hefted the girl's body into the other woman's arms, watching as the other captives assisted her. He puffed a few breaths then turned and started forward again, his tired body shoving against a large, iron candelabra his eyes had not detected in the gloom.

His hands grabbed for it as it fell, but he was nowhere near strong enough to halt its fall after knocking it over, and it hit the floor with an explosive *bang*. Gasps and squeals of fright followed as cold shock pulsed through Sharova's body.

"Run!" he hissed, grabbing Thoran's hand and pulling her along.

Like a cloud of bats erupting from a cave, Sharova led the small group of women from the great hall and throne with its gilt dais and velvet drapery, entering the antechamber outside. The gathering area there was gravely silent, and Sharova was shocked to learn the alarm had not yet been raised.

Where are all the guards?

He paused briefly at the door, pressing his ear to the wood, hearing nothing but the blood roaring through his ears. Sharova reached down, twisting the heavy ring, sure that some guard would slash at his throat. The corridor outside was silent and as dark as the rest of the palace.

Sharova led the women down corridors that should have been kept lit but were as dark as jet stones. So nervous and filled with anticipation had he been on his way inside, Sharova had not even noticed. Now the empty hallways echoed with the whispers of the women behind him and the occasional strange *thump*. Doors that should have had guards stationed outside hung open, the chambers beyond silent as sepulchers.

Sharova put the issue out of his mind, not able to believe his luck, and concentrated on leading the women from the palace.

Still have to escape the grounds.

At the main door – still open as he had left it – Sharova peeked outside. Elegantly manicured lawns and shrubs lay still and fresh in the moonlight. Gazluth's capital, Morantine, lay beyond the walled gardens, and his eyes could see the twinkling lights of hundreds of candles and fires.

"Are we free?" a ghostly voice asked from behind him.

Sharova turned to see the hopeful faces staring back at him and smiled.

"I believe you might just be," he said. "A little more patience and silence as we leave the grounds would be prudent, however."

Running almost in a crouch, Sharova trotted along the gravel pathways, past bushes sculpted and clipped into the shape of beasts and heroes. A maze lay to his right, but he skirted round the edge, not wanting to get caught up in the green twists and turns. Glancing back, he saw the women were lagging behind, especially the few who carried the unfortunate Virine. Having been half starved and treated worse than cattle had certainly not helped, and Sharova slowed his pace until they caught up to him.

"Hand me the girl," he ordered, taking the body from them. "For any who do not know, this is the northern gate." He pointed to a darker patch of night. "Once through that gate you will all have to find your own way." Sharova said grimly.

"Thank you, Fleet Admiral," Thoran said.

Sharova felt his eyes widen when the younger woman hugged him tightly, pressing the warmth of her body against him. Two of the others followed suit, offering blessings and good fortune while thanking him for their lives.

He watched as one by one the former captives slipped from the gate, their forms melding with the night and disappearing from view. It was not long until only he and Thoran remained. He looked at her fine profile, strong yet delicate nose and the long, dark lashes that graced her eyes. His career had left little time for appreciation of the fairer sex, and a pang of regret hit him that he had wasted so many years in service to a mad tyrant.

Thoran caught his look and turned her eyes away in embarrassment.

"What are your thoughts?" she asked in a quiet voice.

"Merely detailing my regrets, lady," he replied. "We ought to leave here and put as many miles between us as possible."

Thoran looked at him with something like awe in her eyes. Sharova could see tears glistening in the moonlight, and his heart broke to see them.

"Do not shed tears, lady," he said. "You are free to return to your home and family,"

"I have none," she said with a wrenching sob. "My home was attacked and burned to the ground. Tiernon had the women and older girls rounded up and put in massive wheeled cages. Then he made us watch his troops slaughter the men. My betrothed died fighting them."

"You could come with me," he said. "If you wish to, of course."

Her tear-streaked face turned to him again, filled with gratitude, and a slight smile turned the corners of her mouth up. She nodded.

"I would like that, Lord," she said.

Sharova stood from the squat he had been in and turned to pick up the young girl's body from where he had braced her against a wall. Thoran's scream split the night when she saw her staring at them with an evil grin plastered across her face.

"A beautiful betrayal, Sharova," Tiernon said in the young girl's voice. Her dead eyes rolled horribly in their sockets as the king turned her head like a puppet master. Her slack-jawed grin sent chills down Sharova's spine.

"Do you like my new toy?" Tiernon asked through the girl. "I discovered something about the dead," the king carried on as Thoran buried her face in Sharova's side. "They are so much more reliable than the living," he added in a dark tone.

Sharova pulled a long knife from beneath his cloak. The girl's dead eyes widened even though they did not focus on Sharova.

"What manner of man are you?" Tiernon asked with false shock. "You have already murdered my little pet and now threaten her with a knife." he chuckled horribly. "And you, woman," Tiernon addressed Thoran. "How ungrateful you are. You were to birth a new race! You would have been the mother of the people, blessed above all. Now," Tiernon added in a vindictive voice, "now you will suffer."

The dead girl took a step towards them, arms outstretched and grinning awfully. Thoran screamed. Tiernon laughed.

***

Besmir sat at the head of a table. Zaynorth sat to his right with Keluse at his left. Herofic, Ranyor and Suranim sat beside them. Opposite the table, seated on mats or the ground, or simply standing with arms folded, were as many of the residents of the tent town as wished to be there. Besmir guessed there might be as many as two hundred, with the majority being women. A few older men dotted the crowd, as well as a few adolescent boys who had grown up fast.

So this is my kingdom? These are my people?

Besmir sighed and stood, glancing at Arteera, who offered him a warm smile. Besmir smiled in return, thanking any gods listening for the woman. He had spent most of his time in her company since the attack, finding himself irritable and out of sorts when she was not around.

"Friends!" he called, his voice rolling across the gathered crowd. "We have suffered a horrible loss at the hands of Tiernon's men. We have buried our dead and must decide what to do next."

Murmurs ran through the gathered people.

"Who did *you* lose?" Someone muttered.

"Who are you to decide what we do next?" An older woman asked.

"They only came here because of you." An elderly man observed, leaning on a crude walking stick.

Besmir ignored their mutterings and continued. These people were grieving, angry and disheartened by the attack.

"I have heard in the past few weeks that some of you have expressed the opinion I should leave." A whisper rippled through the crowd. "I asked you all here to decide your future, the future of your children, your families. I want to hear your voice in this matter."

Zaynorth shook his head in disapproval.

"I know you don't agree with me, my friend, but the people in this land have suffered so much because of decisions made by others, and I can't expect them to just follow me blindly."

"I believe you mean well, Besmir," the mage said, pulling his beard. "And yet I believe considering the opinion of these people, no matter how good they may be, is a flawed plan. They have no conception of what we face, they are only—"

"Only what, Zaynorth?" Besmir demanded. "Peasants? Commoners?"

The mage looked away from his stare.

"I might be of royal blood, Zaynorth, but I grew up in an orphanage surrounded by people just like these." He cast his arm at the crowd. "And one of the biggest concerns they have is not having a voice. If I am to ask them to die for me, I need them to want to do it."

"They need a leader," Zaynorth said. "They need telling what to do and where to go."

Even Herofic turned an expression of displeasure on him.

"What an enlightened opinion, Brother," he mumbled.

"What, you agree?" Zaynorth asked in shock.

"Look at them, Zay," Herofic said. "A handful of broken women with nothing left to give but their lives. What hope can we possibly offer them?" He paused. "I do not know. What I do know is that treating them in the same way as Tiernon will get us nowhere."

"You cannot rule by democracy," Zaynorth grunted, folding his arms.

"I don't intend to," Besmir replied. "Now, can I carry on?" He tilted his head at the old man.

Zaynorth made a disgusted gesture, flapping his hand at the crowd. Besmir grinned and turned back to the people who were all watching their exchange with interest.

"Word will surely reach Tiernon of what happened here. You all aided in the defence of your homes, aiding me in defeating his soldiers." He let his words sink in. "What response do you think this will bring? Acceptance? Do you think he will let this pass? Allow you to live in peace after defying him and killing his men?" Besmir paced before the table, giving them time to think. "No!" he shouted, making a few of the closer ones jump. "Tiernon has proved time and again he enjoys murder, lives to inflict pain and misery on his own people. He will come here in force, with hundreds of men if necessary. An army could descend on you all, burning and killing as it has done before. Yes, the soldiers came for me this time, but next time they will be here for you."

Besmir waited as the women, children and old men chattered and wailed among themselves. Eventually he faced them and held his arms up for silence. Zaynorth watched as they quieted for him, accepting his lead already, and a slight smile creased his lips.

"I, Besmir Fringor, stand before you as the rightful heir to the throne of Gazluth and I make these promises before you all, as borne witness by the gods themselves." Besmir thrust one finger up into the sky. "First, I will make sure that all are fed and protected to the extent of my own ability." He watched as a few of those seated stood up. "Second, I will work tirelessly for the good of Gazluth and her people." More stood at that. "And third," he bellowed. "I will make my uncle Tiernon pay for his crimes against you all!"

A rough cheer rose from the gathered throats, quietly subdued but a cheer regardless.

"Before you are two flags." Besmir pointed. "Red and green. I urge you to think carefully about the choice I now ask you to make. If you are willing to support me, allow me to lead you, stand before the green flag." Besmir pointed once more. "If you desire that I should leave you to your fate, come before the red."

Besmir sat back down, speaking to Keluse to give them all a chance to choose and move without him watching.

"Herofic was moaning about having to find new lodgings," he whispered behind his hand. "Something about never getting any peace thanks to you and Ranyor."

Besmir grinned as he watched the red blush creep up Keluse's neck, her eyes widen and mouth open a little.

"I-I-I...after the attack," she spluttered. "Ranyor...we...are fond of each other."

"Really?" Besmir teased sarcastically. "You hid that extremely well."

"You're not angry, are you?" she asked.

"Gods no!" he said in surprise. "It's about time." He patted her hand and smiled. "You deserve a little happiness." Despair hammered into Besmir then, pulling his face into a mask of doubt. "The gods know there's precious little of that in the future."

Besmir stood again, looking at the two groups that had gathered around the flags he had placed. Excitement and apprehension crashed into him in equal measure when he saw the vast majority had gathered around his green flag. Once more Besmir held his hands up.

"I have one last request," he called to them. "I have given you my promises and now I demand yours. If we are to go forward as a nation, I require your pledge. Your pledge to serve me as your king!"

Silence dropped over the assembled crowd as his words sank in. Zaynorth looked at the milling crowd as they chattered among themselves. A flock of birds flew overhead, crying their woes to anyone who would hear. The old man rose, walking round the table until he stood before Besmir, staring into his eyes for a long moment.

"Zaynorth?" Besmir asked. "Is there something wrong?"

The illusion mage shook his head slowly before lowering himself to one knee before everyone there. He bowed his head to Besmir.

"I, Zaynorth Welforth, pledge allegiance to the land of Gazluth and to you, King Besmir," he said, bringing tears to Besmir's eyes. "Long live the king!" he shouted.

Besmir offered his hand, helping Zaynorth to his feet, pulling the old man into a tight hug.

"You need never kneel to me," Besmir told him as the people moved from the green flag to surround them. "Your knees will never take the strain."

A ripple of laughter ran through the crowd at his comment, those closest relating his words to the rest. Herofic stood beside his brother, a warm smile on his face.

"You'll have to kneel though," Besmir joked.

Herofic stared at him with a flat expression as he grinned impudently back. A hush fell over the crowd as they watched the warrior who had defended their homes smile and bend his knee to their new king.

"I, Herofic Welforth, pledge my allegiance and my life to you, King Besmir. Long live the king!"

He rose, accepting Besmir's arm in a warrior's grip, turning to crook his finger at Ranyor. The rangy swordsman trotted around the table and knelt before Besmir, offering his pledge of oath as well. Keluse followed suit. As soon as she had stood, hugging Besmir and laughing, a figure pushed to the front of the crowd, who spread out a little to watch his progress.

Suranim had suffered a nasty stab to the thigh during the attack, but he limped across to stand before Besmir, the bloody bandage clear for all to see. He stared at Besmir with hope in his eyes and started to lower himself, but the king caught his arms.

"There is no need," he said.

Suranim stepped back from Besmir, holding his arm out to Herofic, who helped him kneel. Besmir's heart beat faster, his chest filling with pride for these noble people as they all began to kneel before him. Even those who had chosen to stand before the red flag grudgingly knelt before their new king.

Zaynorth stepped forward, holding his arms aloft and calling out loudly, "Do you pledge your loyalty to the rightful king?"

"Yes!" they shouted in unison.

"And do you swear your solemn oath to obey his commands and edicts to the best of your abilities?"

"We swear!" the crowd shouted.

Besmir swallowed, the lump in his throat gritty and hard as he cast his eye over the ragged, the poor and the starved of whom he had just become king.

**

"And how does it feel to be king now, Your Majesty?" Arteera asked Besmir sometime later.

Tent-town residents had pooled what few resources they could find for the impromptu feast that had been organized. Mead had appeared miraculously from somewhere, and Besmir was warm with the brew. Another large fire had been built in the middle of the tents, the ground around it trampled flat by hundreds of dancing feet. A few women had learned to play instruments in their youth and a rude band had formed, playing traditional Gazluthian songs for anyone to sing to.

Besmir regarded the woman before him, realizing again just how beautiful he thought she was. Her hair had gone back to its former lustrous self – long, straight and dark – catching the firelight in warm patches. Her flawless skin appeared to glow in his eyes and her round body called to his on a primitive level.

"It feels good," he said simply, smiling at her.

Arteera looked up through her lashes, making Besmir's head swim.

"All these people," she murmured. "Willing to do your bidding." Arteera ran her hand through her long hair, flicking it from her neck.

Besmir traced the line of her throat with his eyes.

"What would you order me to do, Your Majesty?" she asked in a low voice.

Besmir grabbed Arteera by the shoulders, feeling her delicate bones shifting as she breathed heavily, and pulled her against him.

"Is there anything you would deny me?" he murmured.

"No, my Lord," Arteera breathed against his lips, smiling.

Besmir grinned and dragged her towards the tents.

Zaynorth and Herofic watched the young couple as they giggled their way across to lose themselves in the night.

"Looks as if our new king is about to receive his coronation," the warrior grunted salaciously.

Zaynorth chuckled, tugging his beard and following Besmir with his gaze. Both brothers sat on logs that had been dragged across beside the fire, warming their backs as they shared a bottle of the valuable mead.

"Those used to be the days, eh, Brother?" the mage asked. "Do you remember?"

"Hmm," Herofic grunted in response. "Do you really believe this is all about to work out for him?"

Zaynorth turned to stare at his brother with an expression of shocked displeasure.

"Where did that appear from?" he demanded. "This has been a good night until now. Why must you ruin it with mawkish questions?"

"It falls to us to ask those questions, Zaynorth," he grumbled. "Besmir has no real idea of what he is up against. So, do you think he has a chance?"

Zaynorth sighed, his mind whirling over all the possibilities he could think of.

"I believed so when I left to search for him in Gravistard," he said. "Now we have seen how bad things have gotten here, I... I simply do not know," Zaynorth admitted in a tone of defeat.

Herofic was silent for a long time, making the mage believe he had fallen asleep until he grunted again, rising.

"I can feel the pull of my bedroll," he said. "You need to consider the best course for that lad," he added seriously. "I have become a little fond of him and would hate to see him crushed beneath your ideals."

Without another word, Herofic nodded once and stomped off towards his own tent.

Zaynorth turned and stared into the glowing orange embers of the fire, spirits dancing in the heat mesmerizing and lulling him into a fitful sleep.

Steel grey skies met his bleary eyes when Zaynorth woke with a start the following day. His back ached as he struggled up, searching for the source of the commotion.

"Riders!" someone screamed.

"Soldiers!" another voice split the calm morning, waking the camp.

Squinting at the horizon, he could just make out a column of darkness moving in the distance, and his heart sank to think this might be the end before they had even begun.

Chapter Twelve

Tiernon had used his puppet control of the dead girl's body as a conduit to slam Sharova with lightning, making every muscle tighten in agony. Thoran had been screaming. A high-pitched and piercing sound that reached his ears even through the agony he felt and he hoped she was being spared the same fate as he was.

Eventually rough hands had grabbed him beneath the arms, dragging him along the ground unceremoniously, causing more pain. Shorova had tried to see where he was being taken but none of his muscles obeyed him and his head hung limply only allowing him to catch glimpses of the floor as it passed him by. After an eternity he had been thrown down some stone stairs into a pool of stagnant water, spluttering and coughing as it burned his lungs. Sharova's first thought was that Tiernon had blinded him, and he had lifted his hands to his face, trembling fingers searching for any signs of injury. Relief had flooded him when he found himself intact, but fear grabbed him almost immediately when he wondered just what the mad king had in mind for him.

That had been a long time ago, but his pain would not subside. The skin on his legs was hot and tight to his touch, and he knew infection had set in. Two of his fingers had snapped, and his scream had rent the blackness when he pulled them to reset the bones. Bandages torn from what remained of his clothing had pinned the digits together, relieving the pain a little.

Slowly and painfully Sharova had begun an exploration of his new world, his fingers flowing over the rough, wet stone that surrounded him. The chill ground against his bones made him shiver. He had no idea where he was or how long he had been here save that his beard had begun to grow.

The room was some kind of cell, he decided, cut from the rock and with a rough, wooden door fitted. The wood had swollen, wedging the crude thing in place so effectively, it was as solid as the stone around it. Sharova beat and kicked against the wood, trying to rouse someone, anyone, who might hear him. The silence grated on his ears, driving him mad with the need to hear someone else.

Minutes or years passed in silent darkness, giving Sharova plenty of time to consider his fate. Did he deserve this end? Possibly not, but then he could also argue it was entirely well earned. He had known there was something different with Tiernon when they had first met in his younger years. He had been quiet and introverted then, holding himself apart from others. Yet Sharova had been blinded by his own success and desire to advance to the highest rank in the navy. When the old king had died and his heir disappeared under unusual circumstances, Sharova had merely dismissed it as politics. He would serve his new king as well as he had the old one. He did not have to like him, after all, and would spend as little time in his presence as possible.

"You have brought this on yourself, Sharova." His mournful whisper echoed like thunder in the small cell and he actually jumped.

The irony of being caught while actually doing the right thing was not lost on the former fleet admiral, and a bitter smile twisted his lips when he thought about how close he had come to escaping and saving them all.

Fool to try and keep him from that girl, Virine.

Some spark within him must have wanted to stay alive, clinging to the last vestiges of his existence, as he found himself sucking what little moisture he could from the stone. Dirt and grit coated his mouth and stuck in his throat, but he carried on drinking what water he could.

So I can starve to death.

"Why did you leave me to Tiernon?"

Sharova jerked, his heart beating hard enough to crack his ribs and an icy spike sliding through his core.

"Thoran?" he asked the dark. "Are you hurt? How is it you are down here also?"

"You left me, Sharova," Thoran said accusingly. "Left me to endure Tiernon's tortures."

"No!" he wailed imploringly. "I tried to get you to safety. Tried, but he caught us, remember?"

"It hurts," Thoran moaned. "So much pain. Help me! Kill me!"

Sharova jumped up, throwing himself at the door in a vain attempt to try and get away from Thoran's voice. Part of him understood she was not here, that her voice only existed in his feverish imagination. Yet another part believed her every word.

Sharova was visited by his mother next. A strange visit, as she had passed into the care of Cathantor decades before. He watched as her kind face hovered in the air before him, looking back at her only son.

"Why did you fail, my son?" she asked.

"Mother...no... I..." He watched as a lock of her hair fell across her face.

She brushed the hair away to fix him with that same gaze again.

"We gave you everything," she said, her words cutting his soul. "The finest tutors and education, a place in the royal court, even bought your way into the navy. And for what? So you could end up a traitor, rotting in a dungeon?"

Sharova's mouth tried to form words. but no sound came out. A single tear, all his body could afford, rolled from his right eye.

"No grandchildren for me either," she continued, lashing at him. "No daughter-in-law to pass along my years of experience to. What a disappointment you are, Sharova."

"Mother!" he screamed as her image faded.

More came to visit him in the black eternity of his own personal hell: people he had wronged, men he had trodden down in his ambition to reach the upper echelons, even his childhood dog came to torture him.

Sharova lay in a fevered, twitching heap, screaming and crying as the ghosts of his past paid him a visit to rip pieces from his psyche.

***

Besmir leaped from Arteera's tent partly dressed, tripped over his own clothing and fell to the ground. Ordinarily that would have earned him a ribbing, king or not. Today, however, an air of abject fear lay over the tent town. Women and children cowered in their tents, following his progress through the town with despair and fear in equal measure.

"Soldiers!" a voice continued to wail, as if any remained who did not know.

Besmir cast about angrily, searching for the owner of the voice.

Choke them if I find out who it is.

His foot caught under a tent line, sending him sprawling again, and an explosion of rage filled his chest. More soldiers, probably sent by his uncle to try and kill them all, to put an end to them before he could do any damage. Part of Besmir rejoiced that they had been sent, as it meant his little kingdom was a threat to Tiernon at least as an ideal. Another part feared for what these men might do to a camp filled with women and children. Yet another part of his brain said they would pay dearly for any harm that came to the people under his care.

Besmir caught his first glimpse of the invaders between the tops of a pair of tents. At the head of the party was an immense bear of a man at least seven feet in height. He wore a long coat of chain mail with steel plates added for reinforcement and carried a sword that looked capable of cutting a man in half. Braided hair cascaded from his chin, and within the mail, a cowl hid most of his head. A cloak slung over his shoulders bore some insignia Besmir was unfamiliar with, a pair of crossed swords on a red and white background. He led a group of around ten men, all similarly dressed, who had halted a short distance from the outskirts of the tent town.

Probably to call for my surrender.

With practiced ease, the hunter brought his bow out and slipped an arrow to the string, making sure he had a line of sight on the big man as he approached. He took a deep breath and rounded the final tent, confronting the group who looked surprised to see him and began muttering among themselves.

"What business have you here?" Besmir demanded.

Behind him, he could hear people gathering, and his heart swelled when he realized they had come out in support of him.

"I was in denial when I heard it to begin with," the tall warrior spoke in a deep, rumbling voice that carried past

Besmir to his people. "One who called himself the rightful king, living with a group of women and children."

The giant started across towards Besmir, his armor clinking and leather creaking as he moved. Besmir tensed, pulling his bowstring back and sighting along his arrow directly inside the mail cowl.

"I knew your father," he said, falling to one knee. "Your Majesty."

Behind him the other men followed suit, all kneeling before Besmir even as they held the reins to the powerful horses they had ridden here.

"Who are you?" Besmir asked, relaxing his bow.

The giant looked up, nearly as tall as Besmir even though he was kneeling, and smiled.

"I am Norvasil, commander of the White Blades," he said indicating the small group.

"White Blades?"

Norvasil frowned slightly, the tufts of hair over his bright eyes shifting as if alive.

"Have you not heard of us, Majesty?" he asked. "Has no one ever spoken of our deeds?"

"Not to me," Besmir said. "You may as well get up before that mail starts to rust. Then explain to me who you are and what it's got to do with me."

A wide grin split Norvasil's face then, and he grunted his way to standing again. "By the gods," he bellowed. "Alike in manner as well as looks."

"Norvasil?" Herofic's voice rang out. "I thought I could smell something foul."

The giant's eyes roved the crowd beyond Besmir for the source of the voice.

"Herofic?" he thundered with widening eyes. "From the bowels of which vile creature were you expelled?"

"I believe she called herself your mother, and it was *not* her bowels," Herofic shouted as he trotted across to be engulfed in a massive hug. Besmir watched in confusion as the massive Norvasil tried to squeeze Herofic into submission. The pair laughed and insulted one another freely before the crowd, and a few giggles could be heard. Besmir turned to see many of the women were whispering and muttering to each other, pointing at the newcomers.

"Sire, this degenerate and his crew of little girls," Herofic said when he had finally managed to extricate himself from the cage of Norvasil's arms, "are what remain of your father's royal guards."

"I thought you were part of that," Besmir said.

"He was unable to make the cut, Your Majesty," Norvasil said cheekily.

"I served your grandfather," Herofic said with a warning look at Norvasil. "For some unknown reason your father chose this bunch as guard."

"And yet he was butchered in a foreign land along with my mother," Besmir said.

It had been an observation rather than an accusation. Besmir's feelings for his parents were nonexistent. To him, they were two people he had never known and would never be able to meet. Norvasil, however, paled then reddened as Besmir's words hit him like balls of flame. His expression changed, the levity falling from his features to be replaced with sorrow and loss.

"Your father ordered us to leave him," Norvasil rumbled. "I begged to be allowed to accompany him, but he refused, said our place was at the palace,." Norvasil spat on the floor. "I would sooner defile my own mother than serve that...thing calling himself king." Acid hate laced his every word, and Besmir felt kinship brewing inside him already.

"I meant no offense," he said. "From what I hear, my father made a number of mistakes. Mistakes that cost him and my mother their lives. Will you join us?" he asked.

"We are yours to command, Majesty," Norvasil said worriedly. "We present ourselves before your mercy to—"

"Why, if it is not Norvasil as I live and breathe," Zaynorth said as he made his way through the crowd. "We do not have a stable for you as yet," he added, grinning. His smile faded as he saw the expression on the giant's face. "Is there a problem?" he asked Besmir.

"More of a misunderstanding," Besmir replied. "Seeing as how no one ever told me my father had a dedicated royal guard, I was unaware he told them to remain here while he exiled himself to Gravistard." His voice held a hint of anger.

"That is where he went?" Norvasil wondered.

"And where I was raised an orphan," Besmir said.

Norvasil's eyes crinkled at the corners and he blinked several times, his mouth downturned.

"An orphan," he muttered. "Of course you must have been. I am so sorry."

"It's not your fault," Besmir said, feeling a little guilty for the big man.

"You are gracious to say so, sire. Yet the fact remains it was our duty to protect your family and we failed."

"By carrying out your orders?" Besmir asked.

"Yes, sire," Norvasil nodded solemnly. "For we had a sworn oath to protect your family, even if it was from themselves."

Keluse and Ranyor made their way over, staring at the newcomers. Besmir felt a little smile cross his face when he saw their linked hands.

"Nice of you to join us," he ribbed them. "What kept you?"

Keluse reddened and looked away, a little smile on her face.

Ranyor looked Besmir in the eye, straight-faced. "I must apologize, sire," he said. "For being unable to get here sooner. Had this been an attack, I—"

"Just don't let it happen again," Besmir said quietly to them. "I know what it's like," he said, glancing sideways at Arteera. Ranyor nodded.

"Who are these men?" Keluse asked with interest.

"Apparently they are the remnants of my father's royal guard. That big one in charge is called 'Norvasil,'" Besmir said.

"So why—" Keluse started.

"We've already been through all that," Besmir hissed. "I'll tell you later." He glanced at the giant. "I think he'll eat me if I rake over it again."

He made his way across to the White Blades, assessing their dour mood.

"I'm not one for flowery speeches," he said. "And I don't always think about what I say before I say it, but if you're here in support of me and in particular these people," Besmir cast his arm back at the people of the tent town, "then I welcome you with open arms."

"It would be our honor to serve the son of the man we pledged ourselves to, Majesty," Norvasil said with a bow made awkward by his armor. "To that end," he added, fetching a bone horn from his saddle, and blew a long note, the mournful sound rolling across the grassland towards the horizon.

Besmir waited, following Norvasil and the other Blades' gaze. Eventually his eyes caught sight of another group of people, teams of oxen straining into the traces of loaded wagons and a small herd of goats and sheep.

"The remainder of our force," Norvasil stated quietly. "We did not want to cause panic by advancing in numbers."

Besmir looked at him and shook his head, laughing.

"So you chose to send," he counted, "nine massive armed men, rather than the goatherd?"

Norvasil looked sheepish as he thought about how it must have looked.

"Don't panic, Norvasil," Besmir said. "Pick anywhere you like and set up. Come find us when you're ready and we can have a conversation in a little more comfort."

"As you order, sire," Norvasil said, saluting.

Chapter Thirteen

Tiernon stared at the little man who stood before him, trembling like a bride on her wedding night. General Marthius, head of his armies and the most decorated man Tiernon's father had promoted, reeked of fear. Tiernon reveled in it.

"What?" the king asked bluntly.

"It... I-I-It is... I mean, the attack, sire, it...failed." Marthius flinched as he related the report.

"What are you blathering about? What attack?"

"The one you ordered on the impostor, Besmir, Majesty," the general explained, squirming.

Rage exploded inside Tiernon, burning and cutting him. Beside him, T'noch turned his beastly head to stare at the king.

"As foretold," it hissed. "You must deal with him directly."

"I take no orders from you, fiend!" Tiernon shouted at the presence only he could see. "It is I who countenance your existence here, and I who can banish you back to the hell from which you came!"

"Sire?" Marthius asked, confusion plainly written on his white face.

"Not you," Tiernon growled. "Him." He stabbed his finger at what Marthius saw as thin air.

Tiernon rose from the throne, pacing before the dais and muttering crazily to himself as well as cursing T'noch. Dripping with vile hatred for all things living, T'noch watched Tiernon pace with one pair of its eyes while the other pair monitored the other human in the room. Two of T'noch's minions were approaching General Marthius, unseen, from behind him. A hiss rolled from his throat, filling the air with communication pheromones only they could understand. They backed away, hissing their own displeasure at being denied an easy meal.

Tiernon rounded on Marthius, staring at him with contempt pulling a sneer on his face.

"Tell me what happened," he ordered. "And leave out no detail unless you wish me to feed you to T'noch."

Tiernon watched Marthius struggle with the questions he obviously had, not knowing what a T'noch was. Luckily for the general, he managed to rein his curiosity in, explaining what he had gathered from his spies.

"Our agent in their camp has been keeping a close eye on the one calling himself Besmir, sire," Marthius finished. "She is certain she can slip a knife into him as he sleeps."

Tiernon considered letting this woman, whoever she might be, do just that. It would save him a job he could not be bothered to do, as well as sending a message to any who opposed him that he could get to them at any time.

"You must do this deed," T'noch hissed.

Tiernon spun to stare at the half-formed thing he had summoned.

Gods, how I hate you!

"Your sibilant whispering sets my teeth on edge, T'noch," he said. "And stay out of my thoughts unless you wish to return to hell."

T'noch recoiled, feigning compliance while sucking sustenance from Tiernon's aura to ensure his obedience.

"Marthius, approach me and we shall visit this Besmir. Teach him and his petty band of followers what it is to stand against me."

General Marthius forced himself to step closer to his king, feeling the cold touch of horror when he drew near. There had been something badly wrong in the palace for weeks now, worse than when Tiernon had usurped the throne from his brother in the first place. Now the disappearances, the casual discovery of mutilated bodies in the palace and the general disrepair of the palace itself all pointed to a horrible conclusion for Marthius. He was cursed.

I will end up like Sharova. Left to rot in a cell.

Marthius took the king's offered arm. His flesh had the feel of a corpse, cold and stiff, and it was all Marthius could do to stop himself from recoiling. Tiernon held out his other arm, his hand made into a claw, and Marthius's jaw dropped as he watched something *else* take hold of it.

Inch-long, sickly green talons extended from something that had seven digits. Its skin looked paper-dry, but was dripping with slime simultaneously. The hand, if a hand it was, faded into invisibility just above the wrist, and Marthius came to several realizations at that point.

The thing he talks to is real!

It is some manner of hell beast.

This is my last day alive.

The world faded in Marthius' eyes and he felt a sickening wrench as if he was being dragged sideways by the stomach, his entrails trying to follow.

***

A single figure detached itself from the darkness, its feet slapping on the stones as it moved through the dark of the palace. Thoran had seen more horrors in the last few days than she believed she could bear. From the poor dead girl, Virine, being used as a puppet by the king, to watching helplessly as Sharova was beaten and imprisoned. She had watched in horror, as Tiernon had casually butchered men, women and children on his altar, their screams haunting her both day and night. Worse even than that was the horrible, cold presence that seemed to follow Tiernon everywhere he went. At first she had thought it was the strange, silent guards that accompanied him everywhere, but she had felt it, felt *them*, when Tiernon was out of the room.

When she realized she was alone in the palace, Thoran knew she only had one chance. She took the small lock-picking kit she had picked up after Shorava had left it during his initial rescue from the only place she had to hide it and started to learn how to pick locks.

From observing Sharova previously, Thoran had learned she needed to put the L-shaped wrench in the bottom of the lock and turn it a little. From there, however, she was at a complete disadvantage. She knew there were sections within the lock she needed to do something to, but not how, and had no idea how to tell if she had done the right thing.

Fear sharpened her mind as she recalled how Tiernon moved her from place to place in the palace, stowing her in a different cage and forcing her to witness his atrocities. She had been present when he slaughtered the Lorangian ambassador, slashing his throat in plain sight of numerous other foreign dignitaries. She had been there as he took a naked girl, jabbering and begging for her life, to his altar. She had quieted as soon as he lay her on the surface, her skin dimpling with gooseflesh despite the warmth in the room. Thoran cried out, thinking he was about to rip her virginity away, but what he did was somehow worse. His razor-sharp knife had kissed the girl's flesh deeply, making her back arch, but no sound came from her throat. Blood – bright red and hot – flowed down onto the table, *into* the table, feeding it in some disgusting manner.

Worse still had been Tiernon's expression of utter glee as he sliced the girl apart alive. All the time staring at Thoran, his mad eyes telling her this would be her fate eventually.

As she recalled the harrowing things she had seen, Thoran felt something inside the lock move. She levered it upwards and felt around for more things that moved the same way.

Tension made her sweat, lack of food and water made her weak, and the constant need for pressure on the lock made her fingers hurt worse than when she had broken one as a child. Only thoughts of Sharova and freedom kept her at the seemingly fruitless task.

Time dragged by as Thoran worked, clicking the lock picks back and forth in the lock until she thought she would go mad with frustration.

Then it turned.

Thoran almost cried when her cage opened, swinging away from her on silent hinges.

I hope he forgets about me.

Even as she fled across the throne room, Thoran knew Tiernon would not forget. Even if he did, the cold things with him would chase her down and suck the life from her. Running was her only option, though, so she ran.

With only a general idea where Sharova had been taken and no idea if he was even alive, Thoran made her way down a flight of stone steps, the temperature falling as the light level did too. She made herself retreat and find a lantern, filled with oil and lit, burning her hand on the metal ring at the top before ripping some cloth from her barely existent dress and returning.

At the bottom of the stairs, a door blocked her passage, and she fought to control her breath as fear tried to overwhelm her. There was no telling what lay beyond this door, and certain death rose in her imagination, but if he was in here, suffering, she owed it to Sharova to find him.

Her tiny fingers grabbed the iron ring and turned it with an incredibly loud *click* that echoed from the stone walls around her. She winced and pushed the door open onto an equally dark space within. Bunks lay against the walls in rooms that lay to either side of the main corridor she found herself in. Nothing moved, not the smallest mouse, and the only sound to reach her ears was the guttering of the flame in her lantern.

A body lay in the doorway to one room, twisted and broken so badly, she could not tell it had been human once. Horror tore at her when she considered the force it must have taken to smash a person this badly, but she carried on.

It was some kind of barracks.

Thoran came to a larger room, the walls lined with shelves on which armor and weapons sat for the taking.

Dressed in a pair of scratchy woolen trews and linen shirt that exposed one shoulder and the swell of her breast, Thoran carried on to the end of the corridor. Some kind of office sat here. Wood-paneled walls surrounded her and a desk sat as abandoned as the rest of the place.

Revealed in the glow from her lamp, she could see a door leading into yet another area, this time with a square set into it to see through. Revealed in what little light there was she could see another set of stairs leading down into the blackness.

Thoran opened the door, peering into the dark as her heart beat faster.

I must be beneath the palace.

She descended one slow step at a time, her bare feet feeling the cold biting at them as she went. At the bottom was a set of rooms carved from the rock with doors barring each one. She swallowed and lifted her light up to the metal bars, peering within and expecting to see Sharova's body at any point. Each was as empty as the last.

At the deepest, farthest reaches of the tunnel, Thoran saw evidence of recent works. A hole had been blasted into the rock, leading even further into the ground. Her eyes picked out the soot-blackened shapes of melted rock.

What could have done this?

Yet some part of her mind knew this had to have been Tiernon's doing, and if so, this was where she would find Sharova. Gingerly, she stepped through the ragged hole and down the passage there. Twinkling lights glinted back at her from the walls, and she looked closer to see what looked to be gemstones left in the rock. Thoran wondered why Tiernon had not bothered to exploit this treasure but gave up trying to understand him.

He is mad. Irrevocably, totally, utterly insane.

She almost crashed into the wooden barrier at the end of the tunnel. Her fingers scrabbled at the wood, splinters shredding her flesh, as she searched for a handle or means of opening it, all to no avail. She beat on the wood, feeling its thickness and resilience, but heard nothing. Why would this be here if there was nothing behind it? Thoran put it from her mind, concentrating on finding a way through.

If Tiernon has the power to smash through rock, why does he need to have someone build a wooden barricade?

Thoran considered the point as she trekked back the way she had come, looking for something to break through the wood. In the barracks she found a sword, heavy and rust-pitted, that she thought might work, and trotted back down into the bowels beneath the palace.

Searing pain shot up through her feet and she paused to look. In the dim light cast by her lamp, Thoran saw the soles of her feet had been shredded by the rough floor. She stopped her descent to cut bandages from her voluminous shirt with the sword, wrapping her feet as best as she could before continuing.

She set the lamp down a little way from where she planned to start cutting at the wood, then gripped the sword in both hands and swung it as hard as she could at the wooden barrier.

Agony rolled up her arms as the sword bounced off the wood and slammed into the floor, jarring her elbows and shoulders. Moaning and panting, she slumped to the floor, waiting for the pain to subside.

Thoran tried to lever the heavy planks loose, wedging the tip of her sword between the boards and working it back and forth. The heavy, wet wood refused to give at first, and she leaned more of her weight against the handle until the sword started to bend. Tears of frustration rolled down her face at the realization she was never going to get through to Sharova.

Just when she was about to give up in defeat, one of the thick boards gave way with a scream of wet nails pulling from wood. Hope flared in Thoran's heart. Then her lantern flickered out.

Chapter Fourteen

The men of the White Blades integrated into the tent town well. Many of the women in the camp had lost husbands in the civil war and were more than happy to entertain strong, fit men. Besmir watched his little kingdom as women fought over the men they outnumbered. The men were, unsurprisingly, quite happy about the situation.

He, Zaynorth, Herofic and Norvasil were sitting in a tent Norvasil had insisted Besmir have as his interim palace. In comparison to the one he had been sharing with Arteera, it *was* a palace: spacious and containing furniture.

Arteera was quietly embroidering stags on any scrap of cloth she could lay her talented fingers on as the little group listened to Norvasil's tale.

"After your father left, I had a brief chat with the lads. No one was particularly interested in guarding Tiernon," he said dryly. "So we pinched as much inventory as we could and left." The big man scratched his cheek. "Trekking north seemed to be the best course, and we spent a few months wandering like nomads until word of Tiernon's war reached us." Norvasil drained the wine from his cup and belched. "It was not even a decision we had to consciously make. We lent a hand wherever we could against Tiernon's forces." Norvasil sighed. "Petty skirmishes when I look back now, but I had to stay true to your father, and with him in exile, the only thing I could think of was to attack his enemy."

Norvasil chuckled, running his fingers through his thick beard. Now out of armor, he had pulled the braids from his hair and beard, revealing lustrous curls that drove the tent town women wild.

"I suppose I hoped someone might slip a knife between his ribs, end it all, and your family could come home." Norvasil screwed his face up in thought. "Well, he put an end to that, eh?" He scanned the other men to see if there was judgment in their eyes. Seeing nothing but sympathy, he continued. "We were starting to settle down, put some crops in and starting to make some kind of life trading and running mercenary jobs, protecting caravans and the like, when word reached us there was a man claiming to be the rightful king. A hunter that was feeding the starving and clothing the poor." He grinned at Besmir. "A fanciful tale to be sure, but if there was even a grain of truth to it, we decided we needed to come and help." He shrugged his muscled shoulders.

"And here you are," Besmir said.

"Here we are," Norvasil echoed. "What will you do?"

Besmir rolled his eyes and looked at Zaynorth, who made no comment but pursed his lips to stop himself from speaking.

"We've had a few differences of opinion regarding that," Besmir told him. "Without an army, Tiernon can just roll over us at any time he wants and we're just a target waiting for him to do it."

"Arm the women," Norvasil said immediately.

"That's what I said," Besmir cried, turning an accusatory glare on Zaynorth.

The old mage grumbled something unintelligible and drained his own mug, refilling it from Norvasil's bottle without asking. The giant said nothing about that but carried on talking about the women in camp.

"My men could start to train a small group each, say ten per man, just basic hack techniques." He looked up as he thought. "Each one of those could teach what they have learned to another ten, and before long, you would have a small force," he said.

"Even if that were to work," Zaynorth said dismissively, "with what do you expect them to fight? Harsh words? We have no armory and no smith."

Norvasil grinned and stood.

"If you gentlemen would be so good as to follow me," he said, leading them from Besmir's tent.

They followed him a short distance from Besmir's tent to where they had stowed their wagons. Norvasil leaped up into the back of one, making the whole thing rock on its wheels. Deftly he untied the ropes holding a thick, oiled canvas sheet down and pulled back one corner.

"By the gods!" Herofic muttered when he saw the pile of swords and axes under the sheet. "Where did you come by these?"

"Stole them," Norvasil said. "We have been hauling Tiernon's weapons around for more than a year. The oxen have just about had enough now," he added.

As if it understood his words, one of the massive bulls grazing nearby bellowed a low moo.

"Stop complaining, Zaynorth," Norvasil shouted at the animal.

The old mage stared at him while Herofic tried to stifle his laughter behind his hand. Besmir grinned, looking between Norvasil and Zaynorth.

"Did you really name the beast Zaynorth?" the mage asked.

Norvasil nodded, an impudent grin spreading beneath his beard. Besmir chuckled.

Thunder rolled across the sky, dragging their attention westwards. Zaynorth and Herofic both frowned, glancing at each other worriedly.

"What is it?" Besmir asked.

"Thunder. From a cloudless sky?" Zaynorth said.

Besmir looked, realizing he was right. The sky was a warm azure from horizon to horizon, and a few wisps of white were all he could see.

"So what does that actually mean?"

Zaynorth looked from Norvasil to Herofic then back to Besmir before he answered. "Magic," he said sternly.

From the far side of the tent town the sound of yelling came to their ears. Besmir's heart beat faster, anticipation gripping his chest as he sprinted through the camp, weaving through bodies and the goats that had broken free and were bleating their way between the tents. Besmir could hear Herofic cursing his way along, shouting and extorting people out of his way.

Fright grabbed his chest when he caught the first scent of smoke tainted with the sweet stench of burning flesh. Something exploded to his right, the heat from the fireball searing his face and making him flinch. Besmir swore, ducking and swerving around another tent as he threw his arm up to cover his face.

His panicked run was cut short when he reached the edge of the destruction. Flames leaped from three tents and nausea flooded his stomach as he saw people, *his* people, burning alive inside. Rage burned the sickness away and he grabbed his faithful bow, notching an arrow to the string as he hunted for the source of this violence.

Two figures stood a few feet back from the edge of his town, and Besmir let fly without a thought, his arrow streaking through the air and slamming through the man at the front. He watched as the man's knees buckled, tumbling him back into the one behind.

"Tiernon!" Zaynorth gasped in shock. "You shot him!"

"And I'll do it again," Besmir growled, loosening another arrow at the second man.

This time, however, the missile exploded a few inches from the pair, and Besmir watched as Tiernon got to his feet, grinning madly. The hunter stalked over towards the pair, firing arrow after arrow, each one exploding in a blue flash before it could do any harm. Hate and revulsion rolled through him as he regarded his uncle, realizing he was a blood relation to the maniac.

Tiernon was nothing like Besmir expected. His mind had conjured images of a massive, powerful creature bristling with spiked armor and riding an immense stallion that could breathe flame. The pathetic thing that stood before him was deflated, flaccid as an empty bladder, and looked to be on the verge of death. Skin sagged from bones that jutted painfully from beneath, revealing every aspect of Tiernon's skull. His emaciated fingers jabbed the air like daggers, thin and pointed. A purple and gold silk brocade shirt hung from his thin shoulders, and Besmir could clearly see his collarbone and the top of his rib cage.

Thinning hair fell limply from a translucent scalp, allowing all to see the network of blue veins beneath, and the skin on his face sagged, pulling his lower eyelids down to reveal the raw, red wetness within.

Tiernon viewed the world through minuscule pupils that darted around as if unable to remain fixed on a single point. The kiss of reason had left those eyes long ago, Besmir could see, leaving his uncle utterly insane.

Tiernon watched in fascination as Besmir drew an arrow, aiming it at his chest., recognition and shock pulling his slack features into a gruesome mask as he stood rooted to the spot. Besmir reached him and halted, staring into his eyes with towering rage in his expression, his shoulders heaving with every breath.

"Brother?" Tiernon asked in a whisper. He shook his head to clear his thoughts, focusing on something behind Besmir.

"Zaynorth," he said without surprise. "I did wonder where you lost yourself to. So it is true then, my nephew survived. I can hardly believe the truth of it." Tiernon looked to his left and nodded. "Yes, T'noch, you were right after all."

Besmir frowned, as he was not speaking to the other man who cowered behind him and seemed to be overlooked.

"Leave this place!" Besmir shouted. "Or die where you stand."

Despite the fear that threatened to overwhelm him, Besmir stood his ground, especially as many of his people were watching his every move. Tiernon's awful gaze rolled to him again.

"No, I cannot do that," he spoke gently, calmly, with an almost conversational tone that Besmir thought he might do no more for a second. "I cannot allow you to live, unfortunately, and this little group of slaves will have to serve me now."

Besmir heard a thunderous roar from beside him and spun to see Norvasil hammering a blow at Tiernon with his massive sword. Lightning lanced down the blade when it hit the barrier that surrounded him, throwing the big man ten feet to land in a heap at the feet of the gathered crowd.

"Run!" Besmir bellowed at his people.

He knew nothing would ever be able to reach Tiernon, causing harm, while he had his barrier in place, and despite outward appearances, he had immense powers to draw on and maintain it.

He concentrated, letting his mind soar from his body and grab hold of a flock of passing birds, causing them to dive at the sagging form of Tiernon, blocking his vision. From his lofty view Besmir could see a number of women were dragging Norvasil from the field, and he hoped the big man was unharmed.

Dropping like a stone, Besmir hunted through the grass for mice and other small rodents he could use to distract Tiernon, trying to give his people time to escape at least. Tiernon himself did not bother with Besmir's statuesque body, concentrating rather on burning as many tents and people as he was able to see.

Despair crashed through Besmir as he watched more of the tent town destroyed, homes, possessions and even people burning to ashes under Tiernon's rain of violence. He searched in vain for something he could use, insects if need be, to attack the battlemage.

At the edge of the forest to the northern boundary of the tent town, he caught sight of his stag. The same mighty, proud creature he had brought into camp weeks ago as a sign to the people, a pledge. Besmir flicked into its mind with a blink.

***

Sweat dripped from the toiling woman as she worked in the icy blackness, feeling her way through the layers of planking that had been installed there. Thoran had come to the conclusion Tiernon had had this built, as, despite his immense power, he could only destroy. Even the simple act of creating a barrier to keep Sharova penned in was beyond his capabilities.

Thoran slipped her numb fingers along the jagged edge of the wood, splinters tearing at her as she sought another point to set the sword to work. Her limbs ached as if she had been punched, and unconsciousness was horribly close as she set the sword in place. Thoran hauled herself to her feet and pushed the sword into the wood. She had made her way through four layers of timber so far, the last three in complete darkness, and had no idea how thick this barrier was until she stumbled forward as the blade disappeared between two of the boards.

Hope rose in her chest again as she worked the board loose, wrenching it from the barrier to fall behind her. The smell that wafted from within made her retch, a heavy combination of human waste and putrefaction that meant he had to be dead. Thoran forced herself to carry on, she had to know for certain if Sharova was in here and if he lived.

Eventually she managed to pull enough wood aside to access the chamber beyond and crawled slowly inside, patting the floor gingerly, fearful of what she might find. Gravel and other sharp things met her sore fingertips as she worked.

"Sharova?" she whispered.

Why am I whispering?

Her word echoed hollowly in the tiny space, but she could hear nothing else.

A squeal jumped from her throat when her hand hit something hot, wet and swollen. Her arm jerked back automatically, the skin on her palm crawling and trying to escape. Heart beating hard and breath whistling from her throat, Thoran reached for the thing again.

A leg! It is a leg!

Feeling her way up the body, Thoran ran her hands over damp clothing and through a matted beard until she reached a face. Barely a puff of breath escaped him, and she wondered if this was really Sharova on the verge of death.

With no supplies and no way to get him out, Thoran started to cry. The hopelessness of her situation hit home, and she lay down beside him, weak and spent. Thoran listened to the weak breaths his body dragged slowly in and out, the sound almost comforting.

Just stay with him. Just wait for the end. At least Tiernon can have no claim on you.

"Mama?" Sharova's voice was barely recognizable, hoarse and wasted.

"Sharova?" Thoran said. "Can you hear me?"

"Mama...sorry..."

His tone wrenched at her heart, filled with pain and sorrow, and she wondered what horrors his delirium had conjured.

"Yes, Son," Thoran said, tears flowing down her face. "Now I need you to get up! Come on, Sharova! Up!"

The former fleet admiral moaned as she pulled at him, the pain from his infection ripping through his entire system.

With near constant cajoling and pretending to be his mother, Thoran managed to get Sharova to his feet, one arm thrown over her shoulders, and the pair staggered from his tomb in complete blackness.

Without knowing how long it took, she led the moaning, crying, half-crazed man from within the depths of the earth, birthing them both back into the realms of man when she opened the door that let them back into the palace.

Bright sun flooded the hall, making her squint in agony and confusion. Sharova slumped down the wall to lay in a heap, and shock rolled through her when she saw how wasted and ill he was.

His face and body had shrunk, the former stocky frame gone, wasted to emaciation, and she could see the infection had crawled up his leg, swelling and making it look painfully red. Thoran realized she would not be able to lift him, and he had fallen into unconsciousness, his breathing wet. She struggled and fought to get him on his side, propped against the cool wall, and stumbled off to try and find something to help him.

Sepulcher-like, the palace was completely empty, silent and still. Thoran passed through the halls and chambers like a wraith, not accosted and free. She searched fruitlessly for what felt like hours until finally she reached the former kitchens.

The massive hearth, large enough to stand inside, lay cold, the fires had long since burned out. Foodstuffs and utensils lay in complete disarray, and the evidence of rats lay everywhere. Thoran started a search, looking for anything that she could use and the rats had not nibbled or fouled with their leavings.

A while later she had managed to gather two small jars of honey, some dried and salty meat, and a few desiccated vegetables. Her heart soared when she found a barrel of clean water, slurping the liquid down greedily until her stomach ached painfully. Weariness tempted her to sleep, but she knew she had to get back to Sharova, then realized she had no idea where she had left him.

Working on pure force of will, Thoran made her way back through the palace, looking at the ruined furnishings and scattered items that had once made the place beautiful. She chewed a piece of the meat, her jaws aching with the effort and the salty flavor that assaulted her mouth. Eventually she started to recognize some of the places she had been before and knew how to return to where Sharova lay.

Confusion tore at her when she got back to find his body gone.

Chapter Fifteen

Keluse watched in frightened horror as children burned alive. Their screams of terror and agony ripped at her soul, and she knew they would haunt her for the rest of her life. Madness swirled around her as people ran screaming from Tiernon's destruction of their homes.

Her eyes lit on Besmir, his body planted firmly before Tiernon, directly in his path. Screaming his name, she started forward, wincing as a flock of birds dived straight at the battlemage, swerving off as soon as they had hit his invisible barrier. When the flashes subsided, Tiernon lowered the hand he had used to shield his eyes and carried on throwing fire in all directions. She watched in awe as rats and mice wriggled through the grass to hurl themselves at the same barrier the birds had. Trails of small animals headed for the mage, emerging from piles of logs, the woods nearby and the riverbank.

Besmir!

Keluse realized his plan when Tiernon's attacks paused a second time and she spun, screaming at anyone she could to throw things at the evil man. She drew her bow and started firing arrows, each one making a little flare of light as it exploded against his shield. Ranyor dashed over, hurling anything he could towards Tiernon in the hope it would stop him. Members of the White Blades followed suit, joined by some of the tent-towners when they understood what was happening. Civilians and royal guard alike, all came together in a desperate attempt to stop Tiernon.

A rain of objects hammered against Tiernon's shield, making it flash ever brighter. Plates and cutlery, sticks and branches, anything that was not aflame they used as missiles against him.

Keluse noticed the flashes were reducing in brilliance and one of the larger objects, a battered shield, hammered through to slam into Tiernon's leg breaking his concentration. "He's weakening!" she screamed.

Reaching for another arrow, Keluse's hand grasped at nothing. Her quiver was empty, and despair rolled through her chest.

The sound of thundering hooves came to her ears and she turned to watch as a massive stag galloped across the grassland, headed directly at Tiernon. Her mind made the connection and she cut her eyes to Besmir's broad back in wonder.

Tiernon had thrown his arms up in defence, the slow rain of thrown objects all hitting him now. The odd man behind him took a glancing blow from an earthenware jug, felling him instantly, blood trickling from his nose.

The stag lowered his head, charging at Tiernon, antlers first. Tiernon's hand shot out towards Keluse and the defenders and she watched in dismay as their rain of objects flew in the opposite direction, allowing Tiernon to stare at Besmir with hate. His arm was raised, pointing at the hunter, and something black exploded from his open hand at the same time as the stag smashed into his body.

Tiernon folded in half around the stag's antlers before being thrown high into the air as the great beast tossed its head. Keluse watched as his body made a high arc in the air then disappeared. The stag trembled as if understanding where it was and darted off, headed for the forest again.

Keluse assumed Besmir had released his control of the beast and looked toward where he had been standing. His body lay on the scorched, burned ground, and an ice-cold fist grasped her heart. She scrambled to her feet, racing across the debris and smoking ruins of the tent town towards him.

"Keluse!" Ranyor shouted from behind her.

She ignored her lover, throwing herself down beside the man who had saved her from the evils of her life in Tyrington. Her hands reached for him then halted, as if touching him would make his death real. If she did not touch him, did not feel the lack of pulse, the absence of breath, it would not be real.

Besmir looked peaceful, Keluse decided as she stroked the hair from his pale face. Almost as if a smile tried to play at the corners of his mouth. One arm lay over his chest, the other at his side as if he was asleep, and Keluse almost shook him to try and rouse him.

"Keluse," Ranyor said, resting his hands on her shoulders.

"He's fine," she said as others began to arrive. "Just asleep."

"Besmir!" Arteera screamed as she pelted across towards him.

The dark-haired woman dropped to her knees beside him, laying her head on his chest and sobbing. Zaynorth, Herofic and some members of the White Blades joined the growing crowd of tent-town people sobbing, grief-stricken and pale with shock at the loss of their new king.

Keluse looked from one face to another, searching each for some sign of hope. Zaynorth looked back with pity and grief written on his face. Herofic looked enraged, without a target to unleash his temper on. Norvasil shoved his way through the crowd, took one look at Besmir's body, and collapsed to his knees.

"Not again," he pleaded. "Not another." He bowed his head in grief and loss.

"Quiet!" Arteera yelled, lifting her tear-streaked face to implore them all. "He lives still." She laid her head on his chest again, listening as they all fell silent around him. "I can hear a heartbeat!" she said after a few seconds.

Keluse pressed her fingers against his throat and hovered her ear over his lips. Hope filled her system when she felt the faintest pulse flick over her fingertips, a hint of breath kissing her ear.

"He is!" she cried. "I can feel his heartbeat. Help me lift him."

Hands lifted Besmir's body, all trying to touch the man who had stood against Tiernon for them, offering prayers and giving thanks that he lived.

They bore him through the town to his pavilion, lay him on his bed and stood there, uncertain as to what they could do for him.

"Light a fire," Arteera said. "So he remains warm."

Keluse laid her hand on Besmir's brow, feeling the warmth of life radiating from him.

"He is warm," she muttered, looking at the other woman.

Arteera's face crumpled. "Then what can be done for him?"

"I don't know," Keluse admitted. "Keep him comfortable until he recovers?"

"You think he will?" the other woman asked, hope ringing in her voice.

Keluse looked at her, seeing the same expression on her face that Keluse wore on her own. She loved Besmir as if he were her older brother, but Arteera looked to be in love with him, and she considered how she might feel if it were Ranyor lain low.

"I hope so," she said.

**

Thoran cast about for any sign of the man she had saved, wondering if she had returned to the same place she had left him or somewhere similar-looking. After a few seconds of searching, she knew it was. Damp marks on the stonework showed where he had managed to drag himself off, and she sighed as she followed them.

Luckily he had not been able to get himself too far, and she rounded a corner to see a swollen foot laying at the junction of two corridors. Sharova looked as if he was reaching towards one of the doors, and Thoran moved over to see what was inside.

Beyond the door lay a simple room, bare apart from an old table and piles of dust. She set her pilfered items down on the table and went to check on him, lifting the clay bottle she had filled with water to his lips.

Sharova choked when the first drops hit his lips and his eyes opened, lighting on her for a few seconds but remaining unfocused as he moaned. Thoran dribbled a few more drops onto his cracked lips and watched as he managed to swallow a few.

"This way, Sharova," she said, pulling him towards the door. "This way, Son."

Slowly, the fever-riddled, wasted man dragged himself into the room, and Thoran closed the door. Panting and sliding to one side, she lay there staring at his swollen leg.

Get up, he needs you!

Exhausted both physically and mentally, Thoran climbed slowly to her knees and crawled over to look at Sharova's leg. A deep cut, surrounded by lighter scratches, looked angry, puffy and red. It wept when she touched the hot area around it, bringing a deep moan from his throat. Thoran hardened her heart and pressed her fingers down the length of his leg, forcing the poison from his body.

Sharova screamed, his body jerking away from the pain, but Thoran carried on massaging the pus from his leg as his screams and moans filled the air. Eventually no more would come, and a small trickle of blood flowed from the wound

After pouring some honey on it she managed to rip some cloth from her dwindling clothes and wrapped it around his leg. She scooped a little into her own mouth, wincing at its sweetness as it bit at her mouth.

Fatigue pulled at her and she slumped forward, lying beside the man she was attempting to save.

"I shall look for some more thi..." she murmured, closing her eyes and letting sleep take her.

***

Keluse made her way back through the field of tents, a brace of pheasants over her shoulder. The dead had been buried, the remains of the tents and charred possessions cleared, and life had resumed a hushed routine. Keluse had returned to hunting, as that was what she thought Besmir would wish her to do. A few people called to her as she passed, and she waved at the families and friends as she walked.

She smiled when she saw some of the men of the White Blades living with the tent-town folk, laughing and joking with each other as if nothing had happened. Sadness hit her again as she caught sight of Besmir's large tent and thought of its contents. Keluse could see without looking what it would be like inside. Arteera would be tending Besmir, washing and cleaning his body to prevent sores, pouring honeyed water into his mouth and whispering to him as others poked their heads inside to see if there was any change. Keluse avoided the place entirely, knowing there was going to be no change. His body might cling to life, but his spirit was gone. She could feel the lack of energy, sense the absence of anything that made him *him*.

Ranyor was missing from their tent when she arrived, so she dumped her cargo and trotted through the tents towards the training area the Blades had marked out. Zaynorth had managed to convince people that Besmir would recover, despite Keluse's protests, and they had begun training anyone who was willing to handle a sword or ax, teaching them the basics of combat. Ranyor had volunteered to train his own ten, and Keluse knew that was where he would be.

She rounded the last of the tents to see a massive area filled with women and adolescent boys, each armed and engaged in various forms of combat under the watch of experienced fighters. Easily half the growing camp had volunteered for combat training, and Keluse felt a warm pride growing inside her as she watched them work.

Ranyor stood in the middle of his group, his keen eyes picking up on any tiny mistakes the women might make. Keluse smiled as she walked over towards them, seeing his knitted brow and the serious set of his jaw. He pointed something out to one of the women and she smiled up at him. Keluse halted. That had not been merely a friendly smile.

She was young, Keluse noticed, pretty as many of the Gazluthian women were, with long, dark hair and clear, light skin.

What am I in comparison?

Keluse skirted around behind the group and approached stealthily, losing herself in the mass of people. A few recognized her blonde hair and tanned skin, raising a hand in greeting as she passed. Straining over the sounds of grunting and the clang of metal on metal, Keluse listened to what Ranyor and the girl were saying.

"...to roll your wrist when countering," he said.

"I do not think I will ever be able to get this right," the girl said in a weak voice. "Could you show me again?" Her voice was light and breathy. Keluse watched her expression change, a flash of lust crossing her features.

"No need for that, Dorann," Ranyor said, his voice businesslike. "You will get used to the technique in battle."

Keluse smiled a little when she realized he had no idea the girl was propositioning him, and her look of chagrin sent shivers of satisfaction through her.

"Let us call this a successful day," Ranyor called, turning so they could all hear. "Return at first light tomorrow and we shall continue."

Keluse saw his face light up, a warm smile curving his lips, when he caught sight of her. Striding through the group, he took her hand and kissed the back of her fingers, sending shivers of delight down her spine.

"I thought you were still hunting, love," he said staring into her eyes.

Keluse shook her head, feeling self-conscious in the presence of so many others. Dorann shot a hate-filled look at Keluse as she passed.

"See you tomorrow, Ranyor," she said.

Ranyor ignored the girl completely, his attention focused solely on Keluse. Leading her from the midst of the fighting women, Ranyor retained her hand as they walked, warmth spreading up her arm from the contact.

Heading for the outskirts of the forest, Keluse knew he would make for the small stream that fed the lake the tent town had been built beside. They had found a secluded spot beneath the arms of a willow tree, far from prying eyes and ears, to be truly alone.

Chilly drops hit Keluse when Ranyor jumped into the little pool carved out by the passage of water. He hissed and splashed water over his back, scrubbing the dirt of the day from his skin while she watched in amusement.

"Gods," he gasped. "I forget how cold this is every time."

Keluse chuckled. "You need to be careful around Dorann," she said without knowing she was going to say it.

Ranyor looked up, puzzled, at her own surprised expression.

"Dorann, why?" he asked, flicking water at her.

"Hey!" Keluse cried. "I heard her earlier asking for private lessons." Keluse flicked her hair and put on a high voice, mocking Dorann's speech. "She's after you," she added.

Pain flared in Keluse's chest, a deep ache that made her feel sick when she said that. Ranyor waded through the waist-deep water and climbed up the bank, stripping water from his body with his hands. Keluse felt her eyes crawl over his body as he stood before her, utterly naked.

"Really?" Ranyor asked, his tone skeptical.

"Yes! Most of them were giving you little looks, invitations. Don't tell me you don't see them!" Keluse shouted.

"There is only one woman I see," Ranyor replied calmly. "She sits before me, beautiful and proud."

Tears rolled down Keluse's face then. Hot and unstoppable. She hugged her knees, rocking as she sobbed. She felt Ranyor's strong arms around her and leaned into him.

"I'm sorry," she cried. "I don't mean to be jealous, but when I saw her... I mean, she's all curves and breasts...and what am I in comparison?"

"Everything I have ever wanted," he said simply.

Keluse stared into his eyes, her own tear-reddened and wet, astonished at his words.

"Why?" she asked. "I don't look like them. I'm more like a boy than a woman!"

"I recall a bathtub in which you were a woman," he said, rubbing her back. "I dreamed of your silken hair and smooth skin every night after that. I loved you from the first, even in Gravistard when I coaxed you from beneath that hill," he laughed. "Do you recall? You told Morcath and I to surrender as you were coming out?"

Keluse smiled, her mood lightening a little.

"Yes, then Besmir shot you," she said, reaching to touch the puckered arrow wound in his chest.

Her thoughts turned to Besmir, laid low in his tent, and tears threatened again.

"What's going to happen?" she asked. "To Besmir? To us?"

"I cannot say what Besmir's fate may be," Ranyor said. "As for us, our children will be beautiful beyond imagining." He grinned at her look of surprise. "And rich also. We shall have a long, happy life filled with grandchildren who love us."

"You've spent a lot of time thinking about this, haven't you?"

"Maybe," Ranyor said, smirking at her. "How does it sound?"

"Perfect," Keluse whispered as her lips found his.

Chapter Sixteen

Even the wind cut into him as his eyes fluttered open.
Biting, acid grit rasped over his skin, burning and cutting in
equal measure. A thousand needle points pierced his back
from the ground. Sky the color of complete depression,
starless despite the lack of sun, stretched across his vision and
he sat up, looking around in horrified shock at his
surroundings.

What looked to be a field of ash stretched as far as he could
see, crystals glinting in the light that came from an unknown
source. Blank and featureless with neither tree, hill nor
building to be seen, Besmir turned a slow circle to see if he
could detect anything at all.

Pain rippled up his arms as the hostile wind scoured at his
body, and he held his hands up to shield his eyes. Shock
chilled his whole system when he saw they were a translucent
grey color.

"What...?" His voice sounded hollow and weak in the savage
air.

He looked around, searching desperately for someone,
anyone to help him, but the bleak, blank grey revealed
nothing. Every step sent waves of agony up through his feet,
the needle-sharp ground, like broken glass, shredding the skin.

When he looked, however, his ghostly skin remained intact. He could feel pain without injury.

Trudging through the ashen horror with the very elements ripping at him, Besmir felt panic grabbing at him. What had happened? Was this the afterlife, or some torture Tiernon had conjured? Why was he here?

He remembered taking over the stag, hurling it at the battlemage as he had done with the birds and rats. A rain of objects had been thrown at him too, people from the tent town doing anything to protect themselves. Then the jarring shock as his antlers had slammed into Tiernon and the satisfying crunch as something gave inside his uncle. Besmir had thrown his head, tossing the king up in the air, released his hold on the stag...then woken here.

Acid grit sawed at his naked flesh, and a moan of pure anguish left him as he trudged over the broken glass ground, not knowing if he would ever find anything or anyone else.

It did not matter if he folded his arms; the wind managed to reach every part of him, grinding against his flesh relentlessly. It ripped at his eyes, scoured his nose and throat, burned within his lungs, turning him into a throbbing mass of pain. Every step sent ice-cold needles of agony shooting through his feet and legs, driving him towards the edge of madness.

Time stretched out as he trudged through the endless grey, directionless and without hope of any kind. Nothing changed.

Day and night remained the same colorless, dull grey, featureless and lifeless as far as his eyes could see.

Weariness tugged at him, but there would be no sleep in this hostile place without some kind of shelter, so Besmir concentrated on putting one foot before the other, his head down to keep the air from ripping at his eyes.

After what may have been minutes or centuries, Besmir noticed the ground had sloped upwards a little, a slight incline he was now climbing. He looked up to see an immense hill rising before him, occupying the whole of his vision and climbing into the miserable sky. Despair ripped at him as he began to climb, stumbling as the gradient increased until he was forced to crawl. The ground stabbed into his palms and his knees when he fell, sending savage jolts of agony up his arms now too.

His life became an endless toil of climbing this hill in relentless, searing agony. Throbbing, burning pain tore at every piece of him constantly, and his screams rolled dully over the uncaring landscape as he toiled.

The summit revealed itself to be exactly the same as the rest of this place: flat, grey and featureless apart from a finger of rock that exploded skywards in the distance. With no other option, he stumbled on towards the monolith, hoping someone else might have made their way towards it.

Time became meaningless, blurring as he made his way over the needle-sharp ground towards the rock. As he neared the thing, Besmir's eyes picked out shapes in the distance: pale, dull things that circled the base of the tower endlessly, looking similar to himself.

It was not until Besmir had drawn nearer to them that he realized they were nothing like him. They were twisted, vile things, malformed and skewed horribly. Besmir wondered if they had changed due to the exposure here, but dismissed it, as these things were obviously not human.

Trunk-thick legs supported a body that looked almost square, with numerous appendages that might have been arms, tentacles or wings, for all Besmir knew. Blunt heads lifted to sniff the air, baying when they caught his scent. As one they turned blind eyes on Besmir, screaming and ravening as they started a charge at him.

They flowed from around the pillar, from holes in the ground and caves in the bottom of the rock finger, boiling from the landscape like ants from a nest. Each had a loping gait, using their odd arms to steady and propel them over the ground at a horrible rate of speed.

Besmir fled into the grey with the awful sound of their hunger gaining on him in every passing second. His lungs burned with the poisonous atmosphere, and the searing agony from his ravaged feet made him hobble.

Something cold and wet grasped at his ankle, and he screamed in fear and panic, wrenching his leg away from whatever had him. More pain tore through his muscles as the thing refused to let go. Powerful and desperate, it grunted wetly as another of its kind grabbed at him too. Besmir stumbled, falling to one knee as they swarmed over him, ripping and biting at his translucent flesh.

Teeth ripped at his neck, his belly, his legs. Waves of rippling agony exploded from each wound, fire tearing screams from his ragged throat, as he thrashed weakly for escape. Wet appendages held his arms down as cold mouths bit his fingers, severing each.

Yet somehow, even though the beasts ate pieces of him, they seemed to remain to be eaten again by another mouth. Besmir's world became nothing but searing agony as the monsters ripped and tore at him endlessly, his screams whipped away by the acidic winds.

***

Thoran woke feeling a little better, and to sun pouring in through the window. As soon as she moved, her muscles screamed in protest, evidence of the ordeals she had been through. Sharova had shifted and now lay with his arm over her protectively, a position that made her feel safe for a few seconds. His breaths came somewhat more easily and his heartbeat was stronger, but he remained unconscious and oblivious to her shaking him.

Reluctantly she rolled from beneath his arm and got unsteadily to her feet, weaving like a snake about to strike before finding her balance once more. She sipped water and honey, feeling the liquids refreshing her almost immediately. Sharova moaned and shifted, the tattered shreds of his clothing peeling back from his wounded leg.

Thoran went to him, unwrapping his leg to see the infection had subsided a little. She smeared some more honey on his leg and wrapped it in the last of her improvised bandages. She sighed, looking at him, knowing she had to leave to find more supplies.

The hallway outside was as still and silent as she recalled, but Thoran still kept to the edges of the passageways and hid in as many shadows as she could, bare feet slapping on the cool stones. She ducked into an open door after listening for any signs of life, searching for anything that might be of use. A massive bed, plump and luxurious, commanded one of the rooms, and Thoran dared to lie down on it, reveling in the softness of the feather pillows. She imagined this was all hers, a home she could share with Sharova if he wished, and her eyes had just begun to droop again when she heard the soul-wrenching scream.

Nothing human could have made the sound. It was a drawn-out, bellowing wail that carried on for at least a minute. Thoran felt the hairs rising on her arms as she listened to it, one fist jammed in her mouth to hold back the scream that needed to break free. The howl trailed off eventually, leaving an echoing silence to ring in the empty halls and corridors.

Paralyzed with fear, Thoran could do nothing but remain where she was, all thoughts of Sharova forgotten for a second as her mind whirled around, conjuring horrors that might have been the source of that scream.

Time passed, and with no further howls, Thoran's mind convinced her she had imagined the sound. She rolled from the bed to continue her search of the rooms. One cupboard was filled with linen, and she grabbed a large sheet to make fresh bandages from. Moving back into the main room, she found some old bread that could be revived with water. She paused, considering her options.

Why carry everything back there when I can bring him here?

Sharova moaned when she tried to lift him, the pain from his burning infection still obviously horribly bad. His eyes cracked open, rolling towards her without recognition, but he did not fight. With despicable slowness, she guided Sharova to the new suite she had discovered, putting him on the bed before sinking into a comfortable chair, spent. She still had to return for the honey and bottle, but was relieved to see this room had a large barrel in the corner, filled with rainfall. Water could be directed into a large tub set beneath it, and a hearth sat under that so the water could be heated. Thoran's chest tightened at the possibility of having hot water to wash with, and she made a note to look for flint and tinder on her scavenging treks.

She opened the door to their new suite without listening for danger and almost died when she saw Tiernon hobbling along the corridor away from her. A cold spike of agony shot through her chest when she saw him, even as her mind tried to understand how he could still be alive with such injuries.

The king dragged one leg along the stone floor. Limp and at a horrific angle, she could tell it had been broken by some massive force. His royal robes were ragged, torn and soaked in bright red blood from some injury she could not see. Thoran held her breath as he rounded a corner then ducked back inside the room, slipping the door closed before one of the cold creatures passed and saw her.

She swallowed and went back inside the suite, shaken and worried.

"Get better," she whispered in the direction of the bedroom. "Please get better soon, before he finds us."

***

Tiernon felt the ends of his broken leg grinding against each other, flame licking up his leg from the wound as he dragged his broken body along the Hall of Kings, hanging on to the facsimiles of his ancestors for help.

"Do not look at me that way," he hissed in agony.

His great-grandfather looked back with dead stone eyes, remaining silent as Tiernon moved on, wincing in agony every time his injured leg moved in the slightest.

Not far now. Not far and I can use the altar.

"T'noch, aid me!" he called to the uncaring hall.

Rage built in his wasted chest when the hateful thing did not appear. There would be consequences. T'noch would pay for abandoning him after the stag had charged him.

Tiernon still could not believe what had happened. After realizing the boy Besmir was indeed his nephew, he had been further shocked when a flock of birds had dived at his barrier. Rodents had done the same, and then people had been throwing things at him, draining his power and blinding him with the flashes. He had been unable to take down the barrier for fear of being injured by the things that were thrown. At the same time he could feel his power being drained, the barrier slipping from his mind. Desperately, he had lashed at Besmir with hate, but something, some animal, had charged him. Nausea had hit him as his thigh had snapped along with some of his ribs, the beast's horns piercing his chest deeply. He had just managed to bring himself back here before his body had hit the ground, possibly killing him. T'noch had disappeared when the stag hit.

His thoughts had allowed him to get to his room without noticing the pain, and he fumbled at the door, almost falling in his need to get inside. The altar greeted him like an old friend, tendrils of love radiating from it towards him. Tiernon let himself be carried over to lay on its smooth surface, feeling the cool surface through his clothes.

Instant relief flooded him as the altar infused him with power, healing his wounds and easing his breaths. Yet his leg remained unhealed, the altar using itself up to heal him.

"Woman," he growled. "Come here." He gave the order before he remembered she was locked away.

He sat up painfully, grunting and wheezing, to stare at the empty cage. The king blinked a few times before he realized he had left her in the throne room. He rolled from the altar, screaming when his leg jarred against the floor and bending double as sickness rolled through him from the agony.

"Attend me!" he bellowed to the empty palace. "Where is everyone?" he cried in puzzlement.

Tiernon started for the door, looking for anyone who might be able to assist him. The corridor outside was still and silent, dust motes floating from his passage earlier.

"Hello!" he shouted. "Your king needs you!"

Getting no answer of any kind made Tiernon's rage grow. Every slow, painful footstep he took brought thoughts of dire murder to him, and he actually felt a flutter of pity for the poor soul he met first by the time he reached the throne room.

Something is badly amiss.

His eyes picked out the ragged shape of his throne, the drapes hanging behind it partially fallen and the tall candelabra that had tipped over, scattering dead tapers across the marble floor. Why no one had bothered to clean and restore the room was beyond his comprehension, and he hobbled over to the cage he had the woman in, prepared to ask her what the situation was. Seeing the gate hung open, the cage empty, Tiernon raged, screaming epithets and cursing anyone he could think of.

"T'noch!" he bellowed. "T'noch, where are you?"

Nothing but silence met his ears, and he hobbled across to sit on his throne, exhausted and confused. Concentrating with difficulty on his memories, Tiernon tried to look back on what may have happened here. The palace ought to be filled with servants, ambassadors and dignitaries, their wives and children. There should be music and laughter, food and life, but something had changed this place into a tomb.

His brow furrowed as he sought the answer that so easily eluded him.

"It was I..." he muttered eventually. "T'noch took my mind...but I killed...people...to feed the altar."

Understanding came in the form of a memory of wide eyes and pained screams as people died in agony, their lives flowing into the silver and wood of the table.

T'noch! It was a construction of that vile monster!

Hunger gripped Tiernon's stomach, grumbling deeply, and he wondered how long it had been since he had eaten. Dragging himself wearily to his feet, Tiernon began the long, painful trek towards the kitchens.

My guards! Where are the six?

The king continued his journey in utter confusion, racking his mind for any memories that might be there.

"Where are you going?"

The voice was simultaneously hideous and welcome, a necessary pain he must endure. It brought reason and gave him the answers.

"T'noch," Tiernon said in wonder. "Where have you been?"

***

"I believe it is a lost cause," Zaynorth stated flatly. "You all saw his capabilities here, and now Besmir has been laid low..." He spread his hands in defeat.

A meeting had been arranged for the senior members of Besmir's court. Zaynorth, Herofic, Ranyor, Keluse, Norvasil and Suranim sat around a rough table in Besmir's pavilion. The king himself still lay unconscious in another area, Arteera attending his body.

"Yet I doubt Tiernon will take this defeat lightly," Herofic muttered. "He is likely to return with an immense force to destroy every woman and child here. We should be ready at the least, if we are not to go on the offensive."

"Offensive?" Suranim gasped. "We are simple people, farmers and servants for the most part. Even with the training and weapons, we are not an army."

"We should pack this place up and scatter to the four winds," Norvasil said darkly. "Some might survive Tiernon's vengeance by means of luck."

Keluse listened to them all debating the future of the tent town and all its inhabitants, remaining silent but with Besmir's ideals in the back of her mind. Running had not been in his plans. Nor had sitting idly by and waiting for death to come to them. Besmir had never been one to back down or take the easy path rather than the correct one. Keluse realized she must remind these men of the hunter's disposition.

"Besmir wouldn't just sit and wait for Tiernon to come back," she said abruptly. "You all know that." Keluse looked at their surprised expressions, heat coloring her cheeks.

"Keluse speaks the truth," Ranyor said immediately. "All here swore an oath to serve Besmir as king. His word should remain law."

"And exactly how are we supposed to decide how to proceed?" Zaynorth asked. "With Besmir unable to make the decisions?"

"A vote?" Keluse suggested.

"Never works without a complete government," Herofic grunted. "We need a new figurehead. Someone who can speak for Besmir, lead the people." He looked pointedly at his brother.

Zaynorth shook his head, spreading his hands in a gesture of surrender.

"Do not look to me for this," he said. "I am not a leader of men, let alone women and children."

"You are known to all here," Ranyor told the old man. "As Besmir's adviser and second, they would listen to you."

Keluse watched as the mage's face showed his despair. He tugged at his beard as he looked at them all with pained eyes.

"To lead was never my intent," he said, as if explaining his guilt. "Besmir is king... I..." He trailed off.

"We need a leader," Herofic said. "Those people out there need a leader also. Whether it was your intent or not, Brother, you are that leader." He looked at each member of the council in turn. "Any objections?"

Zaynorth watched his friends and family shake their heads slowly, sealing his fate. He bowed his head, remaining silent for a time.

"Bring me the prisoner," he said eventually.

Chapter Seventeen

Fiends delved inside his body, teeth ripping at flesh that did not disappear. Besmir's mind was consumed in a world of searing, tearing agony from which he could not escape. It was relentless, unending, and he welcomed the moment his mind began to slip into madness, welcomed the relief it would bring.

Screams filled his ears. To begin with they were solely his own, but other voices joined his at some point, high-pitched squeals punctuated by whip-like cracks and the boiling hiss of what sounded like steam.

Besmir felt the creatures flinch as they feasted on his lungs, chewed his intestines and delved inside his immortal body. The pain began to subside as something smashed and burned the demons from his body, sending them screaming from his torture.

He lay on the sharp ground, his eyes squeezed tightly shut until his brain registered the fact he was no longer being eaten alive. When he opened his eyes, another creature stood over him, alternating his amused face between Besmir and scanning the landscape for danger.

"Shall we leave before the Ghoma come back?" It asked in a deep, growling voice.

The creature leaned down, offering its scaled, seven-fingered hand to Besmir. He took it without a thought.

Anything that was not trying to eat him alive was a safe bet, he assumed. Its fingers clamped shut around his hand, holding him like a vice and lifting him with ease from the floor. Besmir felt himself floating above the ground and looked down to see his bare feet were no longer anchored to the world.

The creature turned its horned head to him with an almost kind smile and nodded once before the world melted around them.

Besmir's stomach dropped as if he was falling. Yet his eyes told him he was falling *horizontally*. Flashing across hundreds of leagues of ashen landscape in seconds. His eyes picked out cities. Structures that no human mind could have conceived of were filled with dark writhing forms that reached for them as they flew overhead. He automatically pulled his feet up despite being miles above them, and heard laughter from the creature.

"I will ensure your safety," it said.

They carried on, sometimes skimming the surface of this savage world, sometimes so far above its surface that Besmir could not make out the ground. Fear and exhilaration vied for dominance in his chest as the hunter watched this world pass beneath him.

Eventually the creature slowed, floating down towards the ground which was completely different here than the rest of the world. Trees grew here, although they were grey in both branch and leaf. A grey pool was fed by a small brook that sprung to life from nothing. Something splashed in the water as Besmir looked, and his eyes picked out a glimmering fish, its scales glowing with some kind of inner light. The structure was a simple but elegant thing of wood and stone, larger than many houses he had seen but not palatial. Contrasting layers of grey wood had been alternated to make a pleasing exterior, and a pair of wide doors stood open, welcoming them both.

"Welcome to my home," the creature said. "I was once called Joranas, you are?"

"Besmir," he said, shaking the hand the creature still held.

Joranas frowned deeply, the finer scales around his eyes shifting as if he remembered something important. He let go of Besmir's hand and guided him inside the house.

The furnishings were large and padded with luxurious cushions Besmir sank into gratefully when Joranas bid him to sit. The contrast between this softness and the harshness of the rest of this world was not lost on Besmir, and he began to ask the questions that piled into his mind now that he felt a little safer.

"What is this place?"

"My home," Joranas growled in his deep voice.

"And this whole place?" Besmir asked.

"Are you human?" Joranas asked.

A flash of worry slapped at Besmir then. His head swung to regard the creature warily.

Joranas chuckled. "Do not worry," he said with a smirk. "It is not my intent to injure or consume. I simply need to know your origin in order to adequately explain this place."

Besmir nodded slowly. "Yes, I'm human," he said.

Joranas stood, pacing around his home. Besmir studied him more closely, seeing how his scales moved over each other silently, each one oiled by something his body secreted. Three horns jutted from his head, pulling his skull into an almost triangular shape, and his near-black eyes had oval pupils.

"I also was human when I first came here," Joranas rumbled. "Centuries ago. This form you see has been molded, shaped by this world. It is the only thing I cannot affect."

To demonstrate, Joranas gestured, and a section of the floor bulged upward. The wood planks melted and changed, becoming something else. Besmir's fascination grew as a five-foot-high rabbit appeared before his eyes, ears flat to its body and nose twitching. Every aspect of it was perfect, from the wetness of its eyes to the apparent softness of every hair. It darted from the house, light grey tail flashing as it ran until it reached the edge of the altered land around Joranas's home and exploded into dust, falling like misty rain to the ground once more.

"This place is a conduit," Joranas said when Besmir turned his attention back. "Like a hallway between your world and a place so horrific, so incredibly awful, it would shatter your mind to even see." Joranas gestured and a cup appeared in his hand. "The Ghoma that fed on you were sent by a being that resides there, prototypes if you will, that were sent to try and discover a way for him to get to your world." He sipped at whatever was in the cup.

Besmir licked his lips. Neither hungry or thirsty here, a sudden need had arisen inside him. His throat was dry, his lips cracked, and Joranas fashioned a goblet beside him, the liquid dark and inviting. Besmir grabbed it, gulping down the contents madly. The liquid flowed endlessly, the goblet refilling as he gulped it down, never ending in the same way the brook did outside.

"Just one of the curses here," Joranas said, making the goblets disappear. "You can eat and drink but never feel satiated."

Despair hit Besmir as he grabbed at the goblet, feeling the dust as it fell through his fingers.

"How do I get back?" he asked eagerly.

"Back?" Joranas said in surprise. "There is no back. If you are here, it means you are dead in the world of humans. Your body is being returned to the soil from which it came and your spirit resides here now."

A wrenching sensation grabbed Besmir's stomach. Like intense hunger but a thousand times more painful. An ache that no amount of food could ever remove. He hunched forward in an attempt to ease it, but nothing helped. A low moan ripped from his throat.

"Grief," Joranas said sympathetically. "I take it you had loved ones, friends?" Besmir nodded. "Your soul yearns for them, feels for them, knowing it will never see them again."

"Is this hell?" Besmir groaned.

"It might as well be," Joranas said. "There is no escape, no going back, and everything you once cared for is gone."

Besmir heard the note of finality in his deep growl, but something inside him refused to give up.

"There must be a way," he said, standing. "There must be some way to get back. If this is a hallway between worlds, there must be a door I can get through to go back."

"The door is there," Joranas said. "I can take you to it, but without a body to return to, you will fade into nothing and cease to be." He turned his reptilian eyes towards Besmir. "I have seen it," he added.

"Are there any other people here?" Besmir asked. "Others like me?" Joranas shook his head, waving his horns.

"One other passed this way," he said sadly. "She tried to go back, return to the world of the living as something pulled her there. I watched her disappear. Her spirit faded and disappeared."

"Rather eternal nothingness than this," Besmir grumbled. "I do not understand how you have managed for centuries."

"There are entertainments," Joranas said with a savage, toothy grin. "Entertainments you might just find it worth remaining for."

Besmir frowned in confusion. "What entertainments?" he asked.

"There are a few things you need to learn first," Joranas said. "Let me show you."

Joranas walked outside and held his hands out to the sky.

"As you are probably aware, this plane of existence is...hostile," Joranas said, an understatement. "Yet there are things you can do to shield yourself from the elements here. Clothing and armor can be fashioned with the power of your mind."

"Really?" Besmir asked skeptically.

"How do you think I maintain my home?" Joranas asked. "You must first visualize what it is you wish to create," he added. "Be as detailed as you can. If you wish to have chain mail, imagine every link, every rivet that holds it together. With clothing, you must imagine each stitch, every minute aspect of what it is you want to appear or it will be useless and fall to pieces immediately as you use it." Joranas swung his head towards Besmir. "Can you do that?"

"I can try," Besmir said.

"Try hard," Joranas told him. "Clothe yourself before you return."

The large, demonic figure turned and walked away from Besmir, letting the acidic grit in the wind hammer at him again. His entire being felt as if it was being scoured with grit stones, robbing him of concentration.

"How do I do this?" he screamed into the air.

Besmir looked about but saw nothing. He was alone again. Joranas had gone.

He said to imagine what you want. As detailed as you can. So do that.

Besmir drew in his mind. The leather clothing he once wore in life, constructing it in his thoughts in painstaking detail. He recalled his stitching where it had been necessary to make repairs, the color, even how it felt against his skin. He stood there as the wind cut at him and concentrated harder than he ever had before. It felt as if time stretched off into eternity as Besmir fought to hold the image of his clothing in his mind, but eventually he came to understand the wind did not cut him as deeply, the pain was lessened. Besmir opened his eyes and saw he was clad in the leather clothing he had imagined.

"Good," Joranas said, making him jump. "That took me a great deal longer when first I arrived here."

"What else can I make?" Besmir asked eagerly.

Joranas smiled and gestured, a twenty-foot eagle rising from the surface of the planet. Each feather was lovingly created, catching an imaginary wind. Besmir saw Joranas' creations were made from the fabric of the world itself. "Where is this place?" He asked, carefully crafting a rabbit from the glassy ash around them.

"Somewhere between here and there," Joranas replied cryptically.

Joranas conjured an immense dragon, muscular and powerful, that cooked and ate the rabbit Besmir had perfected.

"What kind of answer is that?" Besmir demanded, angry that his creation had not been allowed to live for long.

"The only one I have," Joranas said, chuckling at Besmir's anger. "As far as I can understand, there are many worlds, many planes of existence. This is one, your world is another, there might be thousands, millions, I do not know." Joranas shrugged his massive shoulders. "But imagine they are stacked atop each other like sheets of parchment." He held his hands out one on top of the other. "There are a few beings that can move between worlds and fewer still that are forced to. Yet even the most powerful, the most accomplished travelers, cannot jump a layer. They have to traverse one world to gain access to the next."

Besmir frowned in thoughtful confusion.

"So my world, here, and the world where the thing that makes the Ghoma is, they are all neighboring worlds?"

"As far as I can tell, yes," Joranas said, sounding impressed. "I have to say you are quite open to this. Does it not confuse you at all?"

"I just watched you create a dragon from nothing but ash and your own imagination," Besmir said. "Confusion is just about all I have now."

***

Joranas kept pushing Besmir in the following weeks, urging him to create numerous objects over and over, perfecting them at speed. He concentrated, willing the world around him to change, bend to his will and become a sword. He felt the hilt forming in his fist and pulled gently, removing a six-foot blade from the planet's surface. He swung it, feeling virtually no weight to the thing.

"Good," Joranas growled. "You are beginning to grasp the basics."

"Basics?" Besmir asked as he changed the sword into an arrow that shot from his hand through a target he pulled from the ash. "What more is there to learn?"

"You are adept at conjuring things that are familiar to you," Joranas said. "Yet what about the abstract? What can you imagine? It is possible to craft anything here," he added.

Besmir thought for a second. He brought forth a gush of water, a grey fountain that bubbled from the ground at his feet, the same height he was.

"Mundane!" Joranas shouted.

Besmir changed his fountain, turning the water into fire. He could feel the heat boiling from it and grinned at Joranas.

"What about a fire fountain?" he asked.

"Better," Joranas said. "Anything else?"

Besmir frowned at the thing's negativity. In the space of just a few weeks he had managed to hone abilities he had not known he had and brought a gout of grey flame into existence where nothing existed before.

"What more do you want?" he demanded angrily, letting the flame fail, the dust falling back to the ground.

"Direct your rage at another target," Joranas said calmly.

"What other target?"

Joranas held his hand out, making the world flow by beneath them as he had when they had first met. Besmir watched in fear as the pillar of rock grew in his eyes, immense and foreboding. He could see the Ghoma gathered at its base, and his spirit recalled the anguish he had felt when they had eaten him alive.

Joranas floated over them, releasing his hand abruptly and letting Besmir fall.

"There are your targets!" he called. "Return if you are victorious."

Besmir watched him wink out of existence as he hit the ground, surrounded by the ravening Ghoma. Some bore wounds from where Joranas had attacked them before, but still remained horribly powerful. They screamed when they saw him, advancing as a unit to consume his soul eternally.

Panic gripped Besmir so tightly, he could do nothing. One Ghoma wrapped a wet appendage round his arm and dragged him off balance towards it. Others joined, preparing to feed, their horrible teeth clacking against each other in anticipation.

Besmir felt something bite at his fingers and the bright pain brought him back to his senses.

He bellowed in defiance, casting a spike through the nearest Ghoma.

It screamed horribly, flinching back from his conjured weapon. Besmir thought and fire ripped from the planet, burning and searing the demonic things but leaving him completely intact. The Ghoma flinched back from him in fright, their cowardice maddening Besmir even more.

"Happy to savage someone who's weak and defenseless but run from someone who can fight back?"

Filled with battle rage and hate for these things, Besmir whipped forward, slamming into the Ghoma with his spirit and shredding them with needle-sharp blades he conjured from the world.

Their screams of pain and fear fueled his rage, and he lashed at them, savagely cutting their malformed bodies into pieces that flopped and flapped like suffocating fish. His incandescent rage was fueled by the loss and grief that gnawed at him.

Arteera. Keluse. Zaynorth. Ranyor. Herofic.

Besmir would smash the life from these things , make these things suffer for what he had lost.

By the time he had shredded and burned the Ghoma, leaving them in mewling piles of raw agony, he was exhausted, panting and spent but satiated for now. He turned and started to trudge away from the pillar but had no idea which way to go to return. The thought hit him that he did not need to walk. If Joranas could fly, Besmir could fly too, and he willed himself into the air, watching as the world dropped from beneath his feet.

It felt more to Besmir as if the world flowed beneath him rather than him moving above it, as if the entire plane of existence bent to his will. The joy of freedom pulled at him, and he willed himself faster, the planet flashing by below him in a grey blur.

He passed the city of grasping darkness, arms reaching for him from the odd buildings. He flew over other weird structures that had been abandoned and lay in ruins, slowly being reclaimed by the planet, until he slowed at the edge of an area of utter blackness.

Besmir landed, staring at the place where the grey planet disappeared into nothing. It was blacker than oil. A gaping, hungry absence that pulled gently but insistently at him, somehow willing him to enter. Deep, ancient evil radiated from inside it – a pervasive, nasty thing that was so completely alien to anything Besmir knew. Its very existence should not have been possible. Yet he could feel something calling him, pulling him in, and he wanted to go. It promised delights beyond imagining, the restoration of his life and an eternity wallowing in pleasures never imagined by any human in history.

Besmir stepped forward, his feet immune to the grating savage surface of the world now. As if controlled by a puppeteer, he took another step towards the edge of nothing.

Something emerged from the absence of everything. Something that was alive with horrible power, an extension of the unimaginable thing that resided there. It birthed wetly from nothing onto the ground before him, squealing and mewling pathetically for a few seconds. Maturing at a disturbing rate, Besmir watched it grow into adulthood before his eyes.

It was a squat ball-shaped thing with a spiked head that waved uneasily atop a long neck. Sucking mouth parts moved endlessly, making a wet clicking sound that frightened and disgusted Besmir at the same time. Insectoid arms flapped at him, and he recoiled as it hissed.

Laughter! It's laughing at me.

It moved towards him, a flowing, rolling motion that reminded Besmir of swallowing, and his revulsion grew. Whatever had created this, whatever warped madness lay at the heart of the nothing, had also been responsible for the Ghoma. Besmir's revulsion turned to hate.

He ripped at it with his mind, tearing and cutting as it writhed and screamed. Fire and green lightning exploded from his hands, burning and lancing through the monster as it tried to escape. The stench of its burning flesh reached his nostrils, and he recoiled from the pungent odor of putrefaction. Besmir continued his assault, unrelenting and merciless, forcing the thing back through the portal into the nothing from which it had been birthed.

"Nicely done," Joranas growled, making Besmir jump. "You have done well, Besmir."

"What was that thing?" Besmir asked as hate radiated from the blackness.

"Not here," Joranas said. "Return to my home," he instructed, streaking off into the distance.

Besmir followed, eager to discover what he had to say. He dropped down beside the pool Joranas conjured for his own pleasure and stepped inside the house, looking at the altered surroundings the horned man had wrought.

"That was called a T'noch," Joranas said as he reclined on a sofa that hovered above the floor.

Besmir had not considered before, but there was no need for any of the comforts Joranas conjured at all. He could float without the aid of a sofa, but brought one into existence for the sake of his mind. He wondered about the strange creature's life as a human. Where was he from? What had he done? Had he been a husband? A father? Besmir had no idea, and his constant probing questions had revealed nothing whether blatant and direct or subtly asked.

"The Ancient One finally managed to produce something that can exist in your world, even if it cannot follow them. T'noch are pieces of the thing that lives in the absence, and anything they encounter, it can experience also," Joranas said. "They are utterly without conscience, remorse or empathy, just as the Ancient One is, and deserve none from you."

"These entertainments you said about," Besmir commented as he thought. "Were they fighting these demons?"

Joranas grinned a savage smile that showed his carnivorous teeth.

***

The raids they led on an almost daily basis were more than satisfying for Besmir. His destruction of the beastly things birthed by the Ancient One became like an addiction, and he killed them relentlessly, changing his technique over time. Initially he chose to end their existence quickly, scything through their different bodies with speed as they snapped at him. Eventually Besmir slashed at the fiends with weapons and powers he fashioned from the planet, wounding them and causing pain, reveling in the agony he caused these inhuman extensions of the thing that resided in the absence of anything.

He grinned at Joranas as they flew towards the oddly shaped citadel, preparing to attack the dark, tentacled, grasping things that resided therein. Joranas frowned and slowed his pace, drawing closer to Besmir.

"What?" the hunter asked with a frown of his own.

"You have been here too long," Joranas growled, laying one of his long-boned fingers against Besmir's brow.

The hunter did the same and felt a raised area beneath his skin, bumpy and hard.

"Scales," Joranas said.

"Well, there's not much I can do about it," Besmir said with a shrug. "And you've thrived here, so…"

"I exist!" Joranas snapped. "Nothing thrives in this waste. It is a purgatory worse than any hell, and I am stuck here eternally." The horned being sighed. "Return home," he said before darting back the way they had come.

***

The interior was still rendered in wood of varying shades of grey, but every scrap of furniture had been removed to make room for the dark mass that hovered above the floor. Slate-grey as a thundercloud but somehow dense, it flowed and swirled before Besmir's eyes in a mesmerizing dance. The hunter had no idea what it was, but he could tell it was not made of the same stuff as the planet. It was not from here.

"What's that?"

"The portal back to your world," Joranas said simply. "It is time you returned."

Confusion hit Besmir as he stared at the thing. "You said I'd fade into nothing if I went back," he said accusingly. "You said my body was dead and I had nothing to return to."

"There is a slight chance I might have lied about that," Joranas said with a smirk.

"Why?" Besmir demanded angrily.

"Think back on when you killed the T'noch as it birthed from the absence. How did you kill it?"

"I burned and shocked it," Besmir said. "Used this planet to rip it to shreds."

Joranas raised his hairless brows in question. "Did you?" he asked. "Did you use the stuff of this planet to kill it?"

Besmir thought back, recalling the feelings of revulsion and hate as he had watched the demon been born.

"It came from me," he said in wonder. "The fire, the lightning...it-it came straight from me!"

Joranas nodded, a smile crossing his face as he clapped his hands together once.

"I knew from the first your body lives," he said, casting a glance at the portal. "Barely, but it does live. You are able to return. But there was need to remain. To stay here and hone the skills you were born with."

"Why lie to me?" Besmir asked as betrayal cut him.

"So you could learn how to control your power, Besmir," Joranas said as he approached the hunter. "So I could teach you as I was unable to do in life."

"What?" Besmir asked in shock as Joranas shoved him into the portal.

"Farewell, Besmir," he said sadly. "Farewell, my son..."

Chapter Eighteen

Thoran's heart soared when Sharova's eyes opened, focusing on her face with recognition.

"Th...oran?" he croaked.

She grabbed their bottle, lifting it to his lips so he could drink. He choked a little, his face screwing up as he coughed and spluttered the water from his lungs.

"You are...more beautiful in the light," Sharova said, warming her chest.

She felt the blush crawl up her neck and looked away.

"Your fever is making you say things you should not," she said.

Sharova grunted and tried to sit up. Thoran pulled him up, wincing as the muscles in her back strained and stretched. Even in his wasted condition, Sharova was a substantial man.

"What is this place?" he asked, looking round the ambassadorial suite.

"We are in one of the palace wi—"

"The palace!" he nearly screamed. "What are we doing here?"

"Laying low, Sharova," she said gently. "There is no need to worry, we have been here for three weeks undiscovered. Tiernon does not venture this way."

"Tiernon," he spat. "Wait...Three *weeks*!" Thoran pitied the look of shock on his face.

"You had an infection that had spread into your blood," she explained. "When I found you, you were delirious and I did not know if you would live."

"You saved me?" he asked in complete puzzlement. "I was in the dark...trapped."

"Yes," Thoran said, explaining how she had found him.

"Thank you," he said. "Those words do not seem adequate, but thank you."

"You saved me first, remember?" Thoran asked with a warm smile. "It seemed only fair to return the favor."

"How is it we have not been found here?" he asked, drinking some more water.

"No one has been looking," she said. "His evil has chased everyone away. The buildings are in disarray, the servants fled and ambassadors left. Nothing alive comes willingly to the palace now," she said, the memories of his slaughter surfacing again.

Sharova lifted her chin, his face blurred by her tears.

"What is it?" he asked gently.

"Nothing," she said, not wanting him to know what she had been through. "I am fine."

Sharova looked at the fine drapes and small stock of food she had secured, the silken dress she wore and expensive perfume that sat beside the bed.

"So I see," he said with a grin. "What shall we do next?"

" I would like to leave," Thoran said. "Once I managed to find you, I was unsure if you would even live but now all I want to do is go."

Sharova scratched his cheek, feeling at the beard that had grown there in surprise. He tried to rise, but his weakened body would not support his weight and he fell back, panting and gasping with the effort.

"Maybe I need to recover a little more," he said, smiling through his pain. "Might I have something to eat?"

"Of course," she said, grabbing some of their meager supplies. "You need not ask."

"A gentleman always asks a lady's permission," he told her. "Although I very much doubt I look like a gentleman at present."

Sharova held his hands up to examine their skeletal appearance, his gaunt face showing distress.

"Well, I am no lady," Thoran said, embarrassed by her low-born status. "Just a woman who sews clothing for a few coins."

She turned away from his stare, pretending to busy herself with something. She stopped when she felt his fingers on her arm, pulling gently, and turned.

"You are wrong," he told her gently. "Of all the ladies I have ever met at court, you are the most gracious, kind, selfless and brave I have ever met."

Thoran felt herself filling with pride at his words, and looked down with a little smile on her face.

"Thank you," she said, feeling genuine praise from another human being. "My lord," she added, raising his status.

"There is never any need to call me that," he said. "Not after everything you have done for me."

"All right then...Sharova," Thoran said, smiling. "What do you think we should do?"

Sharova paused in the middle of chewing a hunk of dried meat as if he had never tasted anything finer.

"There is nothing I am able to do at present," he said. "I will have to get some of my strength back before I can even walk," he added seriously.

"Then that is what we should do to begin with," Thoran said, rising from the bed.

"Where are you going?" Sharova asked.

"We are going to need more than this if you are to get your strength back," she said, pointing at the half-empty jar of honey and thin strip of jerky that remained.

"No,," he said. "It is far too risky for you to be roaming the palace."

"What do you think I have been doing for almost a month?" she asked. "I am careful and quiet. Neither Tiernon or his abominable guards have any clue we are here. I will return soon."

With that, Thoran left Sharova for the privacy of the main room, where she stripped out of the fine dress. It was a beautiful thing to wear, one that made her feel like the lady he thought she was, but Thoran was practical. She unraveled the ball of rags she had spent time assembling, slipping into dark cloth trews and a brown shirt she had pinched at the waist. She slipped a pair of cloth slippers on her feet for silence and grabbed the soft bag she had found to carry her finds in.

She slipped from the suite, cold welcoming her into its arms like a lover. A shiver ran down her spine as she padded silently through the corridors.

How can it be so cold in here?

Sunlight flooded the palace, but Thoran's breath formed a mist before her. She had been methodical in her search so far, working further out from their little suite, building a map in her mind. She had already searched the ambassadorial section of the palace, taking what few items had been left behind. Today she was to venture farther than she had since moving to the suite, down a flight of stairs to the servants' quarters.

Stone steps, worn smooth by the passage of thousands of feet, took her into a darker part of the palace where shadows large enough to hide any predator clung to corners. Her heart beat faster and a greasy sweat beaded on her brow despite the biting cold that numbed her arms and slowed her legs.

What little light there was showed her a world very different to the ambassadorial quarters above. Cramped and tight with crude furnishings and little in the way of decoration, the servants had been forced to share rooms for the most part. Thoran began her search, holding out little hope that anything of worth would have been left down here. She uncovered books stashed beneath mattresses, cheap novels for the most part, a diary that made her face redden with its racy entries and a book of recipes that made her mouth water to imagine.

Room after little room brought nothing of any use, the contents being stripped as people fled Tiernon's mad wrath. In despair, she searched room after room looking for anything that might aid them, help heal Sharova or make life easier for them. One room, larger than most, was filled with cupboards, and Thoran started opening each, her excitement building.

Empty. How can they all be empty?

Weariness and depression sapped her strength, and she slumped on the floor, back against the wall. What was the point? Everything of any value had been stripped from the place, food as well as clothing. Thoran rubbed at her face as if washing, pressing her eyes hard enough to make patterns appear, and thought about returning to Sharova. From this lower angle, a glint of something caught her eye, wedged between two of the stone flags in the floor.

Deciding it was probably nothing but wanting to know anyway, Thoran crawled over to where the floor met the wall and peered between the stones. Something flashed in the dim light, wedged between the stones, but it also appeared as if there was a hollow beneath the flag. Wedged in tightly, there was no way for her to lift the stone with her hands, and her mind worked, thinking back to the rooms already searched. She sprinted back through to the rooms she had discovered the diary in and pulled at the bed frame until a piece of loose wood gave way.

Eager anticipation swamped Thoran as she tried to fit the wood between the stones, annoyance making her frown when it was too wide.

If only I had a knife or sword...

She remembered the rusted blade used to pry Sharova from his prison but shuddered at the thought of trying to find it in the oily blackness down there. If there was no other way, she would have to, but the idea scared her beyond belief.

A nail jutted from the wood, and she battered it against the stone floor to try and release it, hoping it would be thin enough to fit. It loosened, pushing back through the plank until the point sat flush with the surface, but no amount of pulling would make it come. Her fingertips split, blood coating the nail and making it slick. Tears of frustration rolled down her cheeks but she carried on, working the nail back and forth, ripping her fingertips deeper in desperation.

Abruptly it came free, her arm shooting up into the air and holding her prize aloft like a trophy. She jammed it between the flagstones, joy filling her when it fit, and gently levered it back. Pain rolled up her arm when the nail pierced her thumb deeply, but a low grating sound issued from the floor as the stone began to move. She slipped the piece of wood beneath the stone and lifted it, the wooden lever a much better device.

A gasp escaped her when she managed to stand the massive stone up out of the way and saw inside. The small pit had been carefully hollowed out to hold someone's treasures. She found a small statue made from gold and onyx, carved into the image of a beautiful woman. Gold coins sat in a leather purse that she dropped in her sack to count later. More money than Thoran had ever seen was now in her possession, and the pleasure of ownership shivered through her.

Nothing to eat, though.

Nestled at the bottom of the hole sat a silver chain with a diamond-encrusted sapphire drop attached. The size of her thumb, the dark blue gem gleamed, its inner beauty calling to her, and she gripped the jeweled thing tightly in her fist, standing to get back to Sharova with her finds.

It was as she reached the top of the stairs leading from the servants' quarters that she almost died.

Her mind whirled with thoughts of her and Sharova at some grand ball. She wore a flowing gown of dark blue silk, the necklace at her throat, and the love and pride shone in Sharova's eyes as he took her hand, grasped her waist. She did not feel the icy blast that passed her at the apex of the stairs until she had rounded the corner.

Once the sound of booted feet on stone reached her ears, however, she froze, watching three of Tiernon's guards pass her by. She clamped her mouth tightly shut, holding in the scream that fought to explode from her chest. Thoran had been forced to watch the vile beasts as they murdered and slaughtered at Tiernon's command. More living armor than creature, his guards injected more fright into her than the king himself.

Two of them dragged a man between them, his arms caught in their vice-strong grip. His eyes bulged horribly from his face and his rictus of pure fright cut Thoran deeply.

He is about to die and I am fawning over baubles?

"Help!" the captive screamed when he caught sight of her. "Oh please help me! I have children...please!"

The guards ignored his cries, dragging his yelling body deeper into the palace, but they haunted Thoran as she made her way back to Sharova in tears.

***

Zaynorth looked at the man Tiernon had casually left behind when he had disappeared after felling Besmir. Wearing some kind of uniform, creased and dirty from being dragged through the muddy camp, the mage assumed him to be someone important to Tiernon. Once, at least.

"Who are you?" he asked bluntly.

"I am...was General Marthius," he said, not bothering to look up from his kneeling position.

Norvasil and Herofic stood close by, ready to hammer the life from the man at the first sign of danger. "Leader of Tiernon's armies."

His lack of the use of the king's title was not lost on Zaynorth, and he wondered if he could be an asset to them, information if nothing else.

"It would appear you no longer hold Tiernon's appreciation," Zaynorth observed dryly. "Why did he leave you here?"

"Madness, sir," Marthius said with a note of utter despair. "He has emptied the palace with his vile experiments and now only ice-cold fiends from some hell roam the halls."

Zaynorth frowned, wondering if this was some kind of trap.

"Why did you continue to serve him, then?" Herofic grunted from behind.

"H-He has my family," Marthius said, breaking down. "My wife and daughters. Oh gods, please let them be safe. Little Jeron is but a year old."

Zaynorth looked at Keluse, whose eyes had gone round and wide. Ranyor moved over and rested his hand on her back. She turned and buried her face in his shoulder as Marthius blabbered on.

"His schemes are madness! He means to breed people as slaves for his army and navy. Humans!" Marthius wrung his hands as if trying to cleanse them. "And the *things* that he has surrounded himself with...his guards are...are just *wrong*."

"What did you hope to achieve by coming here?"

"Achieve?" Marthius asked in surprise. "Not getting murdered was fairly high on my list. Not having my heart cut out and fed to something that has no business on this world!"

"Why did *he* bring you here?" Zaynorth asked for clarification.

"Tiernon said something about killing Besmir," the general told them. "He said he would make an example of the impostor and anyone who stood with him." Marthius looked around at them all with wide eyes. "I got the impression he thought Besmir was really who he claims to be when he saw him."

Zaynorth grunted, saying nothing, stroking his beard.

"Who spies on us for him?" The old man asked eventually.

"There are none," Marthius lied.

Zaynorth sighed and stared at the kneeling man, his eyes narrowing to slits as he spoke again.

"Tell me the names of those who spy for Tiernon or I shall be forced to have this *antila* bite you. Their venom is deadly but has the impressive side effect of making it impossible to lie. That is until the victim begins to dissolve inside."

General Marthius paled and shook as he looked at the fanged beast only he was able to see. Zaynorth's illusion was so powerful in his mind he could even catch the musty scent the creature gave off. The *antila* hissed and lunged at Marthius who jerked back in fear.

"Grinhol," Marthius said, his eyes flicking from Zaynorth to the image the old man put in his mind. "Serenius, Ferendi, Arteera, Wolach..."

"Sorry, who?" Zaynorth asked.

"Wolach," Marthius repeated. "A carpenter we..."

"No, before him,"

"Arteera?" Marthius asked. "We took her sister..."

Arteera passed through, fetching a bucket of clean water to wash Besmir as he lay in silence behind a curtained-off section. Oblivious to their conversation, she only paid any attention when the kneeling man mentioned her name..

Marthius tried to get to his feet, but Herofic slammed the flat of his hand down onto the general's shoulder, knocking him to the floor. Norvasil leaped across the tent with an acrobatic grace his massive frame should not have been capable of and grabbed Arteera by the throat.

Keluse pulled the curtain aside, revealing Besmir's body, unharmed and asleep, well-tended and cared for, lying on his bed. She lay fingers on his throat, feeling the pulse beat slowly and steadily, and sighed a breath of relief.

"What treachery is this?" Norvasil demanded, shaking Arteera by the throat.

Keluse watched as she made a horrible strangling sound, her head lolling.

"She was our spy!" Marthius shouted. "Our spy and assassin if Tiernon wanted Besmir dead."

Tears rolled down Arteera's face, and guilt punched a hard fist into Keluse's stomach when she thought of all the times she had left him in the Lutheran's care. Nausea rolled through her and she crouched, falling forward and retching.

"I could not!" Arteera cried. "Even though Tiernon has my sister, I fell for Besmir...I love him!"

Zaynorth gaped at them, comprehension coming to him slowly.

"Get her out," he muttered to Norvasil.

"No!" Arteera screamed. "No! Where is my sister? What have you done to her?"

"Where is her sister?" Zaynorth asked once the girl's screams had faded.

"I...I do not know," Marthius admitted. "Some were sent to begin breeding. My wife..." He trailed off into a choking sob. "I cannot stand the idea of her being somewhere like that!"

"Where?" Zaynorth growled through his disgust.

Marthius shrugged, defeated.

"Only the king and his disgusting minions know for sure," he said. "Someone entered the palace and freed some of Tiernon's favorites, so he kept the place hidden." Marthius sniveled. "What are you going to do with me?" he asked.

"I am going to hack off your head once you have spilled your guts," Herofic grunted.

"No," Besmir said from behind, making them all jump. "I refuse to become like my uncle."

Chapter Nineteen

"Besmir?" Zaynorth cried as they all spun to stare at him.

"What was my father's name?" Besmir asked.

"Pardon?"

"My father, what was his full name?"

"Derenir," Zaynorth said. "He was called Derenir Joranas Fringor."

Besmir's head fell forward, and he stared at the floor at his feet.

"How do you feel?" Keluse asked with sheer delight in her voice.

"What happened?" Zaynorth wondered.

Besmir stood, his body feeling weak after being laid low for so long, and looked at each of his friends in turn, his face a mask of guilt and depression.

"I met my father," he said quietly. "In hell."

Besmir stepped from the tent, picking his way through the town, people pointing and whispering as he passed. Some reached for him as he walked, fingers trailing over his arm as if to make sure he was real. The king ignored them all, pushing his way through to walk over to the edge of the lake and stare out over its glassy surface. A fish rippled the surface of the water, its dark shape sleek and smooth. For an instant Besmir wanted nothing more than to drive his mind into the trout, losing himself in the depths of the lake and leaving this painful existence behind.

"Besmir?" Keluse said from behind him, her voice a gentle inquiry.

He turned, looking down at her concerned face, and felt a slight smile twist his lips.

"Keluse," he said, grateful for her presence. "It's time I taught you how to survive in hell. Just in case you ever end up there."

She reached out, taking his hand in both of hers, and listened as he told her what had happened in the other dimension. Zaynorth, Herofic and Norvasil listened from nearby, leaving Ranyor to watch Marthius.

"It felt like I was there for years," he said. "And Joranas said he had been there for centuries." He looked about. "But this all looks similar to how I remember. How long was I gone?"

"About a month," Keluse said.

Besmir shook his head in disbelief.

"Maybe it was all some kind of dream," he said, not even convincing himself. "My mind conjuring it all up while I lay there?"

"If that were so," Zaynorth said gently, "how would you know his name?"

Besmir sucked in a deep breath, the moist air from the lake fresh and clean. The ache in his chest was so intense, he thought it might break him.

"I never bothered to even ask," he said shakily. "Never wondered what his name was. What kind of son am I?"

"One who never knew his parents," Zaynorth said gently. "Your mother was named Rhianne," he said. "Beautiful and strong. Their love was stronger than any I have ever heard or read about." The mage held his arm up and a couple appeared before Besmir.

Close and real enough to touch, the pair smiled at Besmir, the loving smile of proud parents. Besmir stepped forward, reached out, and passed a hand through the image Zaynorth had conjured in his mind. Rhianne's face blurred slightly with the passage of her son's hand but was restored as soon as he had let it drop.

She was slender, tall for a woman, with lighter hair than most Gazluthians, waving gently in the breeze. She boasted flawless skin with just a light dusting of freckles over her small nose and a smile that could melt the coldest of hearts.

She would have made a great queen.

Joranas stood tall and proud, his raven hair cut short and neat with a matching beard, also neatly trimmed, to garnish his chin. So little of this man had remained in hell that Besmir found it difficult to believe they were the same. Yet his eyes were as familiar as Besmir's own and exactly the same in hell.

"Why did he end up there?" Besmir asked, his voice sounding like that of a child. "In hell?"

"I cannot say, Besmir," Zaynorth replied painfully. "I really cannot begin to understand it."

"What of my mother? What of Rhianne?"

Zaynorth looked lost, shrugging and gesturing vaguely. Besmir shook himself to clear his head, yet the pain of discovering his father's soul resided in hell would not leave.

"Well, there's nothing I can do for him now," Besmir said in misery. "But Tiernon? He's got a surprise coming."

"What?" Zaynorth asked. "What surprise?"

Besmir grinned savagely, his teeth almost gleaming as he raised his hand and sent a gout of flame shooting into the lake water. Steam hissed from the lake, its waters boiling and churning. Zaynorth gaped in astonishment as Besmir caught a fish thrown from the water, its flesh cooking even as it flew towards them. Besmir took a bite, savoring the taste.

"Perfectly done," he said. "A few good meals and we can begin."

"Begin?" Keluse wondered. "What are we going to begin?"

"Tiernon's downfall," Besmir said in a gruesome voice. "I'm going to destroy him so completely, there will be nothing but a stain on the earth to mark his presence."

Zaynorth stared at the man he had sought out so long ago. Part of him was scared by the changes wrought by his incarceration in the hell dimension, while another part glowed with a prideful glee that Besmir understood his powers and wanted to use them to thwart Tiernon's plans.

"Start preparing to pack this place up," Besmir commanded. "We leave in two days. Make it known that any who don't want to join us are welcome to stay behind."

Herofic smiled as he bowed to Besmir.

"Your will, my King," he said.

***

Sharova looked at the little haul Thoran seemed so proud of in confusion. He knew this kind of wealth must mean something to her, as she nearly glowed with satisfaction as she looked at it. Yet to Sharova it was just bits of worthless metal. With nowhere to spend any of it, there was little point to having it. Food would be of much more use.

Something inside him, however, something deep and secret, swelled and warmed when he saw how happy she was and made him desire to do anything in his power to see it again.

"Excellent," he said, watching her smile grow. "Now if we could spend it..."

Thoran's face fell as the realization hit her.

"You think I am silly," she said. "A childish, silly girl who has been seduced by some glittering coins."

"No," he said gently as she folded her head forward, face crumpling.

"My life was a misery before this," she said sadly. "My mother, sister and I just managed to scrape by after my father died. Living in squalor and poverty with the war going on. When Tiernon came and started to burn everything, what little we did have was gone." She took a shaky breath as the suppressed memories surfaced. "I watched my mother die," she said, turning her haunted eyes to Sharova. "She was trying to save a child trapped in a burning building. As soon as she went in there, the roof collapsed, crushing her under burning timbers."

A low, wailing groan wrenched from her chest, and Sharova realized she had not had the opportunity to grieve yet. Awkwardly, he reached for her, pulling her shaking frame into his thin arms and rocking her as she wept.

"I am sorry," Thoran said when her crying eventually subsided.

"There is no need," Sharova replied, guilt smashing into him.

He had devoted his life to serving in the navy, working his way up through the ranks until he made fleet admiral, second only to the king. For what? To cause hardship, sorrow and loss to people like Thoran? Hate for his actions and for everything Tiernon stood for burned inside him, and Thoran looked at him with a little fright.

"What is wrong?" she asked, pulling back.

"What is wrong is that I served the man that did this to you," he admitted. "I was complicit in his schemes and plans to subdue the populace by force. It is I who should be sorry."

"I know," she said, shocking him. "But you changed, right? You came to free us from that cage, save us from being forcefully impregnated."

"I was the cause of your pain, but you saved me still?"

"Tiernon is my enemy and the cause of my pain," Thoran said.

"But the things I have done…"

"Are all in the past," Thoran said kindly. "It is what you do now that matters,"

"I never had children," Sharova said after a long silence. "Never wed. I was too busy directing ships and managing ports." He sighed and rubbed his scraggly beard. "I always wanted children but the opportunity never arose."

Thoran listened as he spoke, her heart melting at his sincerity.

"You have plenty of time to be a father," she told him.

"I believe that ship has sailed," he said.

Thoran stared at him, realizing he had not intended the pun, and a smile spread over her face, mirrored by his when understanding set in. They chuckled, the laughter growing between them until tears of mirth rolled down both their faces.

"Oh, it hurts!" Thoran said, clutching her ribs. "Make it stop!"

For some reason neither of them could understand, that was even more funny, and they both folded over in fresh gales of laughter.

"Whatever happens to us," Sharova said, "whatever our fate may be, I am glad to have met you, Thoran."

Sharova watched as a blush crept up her neck and face, the color bringing new beauty to her as she smiled.

"Me too, Sharova," she said. "Now I will leave the palace and spend some of this money in Morantine, get some food."

"No!" he cried. "It is far too dangerous. If you were caught..."

"I would not tell anyone where you were," she said defensively.

"I know," he said quietly. "I just...do not know what I would do without your presence," he added, looking away. "We should both go and never return."

"Can you walk?" she asked.

"Slowly," he said. "But yes. For you."

Thoran stared into his eyes for a moment, her expression unreadable, before she stood and helped him to his feet. Sharova felt the weight of his wasted body hammer down on him when his feet hit the floor and he grunted, falling. She caught him and their bodies pressed together, faces barely inches apart, eyes searching the other for some sign.

"We should go," Thoran said, her breath puffing over his face.

Sharova nodded, but a pang of regret sliced up through his chest.

***

"You're a traitor, then?" Besmir muttered to the shackled Arteera. "A spy sent to kill me in my sleep?"

"No!" Arteera wailed, reaching for him. "It is not like that... They wanted me to watch you, tell them what your plans were to begin with." Her pleading tone resonated within Besmir. "They have my sister, Besmir," she wailed. "My only family."

Besmir watched, her anguish and pain cutting at him too.

"You have to believe me I could never have killed you," Arteera fell to her knees, head bowed as she sobbed.

Besmir's hand reached out to stroke her silken hair, feeling as if his chest was being ripped apart.

"Come," he said, releasing her shackles.

Arteera looked up at him in disbelief for a moment then climbed up into his lap and buried her face in his neck, weeping with joy and sadness. Besmir wrapped her in the cage of his arms, tangling her hair in his fist but a grim expression crossed his face and his hand dropped to where his knife lay strapped to his leg.

***

Norvasil strode through the tents, watching as the women and young men packed and rolled their meager belongings into bags, preparing to leave. He had misgivings about their ability to work together as an army, especially as they seemed more intent on gossiping than actually getting any work done. Norvasil chuckled to himself.

Not all that different to other armies, then.

A boy of around six years old jumped from behind one of the tents, armed with a stick that he pointed straight at Norvasil.

"Stop!" he shouted in his shrill voice. "This is my mama's tent!"

Norvasil grinned. Barely taller than his knee, the child showed absolutely no fear whatsoever in the face of his massive enemy. He reached for his sword, easily larger than the boy, and drew it slowly, watching the youth as his eyes went wide in shock.

"Is this a challenge, lad?" Norvasil asked as women started pouring from tents, pointing and laughing. "If so, I would know the name of the warrior who challenges the great Norvasil."

The giant looked down at his tiny opponent, the stick drooping slowly to the floor as he stared at him. He was a handsome lad, Norvasil saw, with bright blue eyes and a round face. Light brown hair, cut short, framed his serious expression as he looked back at Norvasil.

"Daran!" a young woman squealed, emerging from one of the tents.

Norvasil saw where Daran got his good looks from. The mother shared the blue eyes and light hair her son had. Hers was longer, however, pulled back to reveal the slim, smooth lines of her neck.

"I am so sorry," she said nervously to Norvasil. "I have spoken of this to him, but..." She spread her hands.

"I am glad you arrived," Norvasil said sternly, sheathing his massive sword again. "I fear the lad was about to run me through."

Norvasil crouched and beckoned to Daran, who trotted across to him without hesitation.

"You are a brave one," he said as the mother approached. "You will be a strong warrior one day, but this is not a suitable weapon for a great warrior." Norvasil tapped the stick Daran held. "If your mother agrees, I would offer you this."

Norvasil reached for a dagger at his belt, a simple yet serviceable piece of around six inches. Daran's eyes widened in awe as he looked at the dagger, and he turned to look at his mother.

"Can I have it?" he begged. "Can I, Mama, please?"

"Please, Mama," Norvasil growled with a grin, bringing a collective chuckle from the audience that had gathered.

She looked around at the people watching then at Norvasil and her son, tilting her head so her hair fell to one side.

"It seems I have little choice," she said with a slight smile.

Norvasil offered the dagger to Daran, hilt first, and the boy grabbed at it eagerly.

"Two conditions come with this blade," he said. "First, you must promise not to attack any friendly souls who come near your home," Norvasil muttered in his deep voice. "And second, you must bind the blade until such time as your mother thinks you are not likely to gut yourself with it." Norvasil stared into the boy's eyes seriously. "Do you swear on your honor to keep these promises?"

Daran nodded eagerly, so Norvasil released the blade, watching as Daran held the blade up before his eyes, pleasure gleaming from his expression. Wordlessly he turned and wandered off, a group of young boys gathering to point and touch the dagger as he went.

"Thank you. I think," Daran's mother said as Norvasil rose. "I am Loraise."

"Norvasil," he said, bowing.

"I know who you are," Loraise said, laughing at his mockery. "Anyway, thank you again for that. Daran is...younger than his years. It takes a rare man to not immediately dismiss him."

"Oh, I am a rare man," Norvasil said, puffing his chest out. "Rare indeed. They write songs about me, you know?" he said in a speculative voice. "At least someone might if they had heard of me."

Loraise chuckled, appraising the big man she had seen teaching his group to fight. Yoranna had sung his praises, marveling at how strong he was, how his muscles bulged. She had not mentioned his charisma and wry sense of humor. It had been too long since she had laughed, and the feeling lifted her spirits.

"Would you like to join me?" she asked nervously. "For some tea?"

"Yes. Yes, I would." He grinned at her, offering his arm. "Lead on, my lady," he said. "Step aside!" he called loudly. "A rare man walks among you! Step aside there!"

The few people there laughed, especially when Loraise reddened at the attention, but a little smile crossed her face.

Chapter Twenty

"By all that is holy!" a guard said as he rubbed his hands for warmth. "The cold is enough to freeze off my vitals."

Stationed at the top of twenty feet of stone wall with only a two-foot-wide walkway and chest-height parapet between him and his fellow guards, the icy wind had blown up from nowhere. Grey dawn light added a leaden gleam over every surface, the single exception being the brazier full of coals glowing under a makeshift roof at the intersection of two walls. The cold drilled through his light leather and plate armor, seeped through the woolen undershirt and into his very bones, making him ache deeply.

"Fell off years ago, I heard, lack of use!" one of the other men said, bringing raucous laughter from the guards.

"Wore it down is more like." the first voice said.

A dull *clink* came to his ears and he turned, peering into the grey that surrounded them. "Did you hear that?" he asked.

"No," a few of the others told him.

"You hearing ghosts again?" the second guard teased.

"The White Lady is real, I say!" the first guard hissed. "Seen her in the great hall with these two eyes I did." He turned his eyes back to the gloom. "No, this was out there." He nodded at the bleak emptiness.

"Nothing out there but a few trees, the odd bird and..." the second guard wiggled his fingers. "Spooky ghosts," he added in a spectral moan.

The others laughed at their companion's superstitions, always telling them stories concerning ghosts and spirits of some kind or another.

"If there is nothing out there, why are we up here?" The first guard asked, holding his hands out to the brazier. "Why is the town sealed up tighter than a nun's undergarments every night?"

"Pah. The mayor is frightened of his own shadow!" The second guard spat disdainfully. "This is an easy job and guaranteed pay for doing very little. You would do well to remember that," he added, leveling a finger at the other man's chest.

A loud cracking sound issued from the grey, and they all turned to see what it was.

"Heard that then?" The first guard asked in a self-satisfied voice.

They all gasped when their eyes picked out the army that had appeared at the town's gates. Silent and neatly arranged in columns, they stood there, menacing and threatening, their leader astride a massive, black stallion that pawed at the ground in anticipation.

"Nothing out there?" The first to speak asked in a shaky voice.

"Send word to the mayor!" he barked. "Sound the alarm!"

A horn shattered the silence, soon followed by another, then more. Soon, men were pouring from the barracks, some half-dressed and stumbling, tripping in their haste to get ready. They stared around in confusion, not knowing what was going on.

"What is your business here?" The guard bellowed down to the army below.

"Isn't it obvious?" the leader called in a sarcastic voice. Nervous laughter rippled through the army at his back.

"Who are you?"

"I am Besmir Fringor, rightful heir to the throne of Gazluth and your king!" the figure shouted.

The army of women at his back cheered and screamed, bashing their swords against their shields.

***

Besmir waited for the baying women to quiet. Another figure appeared beside the first, older and rounder, showing the signs of easy living. Disheveled and flustered, he had obviously been woken and dragged out into the cold morning to address the invading army he had never really expected to have to deal with.

Besmir smiled from atop his horse as the newcomer conferred quickly with his guard before leaning over the wall.

"Excuse my ignorance," he called in a strong voice. "But I was under the impression Tiernon is king."

"The usurper that betrayed and murdered my parents?" Besmir thundered "His life is forfeit. He will see a traitor's end."

"Excuse my ignorance again, but what evidence do you have to support this claim?"

Besmir turned, looking at his small army. He had promised there would be no violence this day, promised the town would capitulate without bloodshed and seen the relief in their faces.

"Evidence!" he cried to them. "The man wants evidence!"

A ripple of murmurs echoed through the army as more people flooded to the walls to peer down at the invading force.

"What is your name?" Besmir called.

"Yoran," the reply floated down.

"Yoran," Besmir repeated. "Here is your evidence."

Silence fell over the town and the army, all eyes fixed on Besmir in anticipation of what he might do. From somewhere inside the walls a lone dog howled, a lonely baying sound that spoke of loss and misery. Another hound wailed, joining its voice with the first. A third dog began to wail then, followed by even more. Within the space of two minutes Besmir had more than thirty dogs baying and howling.

Yoran looked back at his town in horror as rats began to boil from cellars and dark waterways, scratching and biting. People screamed as their animals started yelling and neighing, barking and yowling. Rats continued to appear from the earth, jumping from below roofs and running from drains. Minor chaos started in the little town as Besmir sent his mind dashing from one animal to the next, driving them into a frenzy. Men and women ran from the sea of rats, unwittingly allowing themselves to be herded up against the inside of the walls. A few individuals realized they had been cut off and immediately set about opening the gate in a panicked attempt to escape.

Besmir watched in satisfaction as the large gates opened, the sweat pouring from his brow. The expression on the first man was priceless. Utter shock and fear exploded across his face when he saw the army outside the walls. He turned to see the rats then turned again to look at the army, confused as to what to do.

Besmir steered the rats past the fleeing citizens and out into the wilderness beyond the town. He looked up at the astonished faces peering back at him.

"There is your proof," he said before falling from his horse and crashing to the ground.

***

Sharova watched Thoran as she packed the few things she wanted to take. He had convinced her to leave the dress behind; wearing her foraging clothes would be much less conspicuous. Her face had fallen when he suggested it, but she had seen the logic and now he waited as she fretted about something minor and worthless. A smile spread across his face when she started to clean and clear the room, tidying the mess they had made but leaving anything that had already been in disarray.

"Thoran?" he said in a quiet voice.

She turned, blowing a strand of hair from her forehead, to look at him with a question in her eyes. Sharova looked meaningfully around the room then at the window to the palace beyond. Thoran followed his gaze, got his point, and looked away, embarrassed.

"It feels wrong somehow...leaving a mess," she said.

"This whole palace is a mess, Thoran. Leaving this room in a shambles is nothing to worry about."

Thoran looked around one last time at the suite she had shared with Sharova, coming to understand this was the end of something important. She grabbed her small sack of belongings and crossed to the door.

"Let us leave, Sharova," she said.

Something inside him liked the way his name felt when she said it, but he pushed it aside.

She is half your age.

He watched as she pressed her ear against the door, listening for any sign of danger. Her delicate fingers wrapped round the handle and turned it gently. She slipped through and disappeared into the gloom beyond. Sharova followed, his legs aching and breath heaving.

Dust filled the air with every footstep as Thoran led him through the passages and corridors of the palace, making him want to sneeze. Cold fright grabbed him when he saw the state the building had been left in. Dusty and dirty, as no one had cleaned for months, things had started to fall into disrepair. Priceless tapestries and paintings hung askew, with some of them almost falling to the floor.

Thoran froze in front of him and he stopped, resting a hand on her shoulder. She turned to look at his hand briefly but said nothing. She held her finger to her lips and gestured to the room beyond. Sharova recognized it as one of the throne room antechambers and listened.

The faint sound of voices drifted to his ears and he concentrated to hear what they were saying.

"...plan must be carried out," Tiernon was saying to someone else. "Before Besmir arrives with his army."

Who is Besmir? And why does he have an army?

"Yes, T'noch, we will cut the life from him and bleed him on the table for your master."

"That is the cold thing he talks to," Thoran breathed over his hand, sending warmth up his arm. "None but the king can see it, but I know it is there I...felt it pass by."

Sharova nodded but had no idea what she was referring to. He shook Thoran gently, nodding in the direction of the outside world. She led the way with him stumbling along as best as he could. Thoran looked back and hesitated, waiting for him to catch up and grabbed his hand, dragging his arm over her shoulders.

Making better time now she was assisting him, the pair skirted around the antechamber, giving the throne room a wide berth. Approaching the main entrance, they both sped up, desperate to escape the confines of the palace into the welcoming daylight.

"Sharova!" Tiernon shouted from behind them. "And the wench!"

The former fleet admiral gaped in horror at the thing that had once been human. His skin sagged, flowing from his bones as if it wanted to escape. The only thing holding it to him was his stained, ripped clothing. A few wisps of hair clung desperately to his scalp, jutting straight out like an explosion. To Sharova's eyes, his former king looked on the verge of death, if not dead already, yet somehow he still lived. Utter madness leaped from his eyes, most of which were visible to Sharova, and the stench that drifted to his nose was pure putrefaction.

"Gods, man!" Sharova gasped in disgust. "What happened to you?"

"You ask no questions, traitor!" Tiernon squealed. "Why are you not dead?"

"How are you still alive?" Sharova wondered.

Tiernon started towards the pair, who backed up automatically, not wanting the rotting, dying thing any closer. Sharova felt the temperature drop, what little energy he had seeped from him, and his knees buckled.

"Sharova!" Thoran cried as he dragged her to the floor.

Tiernon stood over them as his six guards appeared behind him, brooding and evil. A horrible, triumphant smile crossed Tiernon's face, revealing far too many teeth.

"You should have stayed in your prison, Sharova," he said. "Now you will get to suffer. Suffer loss the likes of which you never believed possible. And you will watch as I devastate your little friend here," Tiernon hissed nastily. "Bring them!" he ordered.

Sharova watched helplessly as two of the large guards grabbed Thoran and dragged her away. Her eyes begged him for aid, but he could barely breathe, let alone move, and all he could do was mouth two words: *love you.*

***

"Will you stop fussing!" Besmir growled as Arteera tucked the blankets more tightly around him.

He lay in a large, soft bed the Mayor of Hourtin had provided. After his demonstration with the rats and animals of the town, the mayor had decided his town would be better off hosting the army rather than being hostile, and allowed them to camp outside the walls. Zaynorth, Herofic, Ranyor, Norvasil, and Keluse, along with Arteera and Besmir, had been offered quarters in the town and the gates had been wedged open.

Mayor Yoran had also sent a doctor to examine Besmir after his collapse. With a pinched nose and prominent cheekbones, he had looked a great deal like a cadaver and Besmir had taken an almost instant dislike to the man.

"The patient has overexerted himself," the doctor had said, completely ignoring Besmir. "A classic case of exhaustion brought on by malnutrition," his droning voice had buzzed on. "Some time resting and eating should see the patient well again."

"I'm right here," Besmir had said crossly. "I can hear everything you're saying."

With a small nod to Arteera the doctor had left.

"Of course, my King," Arteera replied in her calmest, most maddening voice.

She withdrew a few feet to sit on a wooden padded chair and picked up a patch of cloth, a needle and some thread to begin embroidering something. Besmir sighed as he watched her.

"I'm fine," he said. "I need to get back to the army and gathering support."

"Of course, Majesty," she said, eyes never leaving her sewing. "Shall I have your armor delivered?"

Besmir stared at her with rising anger. He hated being confined to this bed, especially when the people in his army were sleeping in cold tents. Arteera had gently but firmly denied his every request to leave and rejoin them. She had then disobeyed his orders and his temper had worn short, snapping at her in frustrated rage. Now she had changed her attitude and had adopted this new, infuriating acceptance. She would not use his name, preferring to use his title, agreed with everything he suggested but added sarcastic little jabs and criticisms to almost every sentence and refused to look at him.

Besmir dragged the covers off, feeling a chill hit his skin despite the bright fire blazing in the hearth. He swung his legs out and sat up, gasping as soon as his feet hit the cold floor. An annoying feeling came from his chest, feeling like his ribs and lungs were aflame, something tried to punch its way from his skull, and his bones ached horribly. He coughed. Coughed until his back and stomach ached, his vision swam, and whatever had taken up residence in his head thrashed even more wildly for release.

Stubbornly he tried to rise, leaning heavily on the bed for support. His balance failed him and he fell to the floor, hands slapping the cold slabs.

"Would you like some assistance, Your Majesty?" Arteera asked sweetly, her needle flashing in the sun.

Besmir cursed, at length and colorfully as he tried unsuccessfully to lift himself from the floor. Eventually he gave in and slumped back down.

"Please help me," he said.

"I beg Your Majesty's pardon?"

"Please, Arteera, I'm begging you," Besmir whined, playing the victim. "Please help me back into bed."

The dark-haired woman pursed her lips, not falling for his weak subterfuge in the least but tried to hide her smile as she made a show of folding her embroidery and sorting her needle before turning to look at him again. She shook her head when she saw his cheek squashed against the floor but felt a little pity for his situation. His eye followed her every move as she approached, squatting beside him to help.

"You're a cruel, cruel woman," Besmir muttered as Arteera chuckled at him.

Besmir let himself be guided to the bed, where he lay in its soft embrace, groaning as the aches in his limbs rotated until different bits of his body hurt.

"What did that doctor say?" Besmir asked after another coughing fit shook his body.

Arteera lay beside him, cradling his head on her stomach and stroking his broad back.

"You have a deep infection in your lungs due to weakness and poor living conditions."

Besmir made a noise.

"I hate being ill," he said. "I was never ill in Tyrington."

"You surprise me," Arteera said sarcastically.

"How long have I got?" he asked.

"What, to live?" she asked, laughing.

"I am glad my suffering brings you such joy," Besmir muttered grouchily. "That's nice, though," he added as she ran her fingers through his hair.

"A few days should have you feeling better," she said. "However, the doctor recommended you take your recovery slowly and not overexert yourself."

Arteera looked down at Besmir, realizing he had fallen asleep. She pulled the covers over him and moved to leave, but his arm wrapped around her, pinning her in place so she shifted, getting comfortable. Without knowing she was going to, she started to hum, a sweet melody from her childhood that brought tears from her eyes.

Abruptly Besmir sat up, staring at her with enormous, sore-looking eyes. He searched her face in the same way he had when he thought she was a traitor.

"Besmir, what—"

"When were you going to tell me?"

"Tell you what?" she asked in utter confusion.

"About the baby," he said, laying his hand on her abdomen.

Cold shock hit her like a hammer to the chest, and she actually flinched as if he had slapped her.

"What do you mean, baby?" she asked. "We have been so careful... I-I-I cannot be... How can we have a baby now?"

Panic threatened to overwhelm her, and she had to try to control her breathing as Besmir struggled into a sitting position, pulling her into his arms and resting his chin on top of her head.

"I promise everything will be fine," he muttered in his deep voice.

"But Tiernon…"

"Will *never* lay his eyes on our baby," Besmir stated in a serious voice. "I'll destroy him utterly before I let that happen."

"I am not ready to be a mother," Arteera said. "I have no idea what to do."

"You'll make the best mother anyone ever had," Besmir said.

Arteera sighed, calming a little as Besmir thought about his parents, wondering exactly how much of what he had just promised Arteera he could keep to.

Chapter Twenty-One

"I sent messengers to six of the nearest towns and villages, sire," Yoran said as he lowered his bulk into one of the chairs not occupied by Besmir's council. Keluse watched as the older man rubbed his head, frowning. "Four of the six replied with positive support," he added, sipping wine from a cup. "However, they are the four town leaders I know personally and have had positive dealings with in the past. The remaining two, the town of Vernsar and the village of Fring," Yoran paused, looking at the two women present. "Suffice to say their replies were similarly impolite."

"Pity," Besmir said. "I was hoping for support from all sides. Is it fear of Tiernon that halts them?"

"The information was not contained in their missives, sire," Yoran replied. "However, I do not believe, from what I know of both town leaders, that it is loyalty to Tiernon that turns them from you. It must be fear. We were all punished during the war for siding against the crown," he said sadly. "It has taken a long time to recover, and we will take even longer to grieve."

The room fell silent as all present recalled someone or something they had lost.

"We'll make for Fring village tomorrow," Besmir said. "Make sure everyone knows."

Mayor Yoran looked horrified, his chubby face pale and lips thin as he stared at Besmir.

"Will you attack them, sire?" he asked.

The chubby mayor flinched as everyone in the room turned to stare at him with hostility in their eyes.

"No, Yoran," Besmir said with a chuckle. "I'll not be like Tiernon. There will be no violence against innocent people, no examples made of anyone and no executions," he said. "With one exception," he added.

"Oh," Yoran said, relieved. "So...what is the purpose of visiting them with an army?"

"To give them a choice," Besmir said with a smile. "To ask them to serve me. Or at least beg them not to stab us all in the back as we move on. Like we did here," he added.

Yoran blinked a few times as understanding filled his head. He stood, putting his cup down, and stepped over to stand before Besmir. Slowly he dropped to one knee before him.

"Please accept my apologies, Your Majesty," he said. "For not giving you my pledge of oath sooner. It slipped my mind."

Besmir reached out and accepted the rotund mayor's hand, lifting him from the floor.

"It's perfectly all right," he said. "I never asked for it."

The Mayor smiled. "I will coordinate with the other towns to arrange food and other supplies," he said. "With pride and honor."

"You're a good man," Besmir said. "I'm glad to have you on my side."

Yoran nodded and turned to leave, nodding to the other people in the room as he went.

"Do you think you can trust him to deliver supplies to an army who has marched on?" Herofic asked skeptically.

"Oh, absolutely," Besmir replied. "That little demonstration there?" He gestured to the floor in front of him. "That told me everything I needed to know about him."

Herofic shrugged, accepting Besmir's appraisal of the situation.

Keluse had been watching Arteera as the meeting took place and noticed her hands never strayed far from her belly. Suspicion ground at her, and she approached her as Besmir spoke with Zaynorth and Norvasil about packing up the army and how long it might take to march to Fring.

"How have you been?" Keluse asked, making Arteera jump.

The woman had been lost in her own little world until Keluse spoke. Now she turned her eyes toward Keluse, a question in them.

"Do you love Besmir?" she asked, surprising Keluse.

"What? No," Keluse said in a shrill voice. "Well, like a brother, I suppose, but I'm not *in* love with him. Why?"

She watched as Arteera looked down, stroking her hands over her flat belly and sighing. Keluse thought it might have been a sigh of contentment or sadness, and was at pains to tell which.

"May I speak freely to you?" Arteera asked. "In confidence?"

"Of course," Keluse replied, following her to another room.

"I believe you have guessed," Arteera said. "If not, then you might be surprised to learn I am carrying Besmir's child."

Keluse felt a wash of pleasure roll through her, but grew concerned when she did not see her grin matched by Arteera's own.

"Is that not a good thing?" she asked.

"Would it be good if you carried Ranyor's?" she asked bluntly.

Keluse reddened, still not comfortable with attitudes towards relationships here, but considered her question. While she knew she loved Ranyor, Keluse also knew they were in the middle of a potentially bloody and violent conflict. None of them knew if they would live through the next few days, let alone long enough to raise a child.

"I see your point," Keluse said. "But still..."

"Do not mistake me," Arteera said, her eyes filling with tears. "I want nothing more than to have a family with him." She sniffed. "Yet the circumstances are...less than ideal."

"Less than ideal?" she asked with a chuckle. "That's the kind of understatement Besmir would make."

Both women laughed at that.

"He promised he would keep the baby safe," Arteera said. "But how can he promise such when faced with Tiernon?"

"I expect as he knows I'll be right there beside him, protecting you also. Ranyor too, and Herofic. Norvasil and Zaynorth would also stand before you."

"Not Zaynorth, I think," Arteera replied. "He still believes I am a spy for Tiernon."

Keluse hugged her awkwardly, not used to the physical contact even now.

"I'm sure your sister will be fine," Keluse said, not believing her own words.

"I think not," Arteera said. "But thank you for saying so."

"So...a baby, then?" Keluse changed the subject.

"Yes," Arteera replied, blushing a little. "It is unexpected...and odd, but I like the feeling."

"It looks like it suits you," Keluse said. "Have you had any symptoms yet?"

"Not so far," Arteera said, frowning. "Do you think something might be wrong?"

"Of course not," Keluse assured her. "I'm sure Besmir would know if something were wrong." Arteera nodded thoughtfully.

**

Besmir sat on his stallion, staring in confusion at the fleeing madness before him. They had reached Fring village two days after leaving Yoran's little town behind. Fring was poorly fortified and even more poorly guarded. A few men stood between Besmir's army and the wooden barrier that was supposed to offer protection. They scattered as soon as the extent of the army became clear, spreading fear and panic through the villagers. Women screamed as they carried children to safety in their arms, while old men looked on in utter fear at Besmir, wielding farming equipment and pointed sticks in shaking hands.

Casting his eyes over the small village, Besmir saw it was little more than a gathering of simple huts, many of which were in need of repair. Some of the thatched roofs were falling in, sections sagging in and a few holes appearing. Half-starved pigs rooted in the dirt, desperately hunting for any form of nourishment as scrawny chickens scratched and pecked at nothing.

Two men and an older woman approached Besmir and looked up at him with a mixture of hate and fear. The two men were of middle age, thin and poorly dressed in long, dirty, brown robes. The woman might have been their mother or even grandmother, judging by her ancient appearance.

"What business have you in Fring?" the woman demanded, staring defiantly up at Besmir.

The hunter-king grinned and dismounted, handing his reins to a woman that appeared beside him. On his approach to the old woman he saw she wore a dress of velvet, mud-splattered and tired, a string of wooden beads hung from her wrinkled neck, and her thinning hair was white and curled. She looked stern and proud, barely accepting the arms the two men offered, preferring to stand on her own.

"Great Lady," Besmir said. "I offer you my greetings and good tidings."

"Offer me nothing at the head of an army," she spat hotly. "Leave here! Fring has nothing more to give."

"My name is Besmir, rightful heir to the throne of Gazluth a—"

"I care not for who you think you are!" the old woman said.

"Margarey!" one of the men said. "You need to show the king some respect."

"Pah!" Margarey spat, her toothless mouth flapping. "He is no king of mine!"

"Perhaps you'd feel better having a visit from Tiernon," Besmir said, staring into her eyes. "I've seen what he does to little villages like this." Besmir pointed with his chin. "It's horrible to see the women and children burned alive in their homes. I offer a more peaceful way of life."

"I have seen the ways of men," Margarey said. "Whether they offer peace or war, the outcome is always the same. Take what you will by force and leave us, you will."

Besmir shook his head in disagreement but raised his voice so the villagers gathering behind Margarey could hear.

"You're wrong about us. Ask any of my warriors, all proud women and young men like yourselves, each will tell you the same thing. I offer my protection from the evil Tiernon who murdered my parents and thought I had perished too—"

"We need no protection from Tiernon," Margarey shouted, her voice loud and strong enough to carry to the crowd. "We need food in our bellies and homes to keep out the cold of winter. Will you give us that, King?"

Besmir grinned at the old woman, staring at her for so long even she started to feel apprehensive. Margarey and the others in the small village gasped and stared, pointing at the mass exodus of animals that marched straight at them. Rabbits, hares, squirrels, fowl of a number of varieties and even a small deer trotted peacefully from the wilds around the village.

"Catch them!" Besmir cried in a hoarse voice. "Feast on the bounty I provide."

Zaynorth and Norvasil had approached Besmir as soon as they realized what he was doing, ready to catch him if he were to collapse. Still weakened by his sojourn in hell and recent infection, Besmir staggered when he returned to his body, but managed to keep his balance in front of Margarey.

"Maybe you ought to come in," she said, reappraising Besmir. "Welcome to Fring, Majesty."

Besmir smirked at Zaynorth, who merely shook his head as the three followed her staggering gait between the celebrating villagers.

**

Sharova's world had shrunk to become a single, throbbing agony that rippled up his arms and into his chest with every heartbeat.

Initially he had thought Tiernon had found some small measure of kindness in his heart, as both he and Thoran had been fed and watered, despite being caged. Sharova had watched as the king had sacrifices brought to his chambers, casually butchering them on the vile altar that dominated the space. As the days passed and Sharova regained a little strength, he started to notice the air became colder with each sacrifice, every lungful of his breath frosting in the air.

"It is those *things*," Thoran said when he mentioned it to her. "Have you not felt them?"

While he had felt cold chills, Sharova's mind had convinced him they were symptoms of the overall cold and his poor health. When Thoran put it into words, however, the revelation hit him hard.

"Are they spirits?" he asked, making a protective sign over his heart.

"I do not know," Thoran admitted. "All I do know is they are evil, horrible things."

From that point Sharova had watched Tiernon with a keener eye, bearing the cold things in mind. The king's madness was so complete, so deep and all-encompassing, Sharova was convinced these invisible creatures had something to do with it.

Days ran into weeks as poor souls were led to the altar for Tiernon to casually butcher. Each time a fresh victim was dragged screaming and crying into the room, Sharova took Thoran into his arms and they both huddled at the farthest corner of their cage until the soul-rending screams of terror faded. Even then the pair huddled in the cage, partly for warmth and partly for comfort, losing themselves in each other's eyes rather than enduring the horrific torments Tiernon exposed them to.

"Why does he do this?" Thoran begged when yet another woman died screaming on the table.

Sharova watched as a pair of the massive guards – further demonic beasts – dragged the woman's remains from the room. Her desiccated husk hissed against the floor like a rough stone, reminding Sharova of his days at sea when deck hands would scrub the wood with heavy stones until the wood gleamed.

"It feeds them," Sharova replied. "Whatever they might be, they feed on suffering, pain, blood and fear."

He had taken her into his arms when her tears had started to flow.

Sharova woke to the smell of decay and rotten things puffing over his face. Blinking rapidly, he saw Tiernon's wasted grin inches from his face and fright chilled his belly, clamping down tightly.

"Do you know the punishment for treason, Sharova?" the king whispered in a terrible voice.

"No," Sharova said.

"Sire!" Tiernon bellowed, straightening his back. "No, sire! No, Majesty!"

Tiernon screamed the words over and over again, his eyes blazing with anger as he stared at Sharova.

"Say it. Say it. Say it."

"No, sire," Sharova said meekly.

A grin spread over Tiernon's face again, revealing blackened and rotting teeth that must have been an agony in his mouth. The king seemed not to notice, however, looking down at the former fleet admiral with a benevolent expression.

"In times gone by, a traitor would be publicly flogged and displayed for all to see. People would be free to throw feces and rotting fruit at them while they baked in the sun. Three days would pass in this manner before they were released and dragged behind a team of horses up into the foothills of the Atranus mountains." Tiernon squatted before Sharova, his once beautiful clothes now filthy and ripped, covered in things Sharova's mind shied from. "If still they lived, their legs and arms would be snapped and they would be left for the beasts to eat alive." Tiernon smiled, making Sharova's insides writhe with cold fear. "I have chosen to be kind to you, Sharova, as a king must sometimes be, and so you will suffer a different fate. Guards!"

At the barked command, two of the tall, armored guards shoved their way into the cage and grabbed his wrists, careful not to touch Tiernon in any way. Ice cold and far too strong to be human, they dragged him from the cage, holding his arms out against the wall and stretching them painfully. Tiernon walked across casually towards him with the sound of Thoran's screams as his fanfare. The king stared into his eyes as he raised his hand, bringing a glowing orb to life. He slapped the orb against Sharova's wrist, making agony explode along his arm and into his chest. Sharova felt his heart beating hard and for a moment he hoped it would fail, granting him sweet release from this torment.

Thoughts of Thoran pulled him back from the brink of slipping into his own madness. What would happen to her if he died or let his mind slip? His eyes rolled towards her as Tiernon slammed a second orb into his other wrist, seeing her huddled in the farthest corner of the cage, her hands clamped to her mouth and eyes wider than he had ever seen.

Sharova managed to turn his head and see what had been done to him. His hands had somehow fused with the stonework of the wall, and Sharova's eyes bulged in horrified fascination as he tried to make his fingers move. With no sensation from his wrists downwards, a horrible numbness spread. The skin on his arms actually changed to take on the grey tone of the stones it had been merged with, feeling hard and crusted.

The guards released him, stepping back from where he was fixed to the wall and entering the cell again. Sharova's heart fell when he realized what was about to happen, and a low moan escaped his tortured chest. Thoran's screams ripped at his soul as she was dragged from the cage and brought before Sharova. He looked down at her, his sorrow echoed in her eyes.

"Sorry," he whispered.

Tiernon chortled like a child hearing a weak joke and grabbed Thoran by her upper arm. The sight of his skeletal fingers digging into the soft flesh of her arm made rage explode inside Sharova, and he growled.

"Take your filthy hands off her!"

Tiernon turned his own eyes to Sharova, a grin spreading over his face as he tore the ragged clothing from her. Redness crept up Thoran's neck when she found herself exposed to Sharova's gaze and she looked away, embarrassed despite the horrible circumstances.

Tiernon shoved Thoran bodily onto the sickening altar, the silver inlay glowing a sick blue as if in anticipation of being fed. Sharova felt a wash of shame run through him, followed by a guilt that bit deeply into him. What kind of man allowed this to happen to anyone, let alone a woman he had feelings for? Hot tears of frustration rolled down his cheeks as he watched Tiernon push Thoran down onto the altar. All the fight seemed to leave her as she sank down on the wooden surface, the light leaving her eyes as she went limp.

Sharova thrashed against the stone that held him, his own skin cutting into him where it merged with the granite. He lashed out with his foot, kicking at Tiernon when he came in range, but it was like kicking a bunch of sticks. The king laughed at his effort as a freezing wind caressed his chest and abdomen, pulling at his very life force.

"Enjoy your last few hours, Sharova," Tiernon said with glee. "I shall return soon to butcher your little woman."

Sharova watched as Tiernon ran his hand down Thoran's naked thigh, leaving the room with his guards.

"Thoran!" he shouted. "Thoran, wake up! Fight it! Fight it, my love!"

Her head rolled slowly towards him as if underwater, and her eyes struggled to focus on him. Almost as if she had been drugged, Thoran smiled serenely up at him, her lips an inviting bow. Sharova's heart sank as he realized she was in no condition to do anything, and the pain in his chest grew.

Chapter Twenty-Two

Besmir's army grew slowly as his campaign to unite Gazluth continued. Most of the outlying villages, towns and cities realized siding with the rightful king of the land was in their best interests. News of his benevolence, kindness and charisma spread before him, and many of the settlements welcomed him with open arms, parades and celebrations. Some had prepared grounds for the army to pitch their tents and provided food for them all. Many of the people who had been affected by Tiernon's violence and civil war joined the army, showing their support for this new king who walked among them.

It was not until they began drawing closer to the heart of Gazluth, nearing the capital, Morantine, that any real resistance appeared. One walled city had built up their defenses and refused Besmir entry when he asked. Camping around the outside Besmir's army was subdued, their buoyant mood dissipating with the opposition.

"Are we really going to have to lay siege to the place?" Besmir asked as he and his companions studied the gray city walls.

"These towns and cities are loyal to Tiernon," Zaynorth said grimly. "It will likely take a show of force to make them capitulate."

Besmir shook his head, wondering what manner of people would be loyal to his uncle.

"We'll cut their supply routes off," Besmir said. "Starve them out."

"That may take months," Zaynorth pointed out.

"We need to give them a show of force," Herofic advised. "Smash down the gates and march in as if you own the place."

Besmir felt sickness rise in his stomach. It was one thing to raise an army but quite another to actually order them to attack, to die for him. He looked at Zaynorth, his eyes begging but the old man shrugged.

"It is your order, lad," Herofic said when Besmir turned to him.,

The hunter sighed and stared at the city, its walls lined with people all waiting to see what would happen.

"Form up!" He said in a dark voice. "Prepare to attack."

The citizens inside the walls jeered and called as they watched the ragged army approach. It was not until Besmir lashed the wooden gates with searing flame that they understood he had the same powers as Tiernon. Unfortunately for them it was too late and Besmir's army marched through the burned gates, attacking the token force that met them.

Some of the women who made his original army chose to remain in the places they visited, petitioning him to be released as they had met up with people who offered safety and shelter. Besmir denied them nothing. If they wished to leave, he allowed it. If they offered to join his cause, he welcomed them, all the time progressing slowly towards the capital and Tiernon.

Whether the locations he visited capitulated or chose to remain neutral, Besmir did not allow a single drop of blood to be spilled in his quest. Determined to be as utterly different to Tiernon as he could, Besmir made sure all who followed him understood his army was for defense purposes only.

Besmir crested a rise and stared down into the valley beyond. Farm fields lay in various states of disarray. Some were fields filled with trees, pregnant with fruit, while others were brown with rotten crops that were overripe and ruined. A few people tended the fields, but it did not appear as if anyone was managing them properly.

Beyond that, straddling a sluggish river, Morantine squatted, brooding like a depression, with a smog of hatred hovering over her head. Stone towers and tall buildings dominated the city skyline but very few lights shone from any of them.

Zaynorth approached, shaking his head and hissing. He pointed out some of the pertinent features, adding comments and observations as he did.

"To the west sits the University of Morantine with the golden spire at its heart. East of there is the commercial district where anything might be purchased. That hulk in the center is the palace."

Besmir focused his attention on the palace buildings, seeing how they were grouped together and surrounded by a high wall. Impossible to see at this distance, Besmir assumed there would be a massive force within that wall, ready to defend Tiernon against any invaders. A ripple of concern gripped his gut, twisting anxiously at the thought of his army being slaughtered.

"It looks quiet," Besmir said.

"Yes," Zaynorth agreed. "Far too quiet. I cannot believe how different things are since last I was here."

"I think we should camp here tonight, send a couple of people inside to see what it's like in there," Besmir said.

"A sound plan," Zaynorth said.

***

A few hours later, Besmir sat in his pavilion staring at his circle of advisers with anger.

"No one else is as capable to get in there and see what's going on!" he nearly shouted at them. "If it's not safe for me to enter, then no one else stands a chance."

"If you were to be caught,," Zaynorth started, "Tiernon could win without ever having to try if you offer yourself up to his city like an animal entering a trap."

Besmir sighed, resting his fists on his hips, and scanned their pleading faces.

"I don't like the idea of sending anyone else in there," he muttered stubbornly.

"Then I volunteer, sire," Ranyor said quietly.

Keluse's head snapped round to gape at him. "No," she breathed. "No Ranyor, you can't mean that."

"I will slip inside under cover of darkness," Ranyor said, ignoring Keluse's words. "See how things are within the city walls and report back tomorrow night."

Besmir considered Ranyor's words. It was obvious the tall swordsman believed he was capable of this task. Just as obviously, Keluse did not want him to go. Norvasil nodded almost imperceptibly, staring into the fire while Zaynorth and Herofic merely waited for him to make a decision.

"Take whatever supplies you need," Besmir said as he watched Keluse's face fall. "Take no risks whatsoever," he added as the tall man stood.

"Of course not, Majesty," Ranyor said, his eyes never leaving Keluse.

"Rest while you can," Besmir told the remaining members of his council. "When Ranyor returns, we attack," he added.

***

"I'm going with you," Keluse said as she trailed after Ranyor through the ordered camp the army had set up.

Tents and campfires stretched off in all directions around them, disappearing into the twilight as soldiers prepared simple meals, took care of their meager arms and armor or chanted quiet songs, imploring the gods for good fortune and health.

"No, you are not," Ranyor stated flatly.

His eyes bored into hers when he turned to look at her, and she flinched under the intensity of that gaze. Fear scored the inside of her lungs, making it difficult to breathe. Ranyor lifted her chin with a gentle hand and stroked the tears from her cheeks.

"Nothing can keep me from you," he said. "Not Tiernon nor the gods themselves stand a chance of standing in my way." He leaned down and kissed her tenderly. "Stay safe," he added, turning from her.

"We will," Keluse blurted before she could stop herself.

Ranyor turned, his frown changing to an expression of utter joyful delight as the information sunk in.

"I can't do this alone," Keluse said, shaking. "You've got to come back to me. Promise!" she said.

"Of course I promise," he said.

Taking her hand, Ranyor led her through the tents to one where Norvasil was busy regaling a group with a bawdy tale he was obviously embellishing heavily for effect.

"Sixty men lay dead and dying at his feet! Sixty!" the immense warrior bellowed to his audience.

"Norvasil," Ranyor said. "A word?"

"Ranyor! Keluse!" Norvasil cried as if he had not seen them but minutes earlier. "Come, join us!"

He lifted an earthenware cup and gulped the contents to the rapturous cheering of the crowd.

"Little time for that," Ranyor said with a smile. "Do you still perform marriages?"

Norvasil's expression changed at that, becoming serious in a heartbeat. He led the pair out of earshot to speak to them privately.

"I have not done so in a long time but yes I still have that privilege," he replied with a smile.

Ranyor glanced at Keluse then back at Norvasil before he said anything. "I wish us to be married," he said. "If you would have me?" he added to Keluse.

Utter shock took her breath and robbed her of her words as she stared at him in the light from the campfire. Tight heat blossomed in her chest as she gazed into his open, honest eyes, seeing the love he had for her.

"Y-Yes," she said. "O-Of course."

"I will need but a few minutes to prepare," Norvasil said in a completely different voice. "Have you rings?"

"Oh," Ranyor said. "Er, no."

"Could you procure some?" he asked. "It is a vital part of the ceremony."

"Let me," Keluse said, darting off through the tents.

***

"How are you?" Besmir asked as he stroked his hands over Arteera's stomach.

"Sick," she said. "All the time. I feel sick during my waking hours then dream of feeling sick when I finally sleep."

"Anything I can do?" Besmir asked, taking her in his arms.

"I do not think so." Arteera shook her dark hair. "Unless you can carry our child for me?"

"I do not think so," Besmir echoed her words. "Have you spoken with other mothers in camp?"

"I am not popular among people here since Marthius exposed my secret," Arteera said sadly.

Besmir sighed and hugged her tightly. "They'll have to get used to having you around," he said. "Especially as you'll be their queen."

Arteera pulled back, searching his face for any sign of jest, but could see none, and allowed a smile across her face. As her lips met his, she heard Keluse calling to them both.

"Come in," she said.

Breathless and flushed, Keluse entered and looked at them both. Arteera could see her expression was a little wild, like a foal about to bolt.

"Whatever is wrong?" Arteera asked in concern.

"Ranyor... I...w-we need rings," Keluse stammered.

"Rings?" Besmir echoed in confusion. "What for?"

Arteera rolled her eyes and shoved him, pushing him from the pavilion without a choice.

"Go find us some rings," she commanded. "Quickly now."

"Yes, Your Majesty," Besmir grinned as he trotted off.

Arteera turned and looked at Keluse standing awkwardly in her tight leather hunting clothing.

"Strip," she said sternly. "You cannot be wed in that." She waved her hand dismissively.

"What?" Keluse asked, aghast. "No!"

"Trust me," Arteera said.

***

Norvasil stood beside a fire, his back straight as he thought over the words that would marry the couple, his eyes glazed in thought..

A clearing had been fashioned with a massive fire built at its center, crackling and hissing as thick logs were consumed by flame. Stars peppered the dark blue and purple sky, the twin moons hanging low in the sky providing a warm glow that added to the firelight. Everyone had gathered around to see what was happening, shocked and surprised to see Norvasil was also able to marry people .

Ranyor stood beside him, nervous under the scrutiny of so many eyes yet anticipating the arrival of his bride-to-be. Besmir stood beside him, having persuaded some of his people to part with prized rings of their own.

Arteera appeared at the edge of the firelight and an improvised band played a traditional wedding tune as she led Keluse into the clearing.

All heads turned to stare, some to gape, at the blonde huntress as she approached the three men. Ranyor stared in wonder at the transformation Arteera had wrought in such a short time.

Keluse had a patchwork dress Arteera had made from scraps, furs, skins and swathes of fabric she had spent months sewing and decorating. With a plunging neckline that reached almost to her slender belly, Keluse showed off far more skin than she was used to, but Ranyor could see she was managing well. Her golden locks had been pulled, curled and piled atop her head, leaving her slim neck and shoulders bare.

Ranyor felt the sensation of falling as he set eyes on her, his stomach flipping over and over with every step she took towards him. The firelight flickered, reflecting from her eyes and making them twinkle as she looked back at him. That she carried his child both scared and delighted him, setting a determination in his chest to protect her from any harm at all.

Arteera led her to him and he took her hand, feeling the slight tremble in her fingers.

"Friends," Norvasil bellowed, raising his arms.

The wrappings around his thickly muscled arms flapped in the wind blowing in from the east.

"Let us gather and witness the joining of this man and woman who have declared their love for each other. In the presence of all, in this place here, let none sunder the bonds which I place. Ranyor, Keluse, please join hands."

Ranyor took Keluse's hand, offering them to Norvasil, who wrapped one of his red bindings around their wrists, running it up their forearms until he reached their elbows.

"Red signifies the blood that ties this couple together, the bond of life and love," Norvasil shouted.

He unwound the white ribbon from his own arm and wrapped it round theirs over the red until their arms were completely bound together.

"I love you, Keluse," Ranyor said as Norvasil turned to the crowd once more.

"The white represents the love of Cathantor that overlays all, sealing the love these two have for each other. What is set today, let none attempt to sunder or destroy. Have you rings?" Norvasil asked.

Ranyor looked at Keluse, who turned to look at Besmir. The king smiled at his apprentice and his friend, producing a pair of gold rings.

"I hope they fit," he said quietly. "I had to make a few promises to get them." He grinned as he passed the rings over.

Norvasil slid the rings onto both Ranyor's and Keluse's fingers, removing the wrappings from their arms. He lifted their clasped hands high so all could see.

"I declare you to be man and wife!" he shouted.

The people around them cheered and clapped, hugging each other and the newlyweds, offering little gifts and tokens.

"I love you too," Keluse said as Ranyor led her towards their tent.

***

Besmir floated above the city of Morantine, his light body able to sense the changing air currents that held him aloft. The raven he had taken control of had been busy pecking the eyes from a dead sheep it had found when he had slammed into it. The taste of rotting flesh still hung in his beaked mouth like a malevolent spirit.

He swooped down towards the southern gate, expecting to find it locked tight and heavily guarded, yet when he touched down atop the granite wall that housed the gate, he saw nothing. The guardhouse sat silent and empty, the gate half open and unmanned. He would have frowned if his avian face had allowed it, but the raven simply tilted its head as a single figure slipped inside the gate, becoming one with the shadows.

Besmir watched as the newly married Ranyor crept through the silent streets. An eerie silence had settled over the city and many of the buildings stood open, ransacked or simply empty. With a jump and flap of his wings, Besmir rose into the night ahead of the swordsman in search of any signs of life.

His mission here was twofold. He wanted to see for himself what secrets the city might hold and saw the sense of his advisers telling him not to go. He also wanted to keep an eye on Ranyor, especially as he had just married Keluse.

As he fluttered over the buildings and walkways, Besmir could see the piles of rubbish and discarded debris looters had left behind as they ransacked homes and businesses. Fire had broken out in a few places. Soot-blackened stones surrounded empty doorways that bled ash into the street.

Besmir landed, strutting back and forth on the cobbled streets, waiting for Ranyor. The sound of footsteps echoed from the stones around him and he turned to see a small group of men approaching. Torches cast weak light that flickered, reflecting off his beady eyes as he twitched his head back and forth.

"Will you look at that!" a voice said. "Crow stood there as bold as day!"

A pockmarked face peered at Besmir in confusion as a second man pushed him aside.

"That's a raven," the second man said. "Not a crow."

"Does it matter?" pockmark exclaimed. "Look at him just stood there!"

"Ignore the bird," the second man grunted. "We need to get out of this cursed city."

Besmir danced out of the way as the two companions stomped past. They were both poorly dressed and armed only with small daggers, making Besmir wonder what had happened to them.

Abruptly Besmir realized they were heading straight for Ranyor, and leaped into the air to warn him. He rose above the buildings in search of his friend, flapping his wings madly when a freak gust threatened to blow him off course. His keen sight picked out Ranyor in the darkness, slinking through the streets. Besmir dropped like a stone, folding his wings to hammer towards the ground before the swordsman. He landed, flaring his wings at the last moment and mistiming it so he hit heavily.

Ranyor turned the corner, his dark eyes landing on the raven as it capered about, trying to get its balance. Besmir could see his confusion as the bird scrambled about in a most un-birdlike way.

"I may be losing my mind," Ranyor whispered. "But is that you Besmir? He asked the bird.

Besmir bobbed his raven body and head vigorously, making Ranyor grin.

Besmir stared down the path Ranyor had been following and spread his wings out wide as if to stop him.

"I take it you do not wish me to go that way," Ranyor said.

Besmir shook his bird head, waving his beak from side to side.

"This is madness," Ranyor said in amusement as he ducked inside an open doorway.

Besmir launched himself into the air, wheeling up and out of the way of the two companions until they passed Ranyor's hiding place.

Moments later the swordsman appeared and slipped along the gap between two buildings and out onto the main road that led towards the palace. Outside the curtain wall surrounding the complex, Besmir could make out several dark shapes moving, and the sensation of horror crept over his feathered scalp. Whatever moved in the darkness was as far from human as it was possible to be, and the sensation that flowed over the raven's body reminded Besmir of the absence in hell. Fright crawled through him when he thought about Ranyor coming into contact with whatever these things were, and he leaped into the air, trying to swim through it like a river.

The swordsman was sneaking along the shadows on the eastern side of the avenue leading to the palace, using the ancient oaks for additional cover. Besmir headed awkwardly for him, almost crashing into Ranyor's face, blinding him with his beak.

"Gods!" Ranyor spat, batting at his avian king as Besmir flapped wildly at his face.

Annoyance and shock made Ranyor ignore what Besmir was trying to tell him and he shoved at the bird, knocking Besmir to the ground.

Besmir felt more than saw the creatures that guarded the palace as they approached Ranyor, sucking the life out of the air itself. As he pulled his conscious mind from the bird Besmir just made out the large shape of something that was not human grabbing Ranyor by the throat

***

Ranyor felt the warmth pulled from the air as the raven flew away, cawing madly. He stepped out from behind the ancient, gnarled oak and almost straight into the ice cold grip of a massive hand. Fingers as strong as steel grabbed his throat before he could react, hauling him up into the air and face to face with something from a nightmare.

Set too deep within the metal helmet it wore a pair of dim, yellow eyes gleamed like iridescent pus, glaring at Ranyor. His arm snapped as easily as a twig when the thing twisted it, his drawn sword clattering to the cobbles as he groaned in agony.

Ranyor struggled vainly, pain throbbing in his arm as the large creature carried him towards the palace, its silence almost as eerie as its form.

"I have seen you," Tiernon said when Ranyor was dropped at his feet. "You are part of my nephew's little army."

Ranyor turned his head from the vile stench that wafted from Tiernon's mouth and grunted.

"You will tell me everything I wish to know," Tiernon said. "From his plans to his companions."

"Go die in a hole," Ranyor said through clenched teeth.

"That is unkind," Tiernon muttered. "Perhaps this will loosen your tongue."

Flame crept through Ranyor's veins, wrenching a scream from his throat as he collapsed to the floor. His heartbeat sped up and it felt as if his very blood itched. The one enduring thought keeping him from madness was Keluse's face and he clung to the image as Tiernon tormented him.

"You are strong," Tiernon said. "I can see there is little point in asking you about Besmir so I will just end your life."

Ranyor heard a cracking sound as something vital gave way inside him. Pain lanced up his back, making his spine arch and the base of his skull tingle. His final thought was a regret that he would never get to meet his child.

Chapter Twenty-Three

"Zaynorth! Norvasil! Herofic!" Besmir bellowed as soon as his conscious mind flicked back into his own body.

Arteera stared at him as if he had gone insane, turning over in their bed and pulling the covers up around her throat.

"Middle of the night," she muttered. "Quiet...sleep."

Besmir launched himself out of his pavilion, shouting and rousing the whole camp.

"Ready yourselves! We must march!" he bellowed as he ran through the camp.

Faces began to emerge from tents, bleary-eyed and angry but curious as to what the commotion was. Many had drunk too much in celebration of Ranyor and Keluse's wedding and were still a little drunk.

"Get up!" Besmir shouted. "Wake and ready yourselves for battle!"

Within minutes the whole camp was awash with activity. Women fell from tents half-dressed in armor but attempting to form up as elder children looked after younger ones with wide-eyed fright.

"What is the cause of all this?" Zaynorth asked as he tugged his beard.

"Ranyor is in trouble," Besmir told him as Keluse trotted over.

"Ranyor?" she asked. "What's happened?"

"Something Tiernon's brought here or...created," Besmir said, "took him."

"Tiernon's got him?" Keluse screamed. "*Tiernon!*"

All the fight seemed to go out of her at once, and she collapsed against Besmir, who held her up as he issued commands through Herofic and Norvasil.

Within an hour, the majority of Besmir's army was marching down towards Morantine as the first fingers of light crept over the eastern horizon. Besmir rode at the head of his army, leading by example as he entered the largest city he had ever seen, the scale of the place overwhelming now he experienced it in his own body.

The southern gate was easily fifteen feet in height. As thick as a man and fashioned from iron-bound tree trunks that had been squared, the pair of wooden doors hung partially open, and Besmir had crews open them fully before entering.

The sound of hooves echoed hollowly back from the surrounding stonework, mingling with the nervous chattering from the woman at Besmir's back. The king reined in, turning in the saddle to shout back at them.

"There is nothing to fear within these sections of the city! Nothing resides here, it's at the palace you will face your terrors. Know that I am proud to serve alongside every one of you, and come what may, I am proud to be your king!" He waited as their cheers died down before pulling the bow from his saddle and raising it high. "For Gazluth!" he shouted, spurring his horse forward.

Besmir's army thundered the cheer as they followed their king through the deserted streets and roads of the capital, kicking aside trash as they went.

Besmir looked at the buildings he passed, each one a work of art as well as a functional building.

"Where is everyone?" Herofic muttered as he marched. "That is what I want to know."

Zaynorth turned to stare at his normally fearless brother, noting the grim set of his mouth and the whiteness of his knuckles gripping his ax.

"I have been wondering the same thing," Besmir heard Zaynorth say. "There must have been twenty thousand people living here. Even were they all to flee the city, word would have reached us before now."

Besmir came to the oak-lined avenue leading to the palace gate and looked along its length, wondering where Ranyor had been taken, if he was still alive. Birds flew overhead and he briefly thought about taking one over but dismissed the idea, as he needed to do this in his own body. The hunter king clucked his horse forward, leading his army towards the palace.

Sunlight broke over the buildings at his back, illuminating a scene that turned his stomach and made the whole army pause. Dead bodies lay in random heaps leading up to and through the palace walls. Some looked serene with arms folded, while others lay with their arms outstretched as if begging for salvation.

Rage vied with the horror that crawled through Besmir as he looked at the awful scene. Men, women, children, none had been spared, and lay atop each other like firewood stacked for the winter.

"Gods!" Besmir spat as the wind changed, bringing the scent of death to them all.

He dismounted and let his horse go, the animal shying away from the smell of death. From inside the gate came a soul-chilling howl that was soon joined by others. Something stepped through the gate, dark and horrific in the dawn light. Seven feet of hairy muscle with claws and talons, slavering and insane with blood matting patches of the fur. Remnants of their armor clung to them, although the six forms had no need of any of it. The first through the gate reached into the pile of corpses at its feet and lifted a body by its arm. Limp and lifeless, the girl unfolded in its demonic grasp to hang facing Besmir, her dead face a mask of accusation. The creature hoisted the girl high into the air, dangling her before its maw as a horrible sucking sensation reached his ears and he realized the thing was feeding on her corpse.

Rage took over Besmir at the sight. What right did these things have to kill the people he had promised to protect? What right did they even have to exist in this world? A scream tore from Besmir's throat, and he charged at the creature that held the girl.

The demon tossed the girl's body at him almost contemptuously, but he managed to dodge it with ease. Besmir fired an arrow, catching the thing in the throat. A howl split the dawn light, pain and fright filled, as the beast felt the bite of injury for the first time in this world. Besmir's hands flew as he filled the air with arrow after arrow, one leaving the bowstring before the previous missile had even hit home.

Arrows bristled from the thing as it staggered towards Besmir with claws outstretched. Its muzzle peeled back in a grimace of agony, showing Besmir its jagged teeth. Chest, throat, abdomen and even its face had been pierced numerous times, causing terrible injuries, yet still it plodded towards Besmir as the army watched in utter silence.

Besmir raised his hand as the thing reached him and tried to swipe at him. Its yellow eyes widened when a gout of flame exploded from his hand, engulfing it completely in blue fire. A hissing scream ripped from its throat as Besmir burned the thing alive. The stench of searing hair and cooking flesh washed over him, and he became vaguely aware of some retching sounds from behind him. Besmir's lips pulled back in a grimace of effort and barely controlled rage as he intensified the flame. The demon writhed and mewled in agony, but no one mustered any pity for the vile thing.

A loud popping sound erupted from the thing as its skin burst, spraying intestines and organs over itself and the ground around it. Besmir stared at the other five gathered beasts as they watched him burn their brother alive, a grin spreading over his face. It died in agony, its spilled organs cooking even as it still clung to the last threads of life.

Besmir lowered his hand, staring at the charred, oozing mass of cooked and burned meat before him. Glad it was dead, he felt guilty for torturing the thing so. His guilt dissolved, however, when he saw the piles of bodies again. These things had no mercy in them and deserved none either.

Shouldering his bow, the king drew a sword the White Blades had gifted him. Once belonging to his grandfather, they had secreted it among their stacks of weapons to keep it from Tiernon's hands. Three feet of bright steel flashed in the dawn light as he held the sword aloft for all to see.

"For Gazluth!" he screamed before charging at the group of demons.

"Charge!" Herofic bellowed, hefting his ax.

"White Blades to me!" Norvasil yelled, throwing himself forward as well.

Unorganized and throbbing with fear, the army marched forward to join their king as he hacked and slashed at the ungodly beasts like a man possessed.

The demons themselves appeared confused as to what was happening. Food had never behaved in this manner before. Food ran. Screamed. Died. Never attacked. Never caused hurt.

***

Loraise kept one eye on Norvasil's massive back as she waded in with the other women, hacking and stabbing the unholy beast that screamed and thrashed before her. Shock hammered up her arm every time she dipped her blade into the creature, but she carried on until numbness weakened her to the point she could no longer manage, and she stepped back, panting hard. Although they had three of the things down and dying, her eyes picked out writhing shapes on the ground, comrades and friends that had given their lives in the attack. Neighbors, women she *knew*, lay dead at her feet. Sadness and rage exploded in her chest with equal intensity. One of the demons lay crumpled in a heap atop several of her comrades.

No. You do not share the ground with my friends.

Loraise walked over to where it lay, punctured and broken, blood leaking from hundreds of wounds. It looked pathetic in death. Massive but pathetic, and Loraise felt all fear evaporate as she looked at the thing. Reaching down, she grabbed it by one hand, its dead flesh chill and rubbery, but it was like pulling a root to move a tree. Its arm moved a little but no more. Loraise dropped its hand and fell to her knees, sobbing for the friends she had lost.

Icy shock and panic gripped her when the hand gripped her neck. She wrestled with the demon's wrist as it choked her, sitting up slowly, its dead head rolling limply on its shoulders. Loraise knew it was dead, but her oxygen-starved brain conjured images of the thing being able to come back from the dead, to kill endlessly until the world was a barren waste. Her chest ached, her fingertips tingled, and darkness started at the edges of her vision as the dead demon got back to its feet once more.

"Dead!" it bellowed. "You are all dead!"

Women turned to hack and stab at the dead thing, crowding around it and plunging their swords into it over and over. Long strips of flesh and muscle peeled back to reveal the tendons and bones inside.

"Loraise!" Norvasil thundered as he dashed across the battleground towards the group.

Women turned to see the immense man galloping towards them, broadsword raised above his head, and melted from his path like ice thrown into a furnace. Norvasil leaped into the air, bringing his sword down in a vicious arc that smashed and cut through the demon's forearm, jerking its shoulder out of its socket as well. Sparks exploded where the sword hit the cobblestones, rising in a shower to set fire to the demon's fur.

Loraise slumped backwards, still gripping the demon's severed arm but thankfully able to drag a little air into her lungs. Norvasil knelt beside her, oblivious to the chaos around them.

"Are you well?" he asked gently as he freed her throat of the severed hand.

"I...I thought I was dead...for sure," she croaked in reply.

Norvasil gathered her into his strong arms, bearing her away from the horror and death as Besmir approached the undead, demonic corpse.

***

"You!" It growled in a voice that bubbled.

It pointed its remaining arm at Besmir, who walked across towards it almost casually as his warriors fell back to form a ring of steel around it. Besmir tilted his head, seeing the overlay of Tiernon's features on the demon's face and knew he possessed its body.

"Uncle," he spat. "I've come for you."

"Come, then," Tiernon hissed. Blood bubbled from wounds in the demon as he forced it to speak. "Come and die."

Besmir shook his head and pursed his lips, raising his eyebrows and resting one fist on his hip. He held his grandfather's sword out towards Tiernon, turning the blade slowly so it caught the dawn light.

"Don't think so, Uncle," Besmir said in a conversational tone. "I'm going to hack you to pieces with your father's sword," he added.

"Ranyor sends his regards," the demon hissed. "Withdraw and he will live."

Besmir heard Keluse wail behind him, her pain ripping at him, but he also knew Tiernon would not let Ranyor live whether they fell back or not.

"Why, Uncle," Besmir said in as charming a voice as he could. "It's almost as if you're scared of us." He smiled as the information rippled through his army, and Tiernon growled through the demon.

"I fear nothing!" Tiernon spat. "Nothing!"

"I'm getting bored of this," Besmir said, waving his hand at the demon. "Shall we speak in person?"

Without waiting for a reply, Besmir turned and marched for the palace gate, leaving the bloody wreck to scream behind him.

Several women who remained in a circle around the thing looked at each other nervously. They were all covered in sweat and blood, panting and tired from the short battle but exhilarated to have won, still alive.

"What now?" one asked as she watched the king stalk off.

The others looked around in confusion, unsure now they were alone. A horrible, wet, chuckling sound issued from the demon and they all took a step back.

"Pathetic," it hissed. "Weak women. Serve me, your rightful king, and kill the usurper."

"You heard it, ladies," one woman said as her fear and confusion fell away. "Kill the usurper!"

The four women hacked and slashed violently at the demon's remains, cutting it into pieces and throwing them as far as they could, letting their hatred fuel them.

Chapter Twenty-Four

Thoran floated on a white sea of ecstasy. Something in the back of her mind screamed endlessly this was wrong and she was in danger, but the voice was faint and easily ignored. Delight washed over her entire body, the warm caress of a lover stroking her flesh, bringing her body to life. Rills and shivers rolled over her skin like gooseflesh, making her shiver and writhe in pleasure. Nothing mattered. Nothing but the endless feeling of happiness, joy...

I am naked on that table.

Thoran felt so tired. Just a short nap, a little sleep, and she could wake up in this paradise, refreshed and ready to carry on being loved. Just a little nap...

No! I have to wake up! We are both going to die!

Thoran frowned as Tiernon's vile altar sucked the life from her. The thought of 'we' had pierced the ecstatic bubble she had been in. Her eyes opened a little, unfocused and blurry. Something...some*one* was there, calling to her.

"That is it, Thoran! Fight it, my love!" Sharova cried from his place attached to the wall. His breath came in short bursts, his ribs and arms stretched so far, he was barely able to breathe.

Thoran's body twitched as she tried to move. One leg shimmied over to the edge, her foot falling from the table.

Sharova. Do it for him.

Pain cut into her muscles, her bones, her very blood as the feelings of joy fell from her. Something dark and ancient, distant and timeless, bellowed as she rolled from the altar, her body slapping the cold stone floor painfully. The icy chill brought some sense back to Thoran and she recalled some of what had happened. Reaching out for support, the woman felt the wall beside her and leaned against it, standing on shaky legs.

She took a step, then another. The third step took her foot from beneath her as she tripped over an unseen something, landing heavily on the stone again.

It was a man. Thoran looked at the thing she had fallen over, seeing the ragged holes in his limbs, the blood and scars.

Poor soul. Probably better off, whoever you were.

"Thoran."

She looked up at her name, seeing a figure stretched out on the wall.

Sharova.

His smile was a benign light as he gazed down at her, and Thoran felt a wash of love far deeper and more satisfying than the altar had given her. Tears rolled down her face when she recalled his fate, and she dragged herself across to where he hung, standing to look into his face.

Sharova's flesh was taking on the color of the wall. Granite grey fingers and streaks reached around his body, pulling him slowly into the wall. His breathing was labored and his eyes rolled madly as he slowly metamorphosed into stone. His beard and hair had already changed to grey, some of it molding to the stone behind his head.

"Thoran," he whispered.

"Yes, love," Thoran sobbed.

"You need to go," he said in a strained voice.

"No!" she begged in a tortured voice. "I have to stay with you."

Thoran put her head on his chest, hearing the labored whistle of his breathing, the slowing thudding of his heart, and wailed. His skin was hard and ice-cold, taking on the properties of the stone he was becoming.

"You must," Sharova insisted. "If Tiernon returns, finds you here and not on the altar..." He let the sentence hang.

"But you—"

"It is my time," Sharova said simply. "And I am thankful to have met you...to have loved you." He smiled. "But you must go."

Thoran raised herself on tiptoes, laying herself against him, and pressed her lips to his. They, at least, were still warm, but salty with her tears. With agony in her chest, Thoran stepped back from Sharova, preparing to leave.

Then the door exploded in a shower of hot splinters and dust, making her cough and blink.

***

Besmir stepped into the room that was dominated by a massive table-like altar covered in symbols that hurt his mind. Pure, deadly evil radiated from the thing, warping the space around it. He wrenched his gaze away to look at the naked, crying woman with wide eyes, the man who looked to be sinking into the wall, and Ranyor's corpse.

He knelt beside his friend, feeling for any signs of life, his heart heavy.

"Where's Tiernon?" he asked the naked woman as she blubbered.

"Help him!" she cried. "Help him, please!"

"Where is Tiernon?" Besmir demanded as people flooded the room. A pair of women folded their cloaks over Thoran, who was in no condition to say anything else, and pulled her from the room.

Besmir approached the figure slowly sinking into the wall.

"I t-take it you are the king?" he said, cold making him shiver. "I am Sharova, f-former f-fleet admiral." Besmir nodded slowly. "I t-tried," Sharova added. "T-Tried to s-stop him..."

"Where is he?" Besmir asked.

"Went through that d-door." Sharova rolled his eyes towards a door at the back of the room. "Take care, M-Majesty, he has...th-things. Evil, c-cold th-things."

"Thanks for the warning,' Besmir said. "What of you?"

"J-Just take c-care of Th-Thoran, please," Sharova stammered. "And end th-th-this." He glanced down at himself.

Besmir nodded and reached out to touch Sharova's forehead. Sharova screamed once, then fell silent.

The king hammered the flimsy wooden portal open with a single thought, walking into the bare chamber beyond. Tiernon was huddled in a corner, a wasted thing dressed in rags and barely able to support life any longer. Norvasil, Herofic, Zaynorth and a few others crammed into the room behind Besmir.

There were four creatures in the room. One was attached to Tiernon, locked onto the back of his neck, a pulsing thing that either controlled or fed from him. The other three Besmir knew of. These were the T'noch he had seen birthed in hell. How they had gotten here and what they were doing was a mystery he was not interested in solving.

"You see them?" he asked.

Zaynorth nodded, but the rest shrugged in confusion.

"Give me a second," Zaynorth said as the nearest T'noch shifted, approaching them.

The old man concentrated, putting the image of the creatures into everyone's heads. Norvasil gasped and Herofic grunted as a few of the others cried out.

"I do not know how long I can do this to so many," Zaynorth told Besmir in a strained voice.

"I saw one of these things birthed in hell," Besmir announced. "Zaynorth and I can see them normally, but he's showing them to you by illusion. They can die, but I don't know if you can do anything to them."

The nearest T'noch reached for Besmir, unaware he could see them, and the king lashed out with green lightning as he had in hell. The T'noch died, fading from his vision as the other two advanced. Herofic and Norvasil stepped forwards, each hammering blows against one of the T'noch and hacking pieces off them. They screamed, lashing out at anything within range with their long arms, felling people like trees. Besmir lanced his sword into one, sending lightning arcing down the blade to cook it from the inside. The T'noch screamed, its voice a hot pressure in their ears, bringing pain as it died.

Beside him Herofic and Norvasil were back on their feet and slashing at the remaining creature. Norvasil bellowed as the thing grabbed his arm, twisting and wrenching the bones. Besmir could not attack it with his magic for fear he would hit his friends.

"Fall back!" He shouted at the two warriors.

Yet Norvasil could not. The T'noch had managed to pull him further towards its body, wrapping the big man in a death grip. The muscular warrior's head shot back, his mouth open in a silent scream as the demon crushed him. Besmir grabbed the thing, his skin trying to recoil from the horrible contact. Its rubbery flesh felt hard beneath, as if it covered bones that were as thick as his legs.

Flame leaped from Besmir's hand, searing and cooking the demon's body, making it thrash and scream. It let go of Norvasil who collapsed to the floor so it could pull away from Besmir but when he saw it let go of his friend he increased the fire leaping from his hands, burning it alive. The stench of burning flesh filled the room as Besmir torched the creature, blackening its features until they were unrecognisable.

Before them all, Tiernon rose up. The thing that had attached itself to the back of his neck had become part of him somehow, restoring his body a little and giving him power again.

"Zaynorth!" Tiernon cried as if he was greeting an old friend. "It is a pleasure to see you. A pity you have to die so soon, but..."

Tiernon flicked lightning at Zaynorth, who screamed, his body crashing against the wall..

"No!" Besmir shouted.

He launched himself at Tiernon, power burning from his hands, head and chest. The demon possessing Tiernon flinched as Besmir's magic hammered into him, pure force blasting him against the stonework behind him. Besmir tore at Tiernon with power, ripping wounds open and sealing them again so he could inflict even more pain.

Tiernon laughed in between dire screams of agony. His torso exploded, ribs erupting from his chest as Besmir pulled his lungs from inside. Yet the king had not finished. He healed Tiernon so he could hurt him again, reformed his bones and knitted his skin in order to rend it again.

"What are you laughing at?" he screamed at Tiernon. "What's so funny?"

"You," Tiernon wheezed through the agony. "You are become just like me," he tittered. "Vicious and cruel. You are of Fringor blood, boy." Tiernon spat blood to the floor.

Besmir halted. Tiernon was right. He had counseled against this kind of thing, made sure all he encountered in his long journey knew he was not like Tiernon. Vengeance and torture were not part of his arsenal, and shame colored his face.

"End him, Your Majesty," Zaynorth said, gripping his arm. "Kill him, Besmir."

The old man was deathly pale and his clothing had been ripped. Burn marks darkened the skin of his chest, radiating out in jagged lines, but he lived.

Besmir drew his grandfather's sword and crossed the room to where Tiernon sat in a pool of blood and shredded tissue. His eyes rolled up to Besmir and he grinned.

"Just like me," he gurgled.

Besmir thrust the sword down. Bright steel pierced Tiernon's chest, cutting through muscle and bone easily. The blade passed through Tiernon's heart and into his aorta.

Besmir twisted the blade before wrenching it free. A thick gout of blood exploded from Tiernon as he took his final breath and his smashed body slumped sideways.

Chapter Twenty-Five

"It is done," Zaynorth said with a note of satisfaction in his strained voice. "Yet I am sure the work must now begin in earnest."

Besmir yawned stretching his face as the adrenaline drained from his system. "Surely this is enough for today?"

"Gazluth is weak," Herofic said as he kicked at the gruesome remains in the corner. "Any number of foreign powers might seek to capitalize on the lack of people and undefended borders."

Besmir swore, cursing himself for a fool. Of course killing Tiernon was never going to be the end of his duties. He was a king, with people to care for and lands to tend. Zaynorth spoke the truth: this was merely the beginning.

"We need to destroy that altar for starters," Besmir said irritably. "Get some people in here with axes to chop it into firewood." One of the women in the room saluted and ducked back through the door to issue orders. The sound of metal on wood came to their ears and Besmir smiled as Norvasil struggled to his feet again.

"Sire, we cannot make a mark on it," the woman reported as she stepped back into the room, panting.

"I will deal with it later," Besmir muttered. "Post guards outside the door and make sure no one gets near it, it's lethal."

Besmir finally tore his eyes from the pile of bloodied flesh in the corner and scanned the room more fully now.

Tiernon had cleared every last scrap of furniture from the place for some reason. This had been his bedchamber when he had been sane, but Besmir could think of no reason for stripping it bare. It nagged at him as he wandered around the space, hovering at the back of his mind.

"Something's wrong here," Besmir said.

"Are you serious?" Herofic asked incredulously. "Nothing is *right* here, Besmir."

"It's more than that." Besmir pointed at Tiernon's body. "Look around. Why is this room empty?"

Zaynorth looked, frowning in confusion as Herofic huffed.. The old man leaned against the nearest wall, looking grateful for its cool support. Zaynorth frowned and called out and within a few seconds they were all searching the wall for the source of a breeze he could feel. Norvasil went as far as to hammer against the stone with fists and feet, searching for a hidden exit.

Besmir loosed his mind, sinking through the stones to seek out what was hidden from them. A chasm had been carved beyond the wall, a tunnel leading down into the rock of the planet. He searched feverishly for some way to access it and eventually discovered a latch, the lever hidden in the fireplace. Returning to his body, Besmir triggered the latch and a small section of stonework opened inward.

"If he had a bolt hole," Besmir said as he approached cautiously, "why didn't he use it?"

"Insanity probably had something to do with it," Herofic growled, walking over and looking at the hole suspiciously. "No telling what might be down there," he grumbled.

Besmir grabbed his shoulder as he looked to be about to enter.

"Just a minute," he said.

Besmir sent his mind out into the hole, searching for any signs of life. A lone spider hung in a corner, sitting in the center of its web, but Besmir drifted past, as it was far too small. Farther down the rough passage he encountered a mouse that fluttered nervously along the base of the wall. He dived into it and scurried downwards, searching the area out.

Herofic looked at Zaynorth, scowling at his brother's condition.

"You need to rest," he said. "Before you collapse on us all."

"He needs me," Zaynorth said stubbornly. "I will not abandon him this day."

"Not much good to him if you are dead," Herofic growled.

"Just leave. I—"

"By the gods!" Besmir yelled, his eyes widening. "Get torches. Lanterns, anything to cast light," the king ordered, virtually diving through the hole.

***

Zaynorth staggered after Besmir, worried over his headlong and foolish charge. As he struggled to catch up with the king, a smell insinuated itself into his nose. Perspiration and human waste mingled with the pungent stench of fear as he descended along the passage Tiernon must have cut into the living rock the palace backed onto.

It widened at the bottom, leveling out somewhat, Zaynorth saw as he leaned his hands on his knees and waited for lights to be brought. A pair of soldiers brought a handful of torches each and started to light them from one they jammed in a crevice in the wall.

Besmir took a few and placed them at various intervals around the wall, illuminating the space. Zaynorth felt sickness wash through him when he saw the multiple glints in the darkness, hundreds of eyes staring back at him.

"Don't be afraid," Besmir called in the softest voice he could manage. "Tiernon is dead and you are all free again."

Whispers and mutters ran through the room as the women penned there spoke to each other in disbelief.

"I am Besmir, son of Joranas and Rhianne, and the rightful King of Gazluth," he said. "You are all free to leave this place. Many of you might have family or friends in the world above."

The possibility of finding family spurred one young girl on, and she approached Besmir timidly, tugging at his arm.

"Is it true, M-Majesty?" she asked quietly. "Are we really free to go?"

Besmir looked down at the virtually naked girl, barely in her teens, and nodded. He offered his arm, which she took after a few seconds of staring at it, and led her towards the tunnel leading up.

Zaynorth watched the other women watching her and saw their faces change almost as one. Fear and resignation changed to determination and hope as they filed out silently behind Besmir.

The hunter king made sure every one of the women was cared for, fed, watered and had somewhere to sleep before returning to his own bed.

Arteera took him into her arms, humming and rocking him as he sobbed uncontrollably.

Chapter Twenty-Six

Besmir's baby kicked him in the back and he woke, turning to look at Arteera in the darkness. How she was able to sleep with the child writhing and kicking inside her was a mystery. He turned her gently, curving his body around her back and laying his hand on her swollen belly. As if it knew his hand was there, the baby kicked again, a good, solid kick, and Besmir chuckled.

"Settle down, little one," he murmured, closing his eyes.

The time between his ending of Tiernon and now had been filled with a mixture of sadness and joy. Sadness in the form of Keluse's despair when she found out about Ranyor's death. Sadness as the death toll rose and rose, people discovering friends and neighbors had died in the conflict with the demons outside the palace and sadness at having to bury the slaughtered population of Morantine. Joy came in the form of the whole ordeal simply being over. Tiernon was dead and Besmir lived as the new King of Gazluth. Numerous parties and impromptu gatherings had taken place, especially among those women Tiernon had kept as brood mothers.

He and Arteera had been strolling through the streets, nodding to people they knew and exchanging a few words as they worked. Some cleared debris from the streets, others still carted wagons laden with the dead from the city while others had been setting up a hospital in one of the market squares.

Arteera had stopped in the middle of the street, her eyes fixed on a woman who was wandering aimlessly among the hospital patients. Besmir turned as she bent down, frightened that she was losing the baby.

"Help!" he shouted. "Help over here!"

Arteera grabbed his arm as two women dashed over.

"I am fine," she said. "I am well. I just thought...I believed I saw my sister," Arteera said, embarrassed.

The two women retreated while Arteera stood again. Besmir took her into his arms.

"I'm truly sorry she's not here," he said. "If we find any sign o—"

"Arteera?" a voice screamed from outside the hospital.

They both turned to see a woman with curly hair and wild eyes running at them. Besmir pulled Arteera behind him but she fought past him and ran from the hospital.

"Thoran?" she shouted. "Thoran!" she screamed as the pair met at a run, wrapping their arms about each other and falling to their knees.

Besmir approached a little cautiously, recalling the woman from the altar room where Sharova had been partially absorbed by the wall. The pair rocked and hugged and sobbed in relief as people gathered around them in support.

"I cannot believe you are alive," Thoran said as she wiped tears from her eyes.

"Besmir, this is my sister, Thoran," Arteera introduced them.

Thoran seemed a little awestruck at meeting the new king, but Besmir assured her there was no need to bow to him.

"Look, there really is no need for that," he said. "You're going to be our baby's aunt, after all, you don't need to keep bowing."

The look on Thoran's face was priceless as she stared at Arteera.

"You mean you...?" Arteera nodded. "And you are...?" Arteera nodded again. Thoran squealed in delight. "Oh, I cannot wait until you meet Sharo..." She trailed off, tears springing from her eyes.

"What is it, Thoran?" Arteera asked.

"A man," her sister said. "A good man who saved me and many others...and suffered for it," she whispered.

"We can meet him when he recovers," Besmir said offhandedly as he drained a cup of wine someone had brought him.

"What?" Thoran demanded. "What do you mean?"

Besmir looked at her and realized she did not know.

"He asked me to look after you and end his pain," Besmir said with a smirk. "So I did. I smashed him out of the wall. I'm sorry, I would have thought you were taken to the same place afterwards. I was a little busy, after all."

Thoran barely waited to listen to everything Besmir had to say, jumping up and racing from them back into the hospital to demand the location of the 'stone man'. Besmir grinned at Arteera, who shook her head but smiled.

"Fool," she said. "How could you have forgotten that?"

"Like I said," Besmir replied. "I was a bit busy at the time."

Besmir smiled against Arteera's neck as he drifted off to sleep with the memory in his mind.

***

Keluse sat in the doorway of the modest house she had been assigned, watching people pass her by. She rubbed her chest to try and ease the ache there, but it was like a millstone around her neck, bringing constant, painful pressure.

Nausea rolled through her as well, morning sickness to add to the mourning sickness. Keluse almost smiled at her own joke. Her eyes picked out a woman in the crowd of women bustling about outside her house. She wore a plain dress of rough wool and had poor leather sandals on her feet. Muddy legs ran up to an emaciated body, and her face bore the scars of misuse, bruised and purple. Keluse estimated her to be around fifteen years of age and, despite the wounds, quite pretty. What had brought her to Keluse's attention, however, was the way she cooed and rocked the small bundle in her arms.

Without even knowing she was going to do so, Keluse stood and made her way across the street to where the girl stood, humming a tune to her baby with a serene expression on her face.

"Boy or girl?" Keluse asked, barely recognizing her own voice.

The girl looked up from her bundle and smiled. One of her teeth was missing and both her eyes were purple with bruising.

"My boy," she said in a dreamy voice. "My beautiful little boy."

"Can I see him?"

The girl's expression changed from serene to guarded as she turned away from Keluse, frowning.

"You ain't taking him!" she cried.

"No!" Keluse said defensively. "No, I just wanted to see him. I'm pregnant myself and a little worried," she admitted. "I...I don't really know what to do."

The girl turned, eyeing Keluse suspiciously, but must have been able to see her sincere expression.

"You want me to teach you?" she asked.

"Yes... I...I need some help," Keluse muttered.

"It is right easy," the girl said. "As long as you make sure he is warm and well fed and you love him, you cannot be far wrong. My little Marous here, he got everything he could need in me as his mama," she said, rocking Marous gently.

"Can I see him?" Keluse asked again.

"Go on now, Genne, show the nice lady your baby," an older woman said as she approached.

Keluse turned to see an older woman with a haggard face and worn clothing staring back at her with bright green eyes. She smiled benignly at Keluse but looked slightly hostile for some reason.

The girl called Genne brought her little bundle around for Keluse to see. Holding her baby in one arm, she carefully peeled the edge of his blankets back for Keluse to see inside. Nestled in the blankets was a bundle of dirty rags, twisted and knotted into the semblance of a baby. Keluse looked up into Genne's eyes, realizing with horror something had broken her mind. She stepped back and looked to the older woman who told Genne to go look for her younger brother and addressed Keluse in a harsh voice.

"The old king took her baby," she said. "Before you and your friends turned up. Left her pining for him, half-mad with need, so we made a doll for her. Could not think of anything more to do. Tales of you and your baby will not be helping her, so kindly do not speak of it."

"I'm sorry," Keluse said, tears rolling down her face. "I didn't know!"

"Now you do," the woman said before turning and following Genne.

Keluse stumbled back towards her house and fell into a chair, folding her arms on the wooden table and laying her head on them. Tears dripped on the wood, soaking into the untreated surface as thoughts of Ranyor, Genne and her nonexistent baby whirled around in her head.

"Is there anything I can do?" Besmir asked from behind her.

Keluse looked up at his blurred, concern-filled face and leaped at him, burying her head in his shoulder and weeping so hard, her back ached. Besmir rubbed his hands up and down her back in an attempt to comfort his friend.

"I can't stay here," she managed finally.

"I'll get you somewhere else to live," Besmir promised.

"No," Keluse said. "I can't stay here, in this country. Everywhere I look I see him. Everyone I look at *is* him. I can't be here."

Besmir's heart sank to think the only other person from his homeland of Gravistard might leave. Despite being with Arteera and being surrounded by friends, Besmir felt alone. Yet he understood her pain and vowed to himself he would not stop her if she wanted to leave.

"Anything you need, apprentice," he said. "Anything."

Keluse pulled back, looking up at the man she had followed hundreds of leagues across land and sea.

"If there's any way you can stay, you'll be welcomed with open arms," he said. "But if you really need to go, let me know and I'll see you're provided with anything you might need."

"Oh, Besmir," Keluse sobbed. "I just don't know what to do. I feel lost, so very lost without Ranyor." Her throat closed when she said his name, changing into a squeak.

"Please take your time," he said. "I've come to depend on you more than I should," Besmir chuckled. "Especially as I'm supposed to be teaching *you*."

Epilogue

The familiar scouring, acid wind grated at him when he opened his eyes on the grey expanse of hell. A mixture of horror and expectation rolled through Besmir as he clad himself in the armor of thought the spirit of his father had taught him. He rose into the air and cast about for the familiar landmarks that would point him towards his father's home here. Not long after his arrival, he found the structure.

"Joranas!" he yelled from beside the pond.

"Besmir?" the demonic voice asked in confusion as he appeared at his door.

The hunter king ran across to where his father stood, looking even more attuned to this world than he had before. A fourth horn had sprouted from his head, and his scaling looked to be even heavier, the individual scales thicker. Besmir opened his arms to hug the man who had sired him for the first time ever, but somehow passed through his form.

Besmir turned to see Joranas's arms slowly falling, his head hanging as he realized this was no family reunion.

"What...what's going on?" Besmir asked in a small, disappointed voice.

Joranas turned and offered something that Besmir assumed was a smile to his son. "You are not really here," he grumbled. "Not in spirit at least. Maybe in thought."

Besmir's father lifted his head and bellowed a wordless shout of pure anguish and pain to the uncaring sky. The wretched wail cut at Besmir as he stood there, helpless, a lump growing in his throat.

"Father..."

"It is yet another torture this place brings to taunt me. I can see you, speak to you, but we can never touch. Ah, but the gods are cruel," he muttered. "Come, let me tell you how I ended up in hell," Joranas said as he plodded off into the ashen, grey wasteland. "At the point when the assassin's blade took my life, I was offered a choice."

"Who by?" Besmir asked in confusion.

"Cathantor came to me with an offer."

"Cathantor? The god of the afterlife?" Besmir asked, thinking how many souls he had entrusted to that god.

"The very same," Joranas said. "He lifted me from the world, leaving the agony from my wounds behind and brought me to his realm." Joranas' voice changed, becoming lighter and less guttural. "Oh, my son, it is beautiful!" he said.

Besmir glanced at the demonic face of his father and saw a single tear spring from his eye.

"'Paradise' is the only way I could describe it. It is warm and sunny, everyone lives in harmony with each other, and food appears at your hand if you wish it." He stopped for a second, remembering his visit to heaven. "Rhianne...was there, and I knew the killers had done their job. My only regret was you,"

Besmir's father said, turning to his son. "You were not there, so I knew you lived still.

"Cathantor came to me in all his splendor," Joranas went on as they plodded through the ash. "I cannot begin to describe his aspect, as I believe he appears differently to each individual. Yet his presence is...overwhelming," Joranas breathed. "Imagine, if you can, the greatest ecstasy you have experienced and double, no, triple it. I doubt that even comes close to the feeling you get from being in his presence. He makes you feel the universe rotates around you alone. As if nothing that has existed or *will exist* is as important, as precious, as you. Nothing can ever compare to that feeling, nothing, and an eternity basking in the glow of his love would still not be enough."

Joranas fell silent, and Besmir racked his brain to think of some reason his father would choose to be here rather than in the paradise he had just described. Nothing came to him, so he turned to see the demon regarding him quizzically.

"So why did I give up an eternity in paradise with my wife?" Joranas asked, reading Besmir's mind.

Besmir nodded.

"Cathantor offered me a choice. Remain with him and Rhianne in paradise or come here and safeguard the portal to your world from the things *it* births from the absence." Joranas pointed with his chin. Besmir knew exactly what he was talking of. "In return, he would spare your life from the assassin's blade," Joranas finished.

Besmir nearly doubled from the blow those words delivered. His father had chosen an eternity in hell so he could *live*?

"Why?" Besmir managed to croak as guilt ate through his core like acid.

"As I love you, Son, why else?" Joranas said in a confused voice. "I wanted you to have a chance at life, at love. A chance to experience the hardships of life before entering paradise."

Besmir shook his head in puzzlement and his father chuckled.

"I also hoped you would take revenge on Tiernon as well," Joranas said. "Speaking of which." The demon pointed his seven-fingered hand towards the horizon.

Besmir looked, seeing nothing but grey to begin with. An image resolved in his vision, a jutting finger of rock, and he glanced at his father nervously.

"Come have a look," Joranas said, rising into the air.

Besmir followed, his eyes picking out more details as he flew. At the base of the stone finger the Ghoma had gathered, feasting on something that writhed and screamed on the ground. Besmir landed beside them, knowing they could not injure him this time, and peered at the tortured thing they feasted on.

"A fitting end, no?" Joranas said as he regarded the soul of his brother being endlessly ripped apart and devoured.

Besmir watched Tiernon's face contort in agonized screams as the creatures tore into his soul with their teeth. He reached for Besmir but the hunter stepped away, turning his back on the evil thing that had caused so much pain to so many people.

"How long will you leave him like that?" Besmir asked.

"I have no plans to rescue him any time soon," Joranas said in a dark voice. "I doubt my brother will remain there too long, however. He will realize he can use his powers before long, I think."

"Then what?" Besmir asked.

"Then I shall throw him into the absence," Joranas said.

Besmir shuddered at the thought.

"I'm having a child," he said, changing the subject.

"Really?" Joranas asked, puffing his chest out in pride. "Congratulations," he chuckled. "I am to be a grandfather!"

***

"I am happy for you," Arteera said when Besmir told her of his visit. "And Joranas was pleased to be a grandfather?" she asked, stroking her belly.

"Oh yes," Besmir said, stretching.

Arteera poked him in the ribs and he jerked from her touch. She laughed. "Are you ticklish?" she asked.

"No!" Besmir shouted, guarding his body from her searching fingers. "Hey, stop that!" he laughed as she tickled him mercilessly.

"A good name, Joranas," Arteera said when she had finished torturing him. "If we have a boy..." Besmir grinned.

61758481R00192

Made in the USA
Middletown, DE
14 January 2018